# Praise for David P. Wagner

### Roman Count Down
The Sixth Rick Montoya Italian Mystery

"Wagner's solid sixth Rick Montoya Italian Mystery...explains how he evolved from translator to sleuth... This one will satisfy hungry travelers heading to Rome."

—*Publishers Weekly*

"The tour of Rome, the food and wine, the colorful characters, and the intriguing mystery will keep Montoya fans happy and may well interest those unfamiliar with the series to catch up on the adventures of this engaging translator and sleuth"

—*Booklist*

### A Funeral in Mantova
The Fifth Rick Montoya Italian Mystery

"Following *Return to Umbria*, Wagner's fifth series outing features a likable amateur sleuth who carefully analyzes other people. Rich in details of the food and culture of Italy's Lombardy region, this atmospheric mystery will be appreciated by fans of Martin Walker's French-flavored "Bruno" mysteries. Readers of Frances Mayes's *Under the Tuscan Sun* may enjoy the colorful descriptions."

—*Library Journal*

"Wagner's fifth series entry provides his usual deft mix of art, travel, and suspense."

—*Kirkus Reviews*

"The many details of meals that Rick enjoys on his trip are a highlight, as are the author's appended notes on the food and wines of the area."

—*Booklist*

"This is a book for armchair travelers as much as it is for mystery lovers."

—*Publishers Weekly*

### *Return to Umbria*
The Fourth Rick Montoya Italian Mystery

"Translator Rick Montoya is in Orvieto to persuade his cousin to return home to Rome when he gets drawn into investigating the murder of American Rhonda Van Fleet. Did Rhonda's past in Orvieto, studying ceramics, lead to her death? The setting almost overwhelms the plot, but Rick is a charming and appealing amateur sleuth."

—*Library Journal*

"Wagner skillfully inserts nuggets of local culture without slowing down the narrative pace, and perhaps even more importantly, he gets Italy right. He understands the nuances of Italian manners and mentality as well as the glorious national preoccupation with food."

—*Publishers Weekly*

"With taut pacing and enough credible suspects to keep the reader guessing until the end, *Return to Umbria* makes for an engaging read."

—*Shelf Awareness*

like to visit. As a boy I lived in both Firenze and Napoli, and reading Wagner takes me back deeply and instantly."

—Joseph Heywood, author of the Woods Cop
Mysteries, *The Snowfly*, and *The Berkut*

"If you are interested in Italian art and artifacts, Italian history and culture, Italian food and wine, or even just good storytelling, then *Cold Tuscan Stone* will be right up your cobblestone alleyway. Set in the ancient Tuscan town of Volterra, David P. Wagner's atmospheric debut novel delivers all of the above and more... Simply put, this exciting, intriguing, well-written mystery extends an offer no reader should refuse. *Capiche?*"

—Amanda Matetsky, author of the Paige Turner Mysteries

"Wagner hits all the right notes in this debut. His likable protagonist engages, plus the Italian angle is always appealing. Perfect for readers who enjoy a complex puzzle, a bit of humor, and a fairly gentle procedural. Don't miss this one."

—*Library Journal*, Starred Review

"Like the Etruscan urns he seeks, Rick's debut is well-proportioned and nicely crafted."

—*Kirkus Reviews*

"The intriguing art milieu, [the] mouthwatering cuisine, and the team of the ironic Conti and the bemused but agile Montoya are bound to attract fans."

—*Publishers Weekly*

## Also by David P. Wagner

The Rick Montoya Italian Mysteries
*Cold Tuscan Stone*
*Death in the Dolomites*
*Murder Most Unfortunate*
*Return to Umbria*
*A Funeral in Mantova*
*Roman Count Down*

# TO DIE IN TUSCANY

# TO DIE IN TUSCANY

## A RICK MONTOYA ITALIAN MYSTERY

# DAVID P. WAGNER

Poisoned Pen
PRESS

Published by Poisoned Pen Press, an imprint of Sourcebooks
P.O. Box 4410, Naperville, Illinois 60567-4410
(630) 961-3900
sourcebooks.com

Library of Congress Cataloging-in-Publication Data

Names: Wagner, David P., author.
Title: To die in Tuscany / David P Wagner.
Description: Naperville, Illinois : Poisoned Pen Press, [2021] | Series: A
  Rick Montoya Italian mystery; book 7
Identifiers: LCCN 2020029979 (trade paperback) | (epub) |
Subjects: GSAFD: Mystery fiction.
Classification: LCC PS3623.A35623 T6 2021  (print) | LCC PS3623.A35623
  (ebook) | DDC 813/.6--dc23
LC record available at https://lccn.loc.gov/2020029979

Printed and bound in the United States of America.
SB 10 9 8 7 6 5 4 3 2 1

*This book is for Maria Luz Puente Garcia Somonte Cabeza Wagner, who passed to her sons a proud Asturian heritage.*

*"Drawing is not what you see, but what you must make others see."*

**— EDGAR DEGAS**

# CHAPTER ONE

*"Buon giorno, Nino."*

Giving a serious nod in keeping with his position, Nino Fantozzi acknowledged the greeting of the woman at the cash register. It was, after all, *his* botanical gardens that drew no small number of tourists away from the more famous attractions of Urbino to this narrow street. Many of those same visitors found their way into this bar before or after a delightful visit with nature, his green oasis dropped in the midst of stone buildings and cobbled streets.

Who did the real work of keeping the plants healthy and everything in order? He did, of course, not those botany professors who were more interested in counting leaves than keeping the place neat. Without *his* gardens, this would only be a neighborhood bar, like so many others in odd corners of the city. Not that all the visitors to Urbino put the gardens high on their list of sites, going straight there after seeing the collection of masterpieces at the Palazzo Ducale. Far from it. But it did bring in a certain type of tourist. Lovers of natural beauty was the way Fantozzi characterized those who paid the one-euro entrance fee. In addition, the gardens drew botany students, but they needed only to show their credentials to get in without paying. Nino's boss, Professor Florio, had just yesterday reviewed the attendance numbers, which were considerable. Even those who didn't pay to get in the gardens added to the foot traffic on the street. How many of those people came into this bar?

*They really should offer me a discount.*

He paid and moved sideways where a man behind the counter in a white shirt and black tie nodded a silent *buon giorno* before beginning the noisy process of producing Nino's cappuccino. He had toyed with the idea of having a pastry to go with it but, after glancing down at his stomach, decided against it. The barman placed the steaming cup in front of him and pushed over the sugar bowl. Three times, the long sugar spoon traveled to the cup before Nino picked up his smaller one, stirred the granules into the foam, and took a sip. It was his second caffeine jolt of the morning, the first, prepared at home by his wife, a *caffe latte*, accompanied by two pieces of dried toast. This coffee was considerably better, but he wouldn't say that to his wife.

He drained the cup and patted his lips with a small paper napkin. A moment later he was out on the street, pulling a cream-colored handkerchief from his pocket and cleaning his glasses. Returning them to his nose, he breathed in the early spring air and looked to the sky. It hadn't rained in several days. Perhaps the clouds he saw could bring some needed showers, both cleaning the air and giving his beloved plants the natural moisture they preferred. Urbino's city water was adequate, but it was not the same as rain. Nino walked up the street to a fountain set into the wall just below the entrance to the botanical gardens. The stone papal shield of Benedict XIII hung high above the pool, a reminder to anyone using the fountain who ran this part of Italy in the early eighteenth century. Nino dipped his fingers in the water and dried them on the handkerchief from his pocket.

From another pocket he pulled a large key as he glanced up at the metal letters—*Orto Botanico*—attached to the brick above the entrance. The tall metal door creaked open and then banged shut behind him once he was inside and the key returned to his pocket. The heavy scent of plant life wafted over him as he emerged from the entranceway into the gardens themselves. He cast a critical eye over the path through the greenery with leaves dangling above it on both sides. It would need another sweeping before Manuel Somonte's visit the next day. Nino's boss had insisted that everything be in perfect order for one of the *orto*'s most loyal benefactors, especially noted for the *yucca gloriosa* that Somonte had donated two years earlier. Nino approached the greenhouse where that magnificent plant was housed with other semi-tropical plants donated by the wealthy Spaniard. The glass panes had been cleaned, but from where he stood, the plants appeared to be surrounded by fuzzy halos thanks to the humidity inside.

Nino noticed that the door to the greenhouse was slightly ajar and made a mental note to check its latch and hinges. He pushed it open and closed it carefully behind him, breathing in the earthy odor that was even stronger in the glass-enclosed environment. The yucca's white flowers dangled over the tops of lower plants from its place of honor in the corner. He walked down the narrow gravel path and made a right turn. It was a hardy plant; the only care needed was pulling off any of the jagged leaves that might have turned brown and died. It had to be perfect for the visit of Somonte. Nino's eyes moved from the topmost flowers down to the base when his chest tightened and a wave of nausea washed over him.

On the sandy soil sat the body of the plant's donor, Manuel

Somonte, dressed in a brown suit. He was propped against the plant, his head leaning to one side. His eyes were closed, as if sleeping, but the dark red stain on his shirt said otherwise. A small plaque noted that the yucca was a gift from the generous Spaniard. Above the plaque, written in larger letters, was the plant's Latin botanical designation followed by its popular name: *Spanish Dagger.*

# CHAPTER TWO

Rick Montoya blinked open his eyes when the car left the tunnel and sunlight poured over his face. He rubbed his neck, sat up in the seat, and looked out at the scenery of eastern Tuscany. The terrain was similar to what they'd passed through north of Rome earlier that morning. The wooded hills of the Alpe di Poti, some of them almost a thousand meters high, formed a natural barrier until engineers had gouged through them to shorten the route between Arezzo and Sansepolcro. The road would soon be flatter as it swung north, skirting the border with Umbria before reaching the broad valley below Anghiari. He unsuccessfully stifled a yawn and glanced at Betta Innocenti, whose hands were lightly gripping the steering wheel.

In profile, her smooth neck drew his attention. Did she keep her dark hair short to accentuate the beauty of her neck? Knowing Betta as he did, he doubted it. The cut, almost boyish, was perfect for someone as busy as she, someone who didn't want to spend time on her hair. Having perfect features and thick, healthy hair didn't hurt, Rick thought. Today the earrings were, as always, understated: tiny dots of gold. He tried to remember if he'd ever seen anything dangling from those ears, and could not. He inclined his head toward her and caught a hint of her perfume. Dahlia Noir, the same she'd been wearing when they'd met in her home town of Bassano del Grappa more than a year ago.

She downshifted through a curve. "Back among the living, Signor Montoya? You've been dead to the world since we left the *autostrada*."

He couldn't help lightly stroking the back of her neck before stretching his arms toward the windshield. "I was up late last night finishing an extremely tedious translation so that I would be free to spend a few days with you, *cara*."

"You could have skipped your morning run and slept in. I didn't pick you up until eight thirty."

"Miss my run? Not a chance. Are we there yet?"

A truck going back toward Arezzo passed them as they began climbing a hill into a grove of trees. Their car was a dark blue Fiat, standard issue from the Ministry of Culture where Betta worked at the office of cultural property in the section popularly known as the art cops.

"We are close."

"Tell me about this guy Somonte. I may not have focused on details the other night when you invited me to tag along today."

"You're here to translate when needed, which is the way I justified it to my boss."

"You told me that Somonte speaks Italian."

"I forgot to mention that to my *capo*."

Rick grinned. "Well, all I remember is that he's a rich Spaniard."

"Very rich. Self-made man who started out working in a wool mill and ended up owning it and many others." She eased into a higher gear as the car came off the hill. "He's from northern Spain, Asturias, where there are a lot of sheep."

"I know about Asturias, Betta. I had a great uncle—a Puente, not a Montoya—whose ancestors came from there. It is a rough, mountainous region. I remember him telling me that Asturias was the only part of Spain that the Moors were unable to subjugate."

"Because of the mountains?"

"No, because of the tough Asturianos, if you are to believe my uncle. So what else about Somonte?"

Betta pushed up her sunglasses, rubbed her eyes, and let them drop back on her nose. "Manuel Somonte. Father Spaniard, but his mother was Italian. His parents met when she was hiking the pilgrim trail that goes through northern Spain ending at Santiago de Compostela. Coincidentally, she was from Anghiari."

"Coincidentally?"

Betta pointed across acres of flat fields to a town clinging to the side of the hill in the distance. "That's Anghiari there. Which is why we're driving to Sansepolcro, now just a few kilometers ahead. Manuel learned from his mother to love Italy and feels he has deep roots here as well as in Asturias."

Rick looked, but his view was quickly cut off by the fence surrounding a long warehouse. They were entering an industrial area where factories, gas stations, and big-box stores lined both sides of the road. It was the same as in almost any Italian town, where space in the historic center was at a premium and commerce spread out like lava, taking over farmland in the name of progress.

"And his mother also taught him the Italian language that your boss wasn't told about."

"Precisely. He also got from her an appreciation for Italian art, which is the real reason we are going to Sansepolcro. If his mother's hometown had a museum, he'd likely have donated this work to them. But Sansepolcro is the next best thing, since it's virtually next door, and especially since it was the birthplace of Piero della Francesca."

"Who also did the sketch Somonte is donating, and happens to be one of your favorite Renaissance artists."

"*Bravo.* Which is why I was selected to represent the Culture Ministry when Somonte, in honor of his late mother, hands it over to the Museo Civico of Sansepolcro."

"After which you take a few days off to see the sights with your trusted interpreter. I like this. What else about the guy? Since I'll be meeting him."

"His other passion, besides art and making money from wool, is plants. I'm not sure where he picked that up—it wasn't explained in the bios I read on the internet. My only interest in him is the art, especially this Piero drawing."

"What do you know about the drawing?"

"I'm anxious to see it. It is one of the sketches he made for *The Resurrection,* one of his most famous paintings, which is in the museum here. Christ is seen stepping out of the Holy Sepulcher above the sleeping soldiers. The drawing was a study for the face of one of the soldiers."

"How did Somonte get his hands on it?"

"The drawing surfaced fairly recently, and rather mysteriously, with a dealer in Urbino. Somonte comes to Italy often, buys art, and is a great admirer of Piero. He must have known the dealer, who then tipped him off that it was for sale. That's often the way dealers work—they know the tastes of their best clients. I'm sure it wasn't inexpensive, but it being only a small sketch, he could afford it."

The Fiat slowed for another traffic circle and continued toward Sansepolcro. It crossed the Tiber River, barely as wide as the two lanes of the bridge, and drove under the SS3 highway into the suburbs of the town. The traffic slowed, and they seemed to hit every red light along what had changed from a highway to a street. When the car reached the city walls Betta followed them to the northern side of the city and turned in through one of the narrow gates, ignoring the signs indicating that they were entering a pedestrian zone. After a few turns she pulled up next to the entrance to the Museo Civico. From the glove box she took a large card with the seal of the Carabinieri and placed it against the windshield.

"Here we are, Rick. The last time I was here I was a student, and we had to park outside the walls and walk in. This is much easier. And we're here with time to spare."

The way Betta drove, Rick was not surprised.

The outside of the city museum did not distinguish itself from the other buildings on the block. They all had bars over the windows, though the museum's were more forbidding, and all were covered with the yellow-orange color that was standard throughout the country. Two stone planters filled with bright flowers flanked the entrance, and a discreet banner hung down one side to indicate what was inside. Rick pushed open the door for Betta and they entered a large rectangular room bathed in light from windows built into modern barrel vaults high above the floor. All very twenty-first century, unlike the art collection the museum held. Stanchions and red velvet ropes showed the way to the desk where visitors paid their entrance fees. A woman in a dark business suit talked in a low voice with the man behind the desk. She looked at her watch and then up at the two new arrivals. Her face showed concern, but she forced a smile and approached them.

"You must be Dottoressa Innocenti." She extended her hand to Betta. "I am Tiziana Rossi, the director of the museum. Welcome, and thank you for coming."

"It is my pleasure to return to Sansepolcro, Dottoressa Rossi. May I introduce Riccardo Montoya, who will help interpret for Signor Somonte should the need arise?"

The museum director shook Rick's hand, but the mention of Somonte returned the concern to her face. "I was expecting him and his wife to be here by now. We were going to give him a tour of the entire collection before the formal donation of the drawing." She looked at a man standing in the corner carrying a camera. "This is quite an occasion for us. The mayor and other city officials will arrive later for the ceremony. I hope nothing has happened to Somonte. The drive down from Urbino is not that long, but it does twist and turn."

"I'm sure he'll arrive soon," Rick reassured. "The Spanish idea of punctuality is sometimes different from the Italian."

"I hope you're right. In the meantime please feel free to check out the collection. The Pieros are in hall number five." She gestured toward a ramp that led to the older part of the museum complex. "I'll stay here and wait for Signor Somonte."

They thanked her and walked up the ramp and through a door that had been opened in the wall to connect two buildings whose floors didn't coincide. A few moments later they found themselves in the room that held the most important pieces in the museum. A uniformed guard eyed them carefully. Rick noticed the door-sized glass panel at one end, outside which two people stood peering into the room. He took them to be tourists and, from their dress, probably Scandinavians.

"That's a wonderful feature, don't you think, Rick? There are steps on the street leading up to that little porch where people can look inside without having to pay the entrance fee. At night the painting is lit. It's a way the locals can show their pride for a work that has become a symbol of Sansepolcro along with the town's coat of arms."

Rick turned to see Piero della Francesca's masterpiece on the wall behind him, Christ rising from the Holy Sepulcher—San Sepolcro—while soldiers slept in the foreground. Jesus stared directly at the viewers, challenging them to interpret the penetrating look of his eyes. Was it resignation? Doubt? Determination? Or simple exhaustion? The lips, forming neither a frown nor a smile, offered no help. Behind the figure the landscape was barren on one side and starting to grow on the other. After being dragged countless times through Italian museums and churches as a kid, Rick knew that every aspect of a painting had meaning, and he assumed the background was an allusion to rebirth, as was the brightening morning sky. His eyes were moving over other parts of the composition when Betta spoke.

"This painting shows the connection between the religious and civic life of Sansepolcro. It was commissioned by the city elders for the communal hall and prayed to before each of their council meetings. The name of the town comes from the relics of the sepulcher brought from the Holy Land, and Piero included one right there." She pointed to a crude chunk of stone in the lower right corner of the painting. "Today, though, our interest is connected to him." Her finger moved to one of the sleeping soldiers leaning against the stone sarcophagus.

Rick stepped to get a closer look at the soldier. "That's the one in Somonte's donated drawing."

"Correct. And according to tradition, it is a self-portrait of Piero della Francesca himself."

Rick remembered listening to a former Italian girlfriend talking about the works she had studied as an art historian. Her specialty had been Mannerism, the period that followed Piero and his contemporaries by several decades, but he recalled her using the phrase "according to tradition." He turned to Betta and smiled. "I know enough about Italian painting to know that when they talk about tradition, it probably isn't true."

"Art historians always have differing opinions on just about everything. That's how they make names for themselves. But even if it's not Piero's face, it's still a good story."

"And it makes the donated drawing even more valuable. It looks like they already have a place of honor waiting for it over there."

They walked to a glass case set against the wall, empty except for a small printed card. Betta was leaning over to read the inscription when hurried footsteps caught the attention of the guard. Rick was stepping forward when Signora Rossi appeared, breathing heavily.

"Terrible news," she said when she spotted Betta. "Signor Somonte. He's dead. They just called from Urbino." Her eyes darted to the empty case, and she clasped her hands into a tight knot. "But it's worse. The drawing is missing, and the police believe he was murdered. Do you think someone killed him and took it?" She looked at Rick and Betta. "I must advise the mayor." She turned and rushed from the room.

Betta pulled her phone from her purse. "I have to call my boss." She looked at the guard and retreated to a corner of the room out of earshot.

Rick watched her punch in a number and then gesture with her free hand as she talked in a low voice with the ministry in Rome. He sighed and walked to another of Piero's works, identified as a fresco fragment depicting San Giuliano, taken from a local church. The saint stared over Rick's left shoulder, his face surrounded by thick blond hair and crowned with a disk-like halo. Again Rick tried to read the face the master had created. Fear? Bravery? He would have to look up the hagiography of Giuliano to get a hint. Betta's voice broke through his thoughts.

"Rick, we're going to Urbino."

———

The seventy-one kilometers between the two cities would have meant about a half-hour drive for Betta if the roadway had been like the toll road between Rome and Arezzo. Instead, it would take well over an hour to navigate the two-lane *strada statale* that coiled through the mountains. Making matters worse, a number of trucks plodded slowly up the inclines, and several times Rick had to urge patience, lest Betta try to pass on a curve. There was no need to add to the day's death toll. This pace was agony for someone like Betta, who was used to riding motorcycles. He tried to get her to think about something other than their progress.

"Tell me more of what you know about this drawing, Betta."

"We don't know a whole lot. Provenance usually is not recorded for a simple drawing like it would be for a painting. When it turned up a few years ago in Urbino, the ministry was advised of its appearance. Since there was nothing illegal—it hadn't been reported stolen—my office didn't get involved. Works of art appear all the time in someone's attic or basement, and in many cases there's no way to know how it got there. It could have been in the family for centuries and nobody knew or cared, or it might have been hidden during the war to keep it out of the hands of the Germans. Then someone finds it in a trunk, thinks it might be worth something, and goes to an art dealer. I think that's what happened with this drawing when it was sold to the dealer in Urbino. That's something we'll find out when we get there. If we ever get there."

A straight section of road appeared after a curve, and Betta gunned the engine to pass the truck they had been following for ten kilometers. Rick's head pushed back against the seat, and he gripped the armrest. She groaned as another truck, this one even larger and slower, appeared in the distance.

"But now that the drawing has disappeared, we are involved."

"Art cops to the rescue," said Rick as he tried to relax.

It was early afternoon when they made a final ascent and came around the last section of Urbino's southern walls. A wide parking area spread out to their right. Above it the Palazzo Ducale stood anchored to the highest point in the city. An architectural masterpiece, the palace was built in the mid-fifteenth century by Duke Federico da Montefeltro to be home to one of the most enlightened courts of the Renaissance. Five centuries later, as if in keeping with the duke's support for the arts, it housed the artistic treasures of the Galleria Nazionale delle Marche. Rick leaned forward and looked up at the ramparts of the castle. His parents had brought him and his sister to Urbino when they were children, and he had marveled then at the size and complexity of the palazzo. It was a period when he was sick of being taken to museums, but, thanks to the palazzo's architecture, this museum was different to him. He recalled his sister saying it looked like something out of a Disney movie, which had gotten a laugh from their parents.

The car turned right and drove past the parking lot toward a decorative city gate flanked by columns and topped by carved stone eagles. Just before reaching the wall, Betta slowed, turned, and parked in front of a modern building on the left side of the street. The flags hanging outside, as well as the official seal above the door, told Rick that this was Urbino's police headquarters. The space was reserved for official vehicles, and once again Betta put her pass inside the windshield.

She opened the door and stepped to the ground. "I thought we'd never get here."

The *commissariato* was like so many police stations that Rick had entered, starting with the one where his uncle worked. They all had a certain distinctive smell to them, not unpleasant nor pleasing, just a neutral odor that somehow went with the work carried on inside. Benches lined an entire wall of the large room, but only one person was seated there, a woman dressed in black staring ahead. The other walls were bare, except for the usual bulletin boards displaying official notices that no one ever read. Rick and Betta were greeted by the stare of a uniformed policeman standing behind thick glass directly ahead of the door. If he noticed Rick, it wasn't apparent from his smile or where his eyes were trained.

"You are already making a positive impression," Rick said.

Betta strode quickly to the window and pushed her identification under the glass. "My office in Rome should have called, Sergeant. Regarding the murdered Spaniard."

The policeman looked quickly at the document, stiffened, and pushed it back. "*Si, Signora.* I was told someone from the ministry would be arriving, but I didn't—"

"Just tell us where we can find the investigating officer."

Rick grinned behind her.

"Through that door and at the end of the hall," the policeman stammered. "Let me come out and show—"

"That won't be necessary." She turned on her heel and walked to the door, Rick following behind, trying to keep up. He was at her side when they entered a narrow hallway.

"Loved the way you handled that," he said.

"Let's hope this next cop is more professional."

Rick thought about saying that he couldn't blame the sergeant for noticing a beautiful woman coming into the station but decided this wasn't the time. Maybe later.

The door at the end of the hallway was partially open, and as they got closer they could hear fingers on a computer keyboard. Betta pushed open the door and knocked at the same time. The policeman was seated behind a desk but turned toward a small table where his laptop sat. Stubble covered his face, and his eyes indicated a lack of sleep. He pivoted and surveyed the two arrivals. At first his expression showed incomprehension, then surprise, and finally the face opened into a wide smile.

"The art police headquarters in Rome didn't tell me they were going to send a crack investigative team. I was expecting some bureaucrat art expert wearing an ill-fitting suit." He got to his feet and rounded the desk, giving Betta a warm embrace while squinting over her shoulder at Rick. "You're still hanging out with this guy, Betta?"

"Alfredo," she said, "what a pleasant surprise."

He unclenched from Betta and hugged Rick, the two slapping each other's back.

"Detective Alfredo DiMaio," Rick said, "what have we done to deserve this?"

"I was just going to say the same thing. And that's *Inspector* DiMaio now, Riccardo. How long has it been since the Bassano case? And in the meantime Betta has obviously joined the art cops. And you, Riccardo, still translating and interpreting? I can never remember the difference."

"Still at it," Rick answered.

"Your uncle continues to move up in the police hierarchy in Rome. I am very appreciative of the word he put in for me after Bassano, by the way."

"You deserved it, Alfredo."

Betta spoke. "Has the Piero drawing turned up?"

The inspector sighed. "Do we have to get down to business already?"

Rick shrugged. "She's all business."

DiMaio gestured to two chairs facing his desk and returned to his. He leaned back with a creak when Rick and Betta were seated. "The short answer is no. But as you can imagine, my priority is finding the murderer, and it occurs to me that Riccardo's skills can be of help to both of us, Betta." He turned to Rick. "Do I recall that you are also fluent in Spanish?"

"That was the official reason for my presence, Alfredo, to translate for Signor Somonte if needed. I wouldn't think my services would be required now, given what's happened to the poor man."

"On the contrary. It's his wife and assistant who don't speak any Italian. I had great difficulty communicating with them this morning after we discovered the body, though part of it may just be that the wife is a difficult woman."

Betta shifted in the chair. "Why don't you start at the beginning, Alfredo?"

DiMaio glanced at Rick. "She really is all business, isn't she? I have a suggestion. My only sustenance so far today was a coffee and small pastry very early this morning. I assume you have not had lunch, so why don't I brief you both on what has happened so far at the restaurant next door? It's not the fine cuisine that you two cosmopolitans are accustomed to in Rome, but it will do the job."

"That sounds perfect," said Betta, rising to her feet.

They walked down the hall toward the reception area. It was empty except for a woman dressed in jeans and a turtleneck sweater pacing in front of the desk, a cell phone pressed to her ear. She looked up when the three came through the hall door and walked quickly toward them, stuffing the phone into her pocket.

"Inspector DiMaio?" Her eyes moved between Rick and the policeman.

DiMaio looked past her at the sergeant, who shook his head helplessly. "And you are?"

"Laura Intini." She pulled out a card and pressed it into his hand. "I have some questions about the death of the Spaniard. If you could give me a minute."

DiMaio studied the card while Rick and Betta edged aside. "I put out a written statement this morning, which you should have received."

"Yes, Inspector, of course we did. It was very brief, and we thought that you might have something to add to it. Surely there have been some developments since this morning. As you can understand, this is an important story, and our readers will be anxious to learn more."

"I'm sure they will. Sorry, I have an important meeting now."

She looked quickly at Rick and Betta. "Is it regarding the—"

"I have your card, Signora Intini. If something develops, you'll be the first to know." He walked toward the door with Rick and Betta in tow. "I hate journalists."

The restaurant, only a few steps from the *commissariato*, gave the impression of being a police cafeteria. It was one large, noisy room, its tables mostly filled with men and women in blue uniforms. The ambient noise subsided slightly as the diners watched Inspector DiMaio enter with two strangers, their attention split between Betta's slim figure and Rick's cowboy boots. The room quickly returned to its normally high decibel level, made worse by the cement floor and bare ceiling. One of the waiters, carrying a plate of pasta in each hand, spotted the inspector and pointed with his chin to an empty table in one corner. They worked their way through the room and sat down.

"You come here often?" Rick asked as he looked around the room at all the cops.

"Your sense of humor is still evident, Riccardo."

A waiter appeared balancing three menus, a bread basket, and a bottle of mineral water.

"*Ciao, Mimo. Olive ascolane e un litro di rosso,*" said DiMaio to the waiter, who nodded and disappeared toward the kitchen. "A local specialty, stuffed olives breaded and deep fried. I suggest the *vincisgrassi* for a *primo*—it's another dish you'll only find here in Le Marche, or if you do find it somewhere else in Italy, it won't be as good."

"That's lasagna, isn't it?" asked Rick.

DiMaio wagged a finger. "Don't let anyone in Urbino hear you calling it lasagna, Riccardo."

The wine appeared, a dark red in a ceramic pitcher. DiMaio ordered the pasta, filled their glasses, and offered a toast to old friends reunited. Right behind the wine waiter was one bearing a plate of olives with golden brown breading, still steaming like they had just been scooped out of the frying oil, rolled quickly in toweling, and rushed to the table. Betta spooned a couple of them onto her plate before Rick and Alfredo did the same. They exchanged wishes of *buon appetito* and picked up their knives and forks. The olives were already large, but the stuffing and breading brought them almost to golf ball size, each one yielding two crunchy bites. Betta and Rick agreed that their first taste of Marchigiana cooking was a success.

When the serving dish was almost empty, DiMaio took a long drink from his glass and leaned back. "Betta, now that the edge has been taken from our hunger, we can move on to the business part of this lunch. I will start at the beginning, as you requested. I was called just before eight this morning with the news that a body was found at the botanical gardens. Yes, Urbino has a very fine *orto botanico*, despite its size. The person who found the dead man was the chief gardener and knew the deceased well since he, the deceased, had donated funds and plants. So he told me immediately that it was Manuel Somonte, age seventy-one, a Spaniard with Italian dual citizenship, thanks to his Italian mother. I don't think I need to tell you about Somonte, Betta, since you must have researched him for the event in Sansepolcro, where he was to donate the drawing that you are so interested in finding."

Betta nodded but waited for DiMaio to continue. Rick took a sip of wine.

"When we got to the gardens we found Somonte's body leaning against a plant that ironically he had donated. Our murderer apparently has a sense of humor. Cause of death was a gunshot wound to the chest, and the initial estimate of the time of death is late last night. The autopsy will narrow it down, but that may not help us much. It is certain that he was killed on the spot; there was no indication that the body had been carried or dragged to where he was found. There were no reports of a gunshot in the neighborhood, but the vegetation and high walls of the gardens must have kept the sound inside."

"So he was either forced to go in because the gun was pointed at him, or he knew the person well and trusted him."

"That was my conclusion as well, Riccardo." DiMaio took a drink of the mineral water before continuing. "I couldn't get much out of his wife and the executive assistant this morning since Signora Somonte was almost hysterical, and neither of them speaks Italian. But I did find out that the last time they saw him was at an early afternoon lunch."

"They didn't have dinner with him?" Rick asked.

DiMaio shook his head. "Apparently not. The *signora* is suffering from a cold and had food sent up to the room. The assistant ate in the hotel dining room. They don't know where Somonte had dinner, or if he did at all, but the autopsy will tell us if he ate something."

Rick offered the last two olives to Betta, and when she declined, he spooned them to his plate. "It seems somewhat strange that they wouldn't know what the man did last night. Was it normal for him to wander off by himself?"

"That's what you can ask the wife and assistant, Riccardo. As I said, I couldn't get much out of them and hoped that she would calm down by the afternoon. I had asked for a Spanish speaker from the university to step in, but now that you're here, it won't be necessary. We'll put you on the payroll."

Rick thought for a moment. He had helped the police on various occasions, but it was always pro bono. Having official status in the investigation, even if only as a contract translator, could come in handy. "*Va bene*, Alfredo. I'll charge you my usual hourly rate."

Betta spoke. "Did the hotel clerk see him go out?"

"We called the guy at home," said DiMaio, "since he works nights, and his answer was yes. Somonte had appeared at the desk at precisely seven o'clock, just after the clerk came on duty, and asked to get something out of the hotel safe. That something was a leather briefcase. Somonte signed for the briefcase and left through the front door. The one thing I got out of the assistant this morning was that Somonte kept the drawing in that briefcase. If the clerk hadn't told me, I wouldn't know about your precious work of art, Betta."

"And it's a good thing," Betta said, "since the missing art is likely connected to the man's murder. Unless he didn't trust hotel security, he must have taken it with him to show it to someone." She closed her eyes in thought. "Had the hotel made any dinner reservations for him, or perhaps helped him with directions to walk somewhere?"

"No. I talked to the clerk who was on the desk during the day and who'd chatted with him in the afternoon. Somonte always stayed at the same hotel when he came to Urbino, which was apparently at least once a year, so the clerk knew him. They talked about the big exhibit that's about to open at the Galleria Nazionale delle Marche, since the hotel had a poster for it on the wall. The clerk didn't notice anything different about the Spaniard from the previous stays, and in fact, he said Somonte was in a good mood and looking forward to the exhibit opening."

"Somonte didn't mention the donation of the drawing?"

"I'm afraid not, Betta, and I asked the clerk that. Nor did Somonte say anything at all about driving down to Sansepolcro today."

"When did Somonte get into town?" Rick asked after a sip of wine.

"They checked into the hotel two days ago in the late morning after flying from Madrid to Florence and renting a car."

"What did they do between arrival and last evening?"

"That's something else I hope to get out of the assistant when we talk to him."

The empty plates were removed by yet another waiter who happened to be walking past the table. Service was a team effort, like as in most Italian restaurants.

Betta dabbed at her lips with the napkin. "If Somonte came to Urbino many times, he must have known a lot of people here, so the suspects list could be long. But if the murder was committed to get the drawing, that might exclude many of them. Such as the director of the botanical gardens."

"Who has the delightful name of Salvatore Florio. He showed up at the crime scene about the time I did. I asked him where he was last night, and his alibi was not strong, to say the least, but since Somonte was a donor to his gardens, it would seem that Florio would want to keep the man alive. I'm going to interview him again. I won't need you to translate, Riccardo."

Two waiters appeared. The first held a plate of the *vincisgrassi* in one hand and a bowl of grated cheese in the other, both of which he carefully arranged in front of Betta. The second waiter had the other two plates of pasta, which he put down with considerably less ceremony in front of Rick and DiMaio before he departed with his colleague. The three diners studied their dishes—multiple layers of paper-thin fresh pasta alternated with a rich meat sauce and béchamel—before Betta sprinkled some cheese and passed the bowl to the men. An already-strong aroma was made stronger by the melting Parmigiano-Reggiano.

"May I suggest," said Rick, picking up his fork, "that we speak of things other than murder and missing art while enjoying this wonderful food?"

They agreed, and the conversation turned to when they had met in Bassano del Grappa. Rick had been in town working as a translator for an international conference of art historians, and Betta was helping her father in his art gallery. They were all drawn together when one of the seminar participants was murdered and DiMaio was part of the investigation. Perhaps because they were now sitting in a restaurant, after reminiscing about the murder investigation, the subject of Bassano's cuisine was raised, specifically the town's famous white asparagus. They had not been in season then, so Rick had never tasted them, much to DiMaio's dismay. He urged Betta to take Rick back to Bassano during the annual asparagus festival.

Their pasta course finished, Betta returned to crime.

"One person we must interview, Alfredo, is the dealer who sold the drawing to Somonte in the first place. I asked my office to look it up in our files, and they were going to send me a text." She unzipped her purse and pulled out her phone. "Here it is— Ettore Bruzzone. His address is Via Raffaello 12."

"That's one of the main streets of Urbino," said DiMaio. "Named after the painter, of course, since his birthplace is on it. Now the building is a museum."

Rick recalled when he and his sister were dragged through Raphael's house and wondering what the big deal was. He now kept the thought to himself.

"Are you ready for the *secondo*?" DiMaio asked.

Rick and Betta exchanged glances and shook their heads. After all they had eaten already, they would pass on the second course. The policeman sighed and signaled to the waiter for the *conto*. "Before we get back to the case, should we not find you two lodging for the night? There's a small hotel just up the hill from here that will be perfect. I know the owner, and he'll have a nice room for you if I call him."

Betta folded her napkin and put it next to her empty plate. "That sounds perfect, Alfredo."

"It's on a narrow street with no place to park, so I'll have one of my men take you and your luggage up there."

Fifteen minutes later the patrol car turned off the main street and squeezed along one that could almost have been taken for an alley. The Hotel Botticelli would be described in the tourist brochures as cozy and warm, which was another way of saying it was small. But all the buildings on the street were as small as they were old. The owner greeted Rick and Betta like family and had his son show them to their room on the second floor. The boy was about thirteen and skinny, but he insisted on carrying the two suitcases up a narrow stairway and down the end of the hall. For being in a building dating to the fifteenth century, the room was spacious and included a modern bathroom. No closet, but a tall wood armoire stood wedged between the door and the wall. Rick tipped the boy and walked to the one window to take in the view. Its panes were just high enough to let him see over a sea of orange tiles, their scalloped waves broken by the occasional dark chimney. In the distance the dome and *campanile* of the cathedral formed the two highest points of the city, well above the twin towers of the Palazzo Ducale next to it. Church over state, Rick thought. How the Italians love symbolism. He turned to see Betta hanging up clothes she'd taken from the suitcase.

"Rick, I don't think I need to go along to watch you and Alfredo interview the wife. Why don't I go see the art dealer, Bruzzone? It's the missing drawing that interests my office, and I'd like to hear what he has to say about it."

"You don't think Alfredo would want to go along?"

"I'll take notes and brief him. Since I'm with the art police, it makes sense to divide up the labor this way. It's just a short distance from here, so I can walk to it."

Rick knew from hanging around his uncle that turf battles went hand in hand with police work, and this had the odor of at least a skirmish. Did he have a dog in the fight? Not really, but it could be fun to watch. "Whatever you think, Betta."

# CHAPTER THREE

They walked to the corner and parted ways, Betta turning left to walk up to Via Raffaello, Rick right toward the police station at the bottom of the hill. The steepness had him thinking about what route he would take on his morning run the next day. Always better to begin with a climb and end heading down a hill, so he would likely start in the direction Betta was walking, but he'd try to scout out the town more later. One thing was sure: the residents of Urbino had to be in good shape since it was all a pedestrian area, and inside the walls all hills. But it would not be walking for DiMaio. He was standing next to a police car in front of the *commissariato*, talking on his cell phone. He noticed Rick coming through the gate and nodded. By the time Rick reached him, the *telefonino* was back in Alfredo's coat pocket and he was opening the door to the car.

"Where's Betta?"

Rick got into the passenger seat as DiMaio slipped behind the wheel. "She walked up to Via Raffaello to talk to the art dealer who sold Somonte the drawing. Said you and I should be able to handle interviewing Signora Somonte by ourselves."

DiMaio started the engine and backed out of the space. "I'll talk to Bruzzone later."

Rick didn't know Alfredo well enough to interpret either the comment or the tone in which it was said. The man appeared to be deep in thought, which could be in reaction to Betta's going out on her own or something totally unrelated. A period of silence continued as the car made its way around the outside of the city, eventually pulling up in front of the Hotel Bella Vista. It sat on the edge of Urbino, green hills and valleys spread out below it, and in contrast to the buildings inside the walls, a new construction. DiMaio killed the engine but remained in the seat.

"The initial autopsy report was in when I got back to the office after lunch. It confirmed the cause of death as a gunshot to the chest. Entry indicated the weapon was about level with the wound, not shot from above or below. Small caliber. Stomach contents didn't reveal much. He had some pasta with a garlic sauce and bread, but the coroner suspects that it was from earlier in the day. I didn't think that would be something for us to ask Signora Somonte, so just before you arrived I called the Bella Vista and they're checking to see what he had for lunch. If it matches, then he was killed before he had an evening meal."

Rick hoped that the autopsy was what had been on the policeman's mind, not Betta's decision to interview Bruzzone herself. "What information do you want to get out of the widow right now?"

DiMaio pulled the keys from the ignition. "I have a list, but we'll have to be gentle given the shock of losing her husband. She was almost incoherent this morning. The assistant may be of more help." He opened the door, stepped onto the street, and strode up the stairs of the hotel with Rick behind him.

In his travels around Italy on his interpreter jobs, Rick had observed that hotels usually fell into one of two categories. The first was the type where he and Betta were now staying, an aged, repurposed building. In it the rooms were of all sizes and shapes, no one like another, including the furniture, and the bathrooms were squeezed into corners or carved out of adjoining space. Those were the hotels he preferred because they always had uniqueness and charm. The Hotel Bella Vista was the other type: modern, usually built outside the historical center, and mostly of glass and cement except for decorative stone in the reception area. The rooms were American style, opening off a long hallway, alike in their rectangular shape with the bathroom just inside the door. Furnishings were exactly the same in every room. The new hotels were efficient to build and run, there was no doubt about that, but Rick would take old and quirky over new and boring any day. The hotel Somonte had chosen was new and boring, beginning with the reception and waiting area lit by a garish chandelier, its light bouncing off the polished floor. Rick's eyes moved around the sterile space while DiMaio spoke to the clerk at the desk.

DiMaio turned back to Rick and jerked his thumb toward the far end of the room where two sets of doors opened to the restaurant and breakfast room. They walked past a clump of cushioned chairs and pushed open glass doors to enter the space where breakfast was served in the morning, coffee and other drinks the rest of the day. At the far end a long counter stood in front of a mirrored wall, with glasses, bottles, and the required espresso machine lined up neatly below it. All of the small tables with tablecloths were empty except one where Isabella Somonte and Lucho Garcia sat immersed in conversation. A clear glass tea mug rested next to a small pot in front of the woman. She was not what Rick expected.

The widow Somonte was, at the very least, twenty years younger than her late husband. Her features were sharp, with too much makeup for Rick's tastes, especially since she had enough natural beauty to not need it. He had the feeling that holding on to her good looks as long as possible was the woman's top priority. While she could not be faulted for not packing mourning clothes on the trip, he was surprised by the garish outfit she was wearing. Tall leather boots stopped just below her knees, a leopard-skin print skirt just above them. The high collar of a pea-green angora sweater came up to her dangling earrings, and everything was topped by long, blond hair. This was not an outfit, it was a getup.

Lucho Garcia was a contrast with his boss's widow. To begin with, he was younger, probably in his late twenties, and his clothes were subdued to the point of drabness: white shirt with a conservative striped tie, blue blazer, gray slacks. He wore his hair long, just covering his ears, which, along with a clean-shaven face, accentuated his youthful looks.

As Rick sized up the two, he wondered, given the age of the deceased, if they shared something more than a connection with Manuel Somonte, and then berated himself for such cynicism. Señora Somonte looked up and noticed the two men coming to their table. She squinted at Rick, from which he concluded that she needed glasses but was too vain to wear them.

Rick introduced himself in Spanish, explaining that he was a professional interpreter and was there to help the inspector. Garcia asked if they wanted coffee or something else to drink. Rick and DiMaio declined and sat down. DiMaio took out his notebook and nodded to Rick.

"May I offer my deepest condolences, Señora," Rick began, causing her to remove a tissue from her pocket. He expected it to go to her eyes, but instead she blew her nose and stuffed it back into the pocket. "The inspector knows this is a difficult time, but—"

"Has he found my husband's murderer yet, or not?" The voice was hoarse, but he couldn't tell if that was her normal way of speaking or caused by her cold.

"Not yet, Señora, which is why he wanted to talk to you again. He's hoping you can help in the investigation." Rick quickly translated the initial exchange for DiMaio and returned his attention to the woman. "Can you tell us about your husband's activities after you arrived here from Spain? Who he might have met, where he went in Urbino?"

While they waited for an answer, she once again took out the handkerchief from her pocket and dabbed at her nose, all the while staring intently at Rick. He assumed she was gathering her thoughts for a long discourse. Instead, she rose to her feet. The other three men stood as well.

"I thought you were coming here to tell me who did this terrible act to my beloved husband. Instead you have done nothing and then you want to interrogate me. I will have none of it. Lucho can answer your questions. I am ill and will return to my room." She took two steps, stopped, and turned. "It is that cursed drawing. If not for it, Manuel would be alive today." She walked quickly to the doors, her boot heels clicking.

"It appears," said DiMaio, "that Signora Somonte does not wish to answer any questions. That is unfortunate."

Garcia turned to Rick. "Please tell the inspector that Señora Somonte is not herself because of her illness and of course the loss of her husband. I'm sure anything you needed to know from her I can tell you, since I was Señor Somonte's special assistant." He spoke with the thick Castilian lisp that would have raised eyebrows among Rick's Chicano friends in New Mexico.

"Tell him we will have to talk to her eventually." DiMaio was not happy.

Rick told him, and then repeated the question asked of the widow. What followed was Rick's normal consecutive interpretation routine, moving between Garcia and the policeman.

"Señor Somonte has been to Urbino many times, and knows several people, most of them connected to his love of Italian art. We arrived in Urbino the day before yesterday, in the afternoon, in the rental car we picked up at the airport. After checking in here, he struck out on his own while the señora went to the room and rested. The cabin pressure had made her cold worse. I stayed here and made business phone calls that he had requested."

"Did he say where he was going?"

Garcia leaned back in his chair. "Not directly, but a few days before I had put calls through for him to two of his acquaintances here in Urbino, so he could have gone to see them. One was Ettore Bruzzone, an art dealer, the man who sold him the Piero della Francesca drawing that was to be donated to the museum in Sansepolcro. The other was a man named Cosimo Morelli, a local businessman. I don't know when Señor Somonte got back to the hotel, but he wanted an early dinner here so I could tell him about the phone calls I'd made. It was just the two of us; Señora Somonte had food sent up to her room. I assume he turned in after dinner; it had been a long day for a man of his age."

"What about yesterday?"

"The only time I saw him was when the three of us had lunch. It was here in the hotel again, because of the señora's cold. But at least she was able to come to the dining room."

"What had he been doing that morning?"

The question made Garcia shake his head. "He didn't say. The conversation was mostly about business, the files I had been working on before lunch. His wife spent the meal looking at her cell phone. One thing he did mention, outside of work, was that he was looking forward to seeing the exhibit that is opening tomorrow night. In fact this whole trip, including the donation of the drawing, was planned around that opening. He had received a special invitation to attend from the museum director."

"We will have to talk to the museum director," said DiMaio after Rick translated. "I'd like to know more about our new widow. Please see what you can get out of him."

"Why not?" answered Rick before turning back to Garcia. "Had the Somontes been married very long?"

Garcia gave a weak cough before answering. "He married her soon after the passing of his first wife, three years ago." He looked from one face to the other. "She had worked as a secretary in one of his wool mills."

The Spaniard shrugged, as if nothing more needed to be said, and it occurred to Rick that if Betta had been along, the man wouldn't have said even that much. He asked DiMaio what else he should ask.

"Ask him if Somonte had a cell phone. We didn't find one on the body. Also, could he have any papers or documents in his room that might be helpful? I don't want to ask Signora Somonte, but we will if we have to."

Rick translated the question for Garcia.

"He always carried a cell phone. *Dios mio*, could he have been killed for a cell phone? As far as papers, there was his notebook. You should find it in his room."

"But we don't want to disturb—"

"No, no, Señor Montoya. He had his own room. Because of his wife's cold, of course."

—

Betta had climbed the steep street, glad that she was wearing comfortable, thick-soled shoes. The afternoon shoppers were beginning to appear, along with tourists who wandered about holding tight to their guide books and maps. Before reaching the corner, she passed a wine bar, a sign on the door indicating that it would open at six, and she thought it might be a good place for them to go before dinner. Often such places had good samplings of *antipasto*, so it might even be perfect as an alternative to a full meal. She passed a tiny *gelateria* and came to the Piazza della Repubblica where the main arteries of Urbino intersected. To the right, Via Vittorio Veneto climbed to the Palazzo Ducale, the most famous building in the city. She turned left up the steep Via Raffaello, passing the facade of the San Francesco church, suppressing the desire to take a quick peek inside. Cultural tourism would have to wait for another day.

Galleria Bruzzone, at number 12, was smaller than she had expected. Her frame of reference for commercial art galleries began with her father's business in Bassano del Grappa. That was a large, well-lit room with sufficient space to hang a dozen paintings easily, whereas Bruzzone's shop was small, narrow, and dark. The few paintings she saw as she entered were miniatures in ornate frames, displayed in a case like rings in a jewelry store. She looked through the glass and decided they were nineteenth century and not Italian. The dates and Germanic name on the title cards confirmed both suppositions, but it was not an artist she had ever heard of. Her office had enough missing Italian masterpieces to deal with; they didn't need to be looking for lost foreign art.

She had heard a bell sound somewhere in the back of the gallery when she came in, and now a door in the rear opened and a man emerged pulling on a suit jacket. He was tall, about the same height as Rick, with a well-trimmed, gray goatee surrounding a kindly smile. He bent forward as he walked, adding some years to Betta's guess as to the man's age. Early sixties was what she decided.

"Good afternoon. May I be of assistance?"

Betta pulled a business card from her pocket and handed it to him. "My name is Betta Innocenti. I'm an investigator with the art police in Rome."

Bruzzone pulled a pair of glasses from his jacket pocket, slipped them on, and studied the card. His face changed to a puzzled frown. "I'm familiar with your office, of course, and certainly hope my gallery is not suspected of dealing in stolen art."

"No, sir, that is not the case at all."

The smile returned. "Why don't you come back to my office and you can tell me how I can help. I am always ready to assist the authorities." He gestured toward the open door. "You'll have to excuse the clutter. I hope eventually to move somewhere that gives me more room to display art, in addition to having a larger office. But that would be a large expense, and also I would lose this excellent location. What better address could there be for selling art than Via Raffaello? His birthplace is just up the street, you know. Have you been?"

"Not yet, but I hope to visit it while I'm here."

He was accurate about size and clutter. The office was really a spacious closet, much of its square footage taken up by a desk with chairs on both sides. A credenza ran along almost all of one wall, its surface shared by stacks of files and a printer. The desk had more papers stacked up and a laptop computer. A corkboard stuck with more sheets of paper, exhibit programs, and drawings took up most of the back wall, and everything was illuminated by gray light from a fluorescent lamp hanging from the ceiling. Betta took the chair that was just inside the door on the right facing the side of the desk. She looked at the bulletin board behind the desk while Bruzzone squeezed around to sit across from her. He folded his hands on the papers in front of him.

"I trust you are aware, Signor Bruzzone, that Manuel Somonte arrived in Urbino two days ago."

"Yes, indeed. I saw him yesterday."

"Perhaps you are not aware that he was found dead this morning."

Bruzzone's face froze. "I...I was not aware of that. How tragic." He rubbed his forehead and spent a moment trying to compose himself. "He was not a young man, but he appeared to be in good health for his age when I saw him. He dropped in, as he always does—or I should now say *did*—when he was in town, to see if I had any pieces of interest for him. I showed him the miniatures in the cases, though I knew they aren't the kind of art he purchased."

"Signor Bruzzone, Somonte was murdered."

The man stiffened and swallowed hard. "*O Dio*. How...? But who would do such a thing?" He stared at the desk and slowly lifted his head to look directly at Betta. "I don't understand. This is a matter for the local police—why would your office be involved?"

"I'm sure Inspector DiMaio will want to talk to you, but I am here because the drawing that Somonte was going to donate to the museum in Sansepolcro has gone missing."

This bit of news seemed to upset the art dealer more than hearing about the death of Somonte. "That is indeed terrible.

Just terrible." His mouth stayed open, but no more words came out.

Betta broke the silence and zipped open the case she was carrying, taking out a notebook. "I thought that since you sold it to him, you could be of help in tracking it down. You could begin by telling me—" She looked past him at the board where a piece of paper at a crooked angle was stuck to the cork with a pushpin. Bruzzone followed her eyes and turned around to look.

"Oh, I forgot that was there. You must have seen the finished work in Sansepolcro. Yes, that is a copy of the drawing. Before I sold it to Somonte I made the copy and stuck it up there to remind me of the sale. Such transactions have been few and far between for me lately." He reached behind him and pulled it from the wall, the pushpin falling onto the floor. "Would it be of help to your investigation? Perhaps you could show it around the city to see if anyone has seen it."

"Thank you, but I have pictures of the drawing itself on my telephone."

He pulled a pin from another corner of the board and stuck the copy back in its place. "You were saying how I could be of assistance?"

"You could begin by telling me something of the drawing's provenance. I don't think we have anything in our files in Rome."

"Yes, of course. This was one of those cases that we art dealers dream about. Out of the blue an old woman walked into my shop and offered it to me. She said she came upon it in a trunk in her storage shed and wondered if it was worth anything. Can you believe that?" He shook his head slowly as if he still couldn't believe it himself. "I studied it carefully, consulted a specialist about Piero's various studies for the work in Sansepolcro, and concluded that it was the genuine item.

The woman was unable to tell me how it got into her trunk, of course; it had been there for centuries. There is simply no way of knowing that kind of thing. But she and I were the beneficiaries of the find. It wasn't the same as discovering a full painting by the master—that would be worth millions—but for a dealer like me, such a drawing was a once-in-a-lifetime transaction."

Betta had pen and paper in hand but had written nothing. "Can you give me the name and address of this woman, to put in our files?"

"I'm sure I have it." Bruzzone got up from the chair and squeezed past the desk to the credenza. He opened its door and pulled out a small filing box that might have started its life holding a new pair of shoes. Back at the desk, he opened the box and shuffled through a line of cards. "Here it is." He passed a card to Betta, who wrote down the information and returned it to him.

"Interesting that she lives in Monterchi. That's near Sansepolcro, which would make sense."

"Yes," Bruzzone said, "at about a dozen kilometers, it's easy to reach from Sansepolcro, even in Piero's time. Also, Piero's *Madonna del Parto* hangs in a museum in Monterchi, so there's a strong connection between the artist and the town. Not as much as he had with Sansepolcro, his birthplace, but enough so that it is not surprising the drawing turned up there."

It crossed Betta's mind that a person in Monterchi could have wanted the drawing, someone unhappy that it had not stayed in the town. Unhappy enough to commit murder to get it and then not be able to display it? That didn't make sense.

"When you recover the drawing," said Bruzzone, "it will be turned over to the museum in Sansepolcro, I assume?"

Betta tapped her pen on the notebook. It was an interesting question and not something she had considered. "I don't know if a document was signed already formalizing the donation. If not, I would assume that the drawing would become the property of the heirs, most likely Signora Somonte."

Bruzzone leaned back and folded his hands in his lap. "In that case, she could then go ahead with the donation as her husband had wished, or keep the drawing herself, or sell it."

She saw what he might be getting at and didn't want to go there. "Those questions are something the ministry's legal department would have to work out, so I shouldn't speculate. My assignment is to find the drawing." She closed her notebook.

"I understand. I can't help thinking that there are those in this city who were not happy that it was going to Sansepolcro and now might try to convince her to keep it here. I'm talking, of course, about the Galleria Nazionale delle Marche. Vitellozzi was very upset when he found out that Somonte was going to send the drawing down to that small museum."

"Vitellozzi?"

"Annibale Vitellozzi, the director of the museum. I'm sure you'll meet him in the course of your inquiries."

Betta reopened her notebook and wrote down the name. "That's very helpful, Signor Bruzzone. Is there anyone else you could suggest I talk with?"

He stroked his goatee in thought. "Well, someone else you'll likely encounter anyway, since this is such a small town and the arts community is even smaller, is Cosimo Morelli, an extremely wealthy local businessman. Cosimo has the largest private art collection in Urbino, with some very important pieces. When you meet him he will invite you to see them—he always does."

Betta wrote down the name. "Morelli would seem like the kind of person to have purchased Piero's drawing."

Bruzzone nodded, and a smile formed on his lips. "He tried. But Somonte outbid him."

———

Somonte's room was a small suite on the top floor of the hotel with a sweeping view of the hills north of Urbino. DiMaio had gone immediately to the front desk to stop the cleaning staff, or anyone else, from entering the room but was too late. When they opened the door, using a key given them at the front desk, the suite had been made up and everything was in order. Since Somonte had left his key when he'd gone out the previous evening, it was clear that the murder had taken place somewhere else. Nevertheless, something relevant to the crime might have been changed by the housekeeping crew.

The suite consisted of three rooms. The door from the hallway opened to a sitting area, taken up mostly by a sofa and two chairs with a view out of a large window. Against one of the walls was a bar, including a small sink, with glasses and bottles of liquor lining a shelf above and a small refrigerator below. Rick opened the refrigerator and found small bottles of prosecco as well as an assortment of juices and soft drinks. The only item somewhat out of place sat on the bar counter, a half-full bottle of sherry. It was Spanish, and not a label familiar to Rick, though he was not an expert on sherry, let alone imported brands. While he checked out the bar, DiMaio was looking at papers on a desk at the other side of the room.

"This might be something."

Rick put down the bottle and walked to where Alfredo was thumbing through a small notebook, bound in leather, with the name Manuel Somonte and the year stamped on the outside. "This was sitting on top of the desk. Somonte's agenda. The notations for this week are mostly names and phone numbers, likely people he wanted to see during his stay, but unfortunately it doesn't say when or if he met with them. Can you read his writing better than I can?" He passed the book to Rick.

The penmanship was crude with small flourishes on some of the letters, the handwriting of someone from another generation. "I would imagine Somonte kept personal notes here and that his assistant takes care of business-related appointments, probably with a more modern system than scribbling in a notebook." He felt the vibration of his phone and pulled it from his pocket. "It's a text from Betta. She probably didn't want to call, thinking we might still be in our interview downstairs." He read from the phone screen: "I got names of people Alfredo should interview. Shall I meet you at the commissariato?" Rick looked up from the phone. "Are we going back there when we're done here?"

"I think we're done already, Riccardo. I'll take a quick look in the bedroom, but I don't expect to find anything of interest. Maybe the names she has are the same ones in that little book in your hand."

# CHAPTER FOUR

The two names Betta got from the gallery owner—Morelli, the art collector, and Vitellozzi of the museum—were in Somonte's little book, as were Bruzzone himself and Florio, the director of the botanical gardens. DiMaio sat at his desk, his left hand holding open the book and the other slowly writing the four names and telephone numbers on a legal pad.

"The hotel checked the phone records, and Somonte made no calls from his room. If he called anyone on this list he must have done it on his *telefonino*, the same phone that was not found on his body. That was very inconsiderate of the murderer to take it. I would have thought that having the Piero drawing would have been enough." He dropped the pen on the desk and looked up at Rick and Betta. "Well, we have people to interview, it appears. Betta, you talked already with Bruzzone— what did you glean from the conversation?"

DiMaio rubbed his eyes. Rick could not decide if the gesture indicated annoyance with Betta for unilaterally going off to interview the art dealer or simply fatigue.

She already had her notebook on her lap. "The two names, of course. The more suspicious has to be Morelli, the art collector.

It was he who lost out on getting the drawing, so he was obviously not happy with Somonte for that, and hearing that it was going to be donated to a museum might have added salt to the wound." She looked up, waiting for a reaction from DiMaio. When it didn't come, she continued. "The other, Annibale Vitellozzi, is, as I see it, somewhat less likely to have murdered Somonte, but he was surely annoyed that his museum was not chosen to receive the donation of the drawing. That by itself would be a weak motive for murder."

"I agree," said DiMaio. He picked up the phone on his desk and made three short phone calls while Rick and Betta listened. After he hung up the phone for the third time he looked at his two visitors. "I think you got most of that. Florio, the botanical gardens director, will be waiting for me in his office at the university when we're done here. Morelli is in Pesaro on business, driving back tonight. He will come here to the *commissariato* tomorrow morning. Vitellozzi is extremely busy getting this big exhibit ready to open, but he can be interviewed at the museum tomorrow. Betta, why don't you go talk to him, since you're here for the art squad?"

She nodded, and Rick was relieved that Alfredo didn't appear concerned about having an art cop on his turf. The relief didn't last long.

DiMaio turned to a fresh page of the pad in front of him. "Where did Bruzzone say he was around the time of the murder?"

Betta flushed. "I didn't ask him. I was so focused on the provenance of the drawing that I forgot."

DiMaio nodded slowly before speaking again. "And what did you learn about the drawing?"

"It was discovered in Monterchi," Betta said quickly. "I thought it would be useful to go down there and talk to the woman who found it and sold it to Bruzzone."

Another nod from the policeman. "I fail to see how that would be relevant to my investigation, but I'm sure the art police would like to know more about this drawing. You two can drive down to Monterchi after talking to Vitellozzi at the museum."

The awkward silence was interrupted by a knock on the door. "*Avanti.*"

"Excuse the interruption, Inspector." It was the uniformed sergeant they had passed at the front desk on the way to the office. "There is a woman in the waiting room who insists on seeing the officer in charge of the murder investigation. Her name is Pilar Somonte."

The words jolted DiMaio. "The daughter. I was told Somonte had a daughter, but I didn't expect her to show up here. Bring her in, Sergeant." Rick and Betta got to their feet. "No, no, Riccardo, you must stay. Thank goodness you're here to inter- pret. I would have had to deal with another Spanish harridan by myself. And, Betta, please sit down as well. This woman will realize that the case of her father's death is so important that we have brought specialists up from Rome." He stood up, rushed to a corner where another chair sat empty, and carried it to the front of the desk next to Rick. "There, that's perfect. You can do your interpreting magic."

The door was pushed open by the sergeant, and Pilar Somonte entered.

It might have been a very distant Viking visitor to northern Spain who was responsible for her golden blond hair—it was not a dye job. She wore it shoulder length but held back on one side by a gold barrette that exposed a matching gold earring. Her lightweight wool sweater and matching skirt, as well as her slim figure and features, could have walked off the runway at a Milan fashion house.

Rick, who along with DiMaio was standing, approached

and shook her hand. "My name is Ricardo Montoya," he said in Spanish. "Inspector DiMaio has asked me to interpret. May I also present Betta Innocenti from Rome who is assisting on the investigation. Let me first express our deepest condolences on the loss of your father."

After shaking Rick's hand she looked at Betta, then at DiMaio, but didn't move. Her expression was one of incomprehension, making Rick wonder if he'd spoken the words correctly. Then she smiled.

"Thank you, Riccardo. I very much appreciate the offer, but I don't believe your services will be necessary." Her Italian was almost without accent. She walked first to Betta, then to DiMaio, and shook their hands before sitting in one of the chairs. "As you probably know, my grandmother was Italian, and my father always maintained a strong relationship with this country. He insisted that I learn Italian at the *liceo* and then sent me to Florence for a year to study design."

DiMaio finally found his tongue, but barely. "So that's why you speak Italian so well, Signora."

"*Bravo*, Inspector. But please call me Pilar." She looked at Betta and Rick. "We all seem to be about the same age here, so why don't we dispense with the formalities?" When they agreed, she continued. "Riccardo, I detected an accent in your Spanish that is certainly not from Spain."

"You are correct, Pilar. My father is from America, New Mexico, and I went to university there. My Spanish reflects that. And I go by Rick."

"And Betta, you work in Rome, but are you from there originally?"

"No, Pilar. I am from Bassano del Grappa, in the Veneto."

"Bassano. A delightful city. I love your famous covered bridge over the Mincio."

Rick had expected that they would be the ones putting Pilar Somonte at ease, but it turned out to be just the opposite. DiMaio was enthralled.

"Alfredo, I'll find out about you later since you must be anxious to get down to the case at hand. I should say here at the outset that I have been expecting for a while to get news of my father's death, since he was not a well man. Naturally, I thought his illness would be the cause of his demise, so it was a shock when Lucho called to tell me he had been murdered." She took a breath to maintain her composure before continuing.

"Driving here from the airport, I recalled something my father said to me just after he was diagnosed with the illness he thought would eventually take his life. We were sitting in his office, just the two of us." She held the back of her hand over her mouth for a moment. "He began by telling me something I'd heard so many times before, how much Italy, and especially Tuscany, meant to him. His mother was born in Anghiari, at the eastern edge of Tuscany. It was thanks to her, he said, that he held such a deep love of Italian art. He pointed to an old photograph he always kept on his desk, of him and my grandmother, taken on a visit to Anghiari when he was a boy. As he looked at the two figures he said, 'When it's time, I want to die in Tuscany.' I told him that he wasn't going anywhere for a while, or some such platitude, and we changed the subject. But what he said that day has always stuck in my mind, and I've often thought that he may have been talking more to the photograph than to me."

A difficult silence was broken by Betta. "Urbino isn't Tuscany, but there are few places in Italy identified as strongly with art as this city. He came here often, didn't he?"

"Yes. Yes, he did." She waved a hand in the air, pushing away the memory, and turned her attention to DiMaio. "But I don't

want that story to give you a false impression of my relationship with my father, especially in the last few years. I must tell
you that ever since my mother's death several years ago, and his
subsequent marriage to Isabella, my father and I had become
somewhat estranged. It had been no secret that my mother
was dying, but did that woman keep in the shadows and allow
him to deal with it? No, she was shameless in her pursuit of my
father, even while my mother was fading."

She looked at a bottle of mineral water on the desk. DiMaio
got the message, poured some into a cup, and passed it to her.
She took a sip and set the cup down next to her.

"Thank you, Alfredo. I never hid my feelings from him about
his remarrying, and especially to that woman, so, inevitably,
we drifted apart. Our relationship became less father-daughter
and more owner-employee, since I am chief of design at the
mills." She crossed one leg over the other and straightened
her skirt over her knee. "Pardon the long explanation, but I
thought you should know. Now, can you tell me how all this
happened? I couldn't get much out of Lucho when he called
me early this morning."

DiMaio carefully went over the facts of the case as he knew
them, without giving too much detail about the condition of
the body. He told her what information he and Rick had gotten from Signora Somonte and Lucho Garcia, and the meager
results from the search of her father's room.

"We are now at the point of interviewing others who might
have seen your father before he was killed. Since the missing
drawing may be the motive for the crime, Betta was sent here
from Rome to assist in the case. She works in the office that
investigates stolen art."

"This is the first I've heard about the drawing going missing," said Pilar. "Lucho didn't mention that detail when he

called. Do you really think my father might have been killed for a drawing?"

"It's very valuable," Betta volunteered. "We have had cases of murders committed or planned for artwork of lesser value."

Pilar shook her head and turned to Rick. "Do you work here at the university?"

"No, I'm a professional interpreter based in Rome. And a friend of Betta."

"Ah." She smiled at Betta and turned to the policeman. "Well, Alfredo, what comes next, and is there any way I can help? Or do you just want me to stay out of your way?"

"You most certainly will not be in my way, Pilar. I was about to go to the botanical gardens to interview the director. I assume you have a rental car? You can leave it here and I can drop you at the hotel on the way. Or have you already checked in?"

She held up a delicate hand. "I won't stay at the same hotel as that woman."

DiMaio looked at Rick and Betta. "I think I can find you a room somewhere else."

—

The botany department of the university was conveniently located just behind the botanical gardens. Windows on the lower two floors of the building looked across the narrow street at the walls of the gardens, not an especially picturesque view, but not one unusual for Urbino inside the city walls, where buildings were stuffed together. When marauders menaced in the old days it was better to be living safely in cramped quarters than out in the countryside, despite less than ideal sanitary conditions. With the advent of modern indoor plumbing, heating, and air-conditioning, these buildings became fashionable, and had the university not purchased this one years earlier, it might have been out of its price range.

The office of Professor Salvatore Florio had the best view in the department. Through two small windows it looked past the street and over the wall to the treetops of the botanical gardens. For Florio, however, catching the sunlight was more important than getting the full view. The windowsills were lined with pots, as was the floor below where plants spread out into corners, with lamps supplementing the natural light. The three outer edges of his desk bore a prickly wall of cacti, some more menacing than others. It was this sea of greens and browns that greeted DiMaio as he entered the office. His first thought was to wonder how long it took to water the pots every day. It flashed through his head that Florio could easily blend in among the trees across the street. He was long-necked and awkwardly tall, wore a loose-fitting brown wool suit, and had a mop of unkempt hair that constantly needed to be pushed aside so he could see through his frameless glasses.

The professor motioned to the lone empty chair. "Please sit down, Inspector. I hope I can be of some assistance in your investigation. As you might imagine, the death of Signor Somonte was a great shock to those of us connected to the gardens. He was a generous benefactor."

Florio's high-pitched voice went well with his body type. DiMaio carefully maneuvered his way between pots, looked down to be sure the seat was plant-free, and eased himself into its cushion. "Thank you, Professor. Can I begin by asking when Somonte became involved with the gardens?" He moved his head slightly to see around a rabbit-ear cactus that partially blocked his view of Florio.

"Certainly. It was a few years ago. An Italian friend of his discovered his interest in flora and suggested he visit.

Fortunately, I was there that day and we became acquainted. He was impressed with our history—as you may know, the gardens date back to 1806—and also with the plants. He was quite taken with our *acrogymnospermae* collection, especially a spectacular *Encephalartos sclavoi*. Botanists come from all over Europe to see it."

DiMaio had his pen and notebook at the ready but had written nothing. "The plant where his body was found was his donation."

"Exactly. It and other plants he gave us were formally received about two years ago, in a ceremony conducted by the rector of the university. Perhaps you read about it in the newspaper or saw it on the television news."

"That was before my time here." He wrote a few words on his pad. "Who was the person who suggested he visit the gardens that first time?"

Florio rubbed his chin in thought. "Let me think. I believe it was someone from the museum. Vitellozzi? Yes, that's it, Vitellozzi. I don't know his first name. Somonte was very much interested in art, Inspector. I'm not sure if you were aware of that. I have a theory about the murder that I thought of this morning. I think—"

"We are aware of his interest in art, Professor. In fact, a piece of art in Somonte's possession is missing, and possibly that was the reason he was killed."

Florio's eyes widened and appeared even wider through the glasses. "I was not aware of that. Goodness me, that does complicate things—and it destroys my theory. You see, Inspector, I am a careful reader of *gialli*, especially those of the late Andrea Camilleri, so I cannot help but put this murder in the context of others I have read about."

It was not what DiMaio wanted to hear. He didn't need the

advice from someone who had read a lot of murder mysteries, but he remained polite. "When was the last time you saw Somonte alive?"

Florio swallowed hard, making his Adam's apple even more prominent. "I did not mention it to you this morning, what with the shock of finding his body, but I saw him yesterday. He came by the gardens, as he always does when he comes to Urbino."

"Did he seem preoccupied about anything? Was he different from his other visits?"

Florio could not hide his pleasure. "That is a question that Inspector Montalbano often asks witnesses, and I was wondering if you would ask me as well. No, Somonte was the same as ever, very attentive to the plants, asking questions about soil and nutrients. He was very knowledgeable for an amateur botanist."

DiMaio tapped his pad with the pen. "There is something I neglected to ask this morning. Who has keys to the gardens? I assume you do not leave the gate open after hours."

The Adam's apple bobbed once more. "I have one, of course." He opened the drawer and rifled through its contents before holding up a large, copper key and then putting it back. "Others? Our head gardener, Nino. Two women who collect the entrance fees from visitors and sell postcards. After visiting the gardens, people often pick up a postcard or two to send to friends, but they are mostly the older visitors. Young people just take pictures on their phones. We don't mind; it still gets the word out about the gardens, and that's the important thing since we are always trying to get more visitors. Revenue is critical in keeping the gardens going, since they sit on some very valuable real estate."

"Was there a chance the gate was left open yesterday after the gardens closed?"

"Oh, I don't think so, Inspector. I will check, but I'm sure they locked up as they always do."

"I'll need the names and contact information for those other people with keys." He pulled out a card and stretched it over the cacti to Florio's hand. "You can email it to me. That's all of them?"

"Well, Somonte had his key, of course."

DiMaio's head jerked up. "Somonte?"

"Sorry, I was assuming you knew. It was given to him in that ceremony when he formally donated all the plants. It was the rector's idea, like giving him the key to the city. Purely symbolic, of course, since I would let him into the gardens whenever he wanted, but he appreciated the gesture and carried it with him. It was a real key."

"How many people knew he had that key?"

Florio shrugged. "All of us did, of course. But also anyone who had read the story in the newspaper or seen the report on TV. Wait, I can show you." He went to another of the drawers behind the desk, found a tan file, and opened it on the desk. "Here it is."

He passed a tattered newspaper clipping over the cacti to DiMaio. The picture at the top of the story showed Somonte, flanked by Florio and a well-dressed man the caption identified as the rector, the three standing in front of tall plants. Somonte was holding up his key, hanging from a ribbon. Everyone smiled.

DiMaio read through the story, passed it back to Florio, and rose to his feet. "Thank you for your time, Professor. If there's anything else that comes to mind, you know how to reach me."

"Of course. Here, let me show you to the door." He squeezed around the desk. "I will also be revising my theories about this crime. Perhaps I can be of assistance." He pointed to the wall. "Did you see this, Inspector?"

Having been overwhelmed by all the plants, DiMaio had not noticed the framed photograph. A balding, round-faced man sat at a restaurant table behind a plate of pasta, and leaning down over the man's shoulder was a beaming Florio. The look on the man's face said he was not pleased that his meal had been interrupted.

"Andrea Camilleri, of course," said Florio. "I suggested a plot line he could use. He might have been planning to use it in his next book, but of course he passed away. Such a tragedy for mystery readers."

—

The restaurant consisted of one room, rectangular and large, with high ceilings. All the tables were full, but despite the numbers of diners, the noise level was low. It may have been due to the roof design, pitched and strengthened with heavy crossbeams, but more likely it was due to the reluctance of the diners to raise their voices. The elegance of the place—white tablecloths and star-shaped glass chandeliers hanging from the beams—called for polite conversation. This was very different from the *trattoria* where Rick, Betta, and DiMaio had lunch. Adding to the difference was the presence of Pilar Somonte. She was as elegant as before, and DiMaio had shaved and changed into a better suit.

"When he's not watering his plants, he reads mysteries," said DiMaio after describing his encounter with Professor Florio.

Their wineglasses were half-filled with a ruby-tinted Rosso Cònero as they awaited the arrival of the first course. They had made it easy on the cook by all ordering the same dish, *gnocchetti al ragu di cinghiale,* which the waiter said was a specialty of the house. The red wine they'd chosen, he assured them, would be a perfect match for the rich wild boar sauce on the small gnocchi.

"So do I," said Pilar. "Read mysteries, I mean, not water plants."

"But you don't presume to tell us police how to do our jobs because you've read every book by Andrea Camilleri."

"I'm a big fan of Camilleri," said Rick while taking a piece of bread from the basket in the middle of the table. "Except for how Montalbano refuses to talk during meals."

Betta nodded. "I always found that a bit strange myself."

DiMaio shook his head. "Why don't we talk about something other than mystery books? Like Pilar's work in the wool business."

"That's kind of you, Alfredo, but there isn't that much to tell, really. I work mostly with our clients so that we produce the patterns they need in the right fabric texture. They plan ahead, so we're now working on next spring's fashions, mostly lightweight wools like this one." She wore a beige sweater with a subtle blue stripe.

Betta looked at Rick and turned to Pilar. "Will you now have a larger role in the business? Perhaps I shouldn't bring that up."

"No, no, that's all right. My father has left the business to me, which is what I assume you are asking. I haven't talked to the family attorney since flying here, but it's what my father told me a few years ago, after he remarried. That woman will get the house, as well as their summer home on Minorca, along with a sizable number of euros in the form of a trust. She will be able to live comfortably the rest of her life without having to stick her nose into the business. The mill is mine."

Everyone noticed that her voice had hardened.

"It appears that your father didn't leave any detail to chance," said DiMaio. "In my experience, that is not always the case, and sometimes the fighting over an inheritance can go on for years. Even though you and your father were estranged, as you said this afternoon, you should be grateful to him for what he did to avoid such unpleasantness."

"I suppose so, but I'm afraid it was more his need for control, even after he was gone." The table was silent, and Pilar quickly sensed the discomfort around her. "But to answer your question, Betta, I was not expecting my father to live much longer. And because of that I have put some thought into changes I might make when it happened."

"You can make all the changes you like when you move into your father's office," said Rick.

Pilar picked up her glass and studied it. Light from the chandelier above the table rippled through the wine as she slowly swirled it. "I'm not sure I'll take over the office. I quite enjoy my work now, and I may not have what is needed to manage the entire operation. It's always wise to know one's strengths as well as one's limitations."

"So you'll hire a manager."

"That's one possibility, Riccardo."

"I'm guessing you won't keep Lucho Garcia on the payroll."

She thought for a moment before answering. "Actually, Lucho is very good at what he does. He had to be, or my father would not have kept him as his assistant. If I hire a new general manager rather than take over the company myself, it would be wise to keep Lucho in place. At this point, he's the institutional memory. But we'll see."

The pasta course arrived. With four plates, the gamey aroma of the wild boar and tomato dominated the air over the table. After exchanging wishes of *buon appetito*, they began eating.

"Perhaps Montalbano is correct," said Rick, "and we should refrain from speaking while eating this dish." The silence lasted only to the third bite.

"I had a call from Bruzzone," said DiMaio. "Pilar, he's the art dealer who sold your father the drawing. He wanted to know how the investigation was progressing and sounded very agitated."

"He was quite shaken when I told him the news," said Betta.

"My father gave him a lot of business, more than just the drawing. Every time he returned from here, he would show me what he'd acquired. It was one of the few interactions I had with him outside of discussing fabrics, since he knew I love Italy as much as he did. It's understandable that Bruzzone would be upset, losing such a good client."

"Did Bruzzone have anything new to add?" Rick asked.

"I didn't talk with him very long. I set up a formal interview for tomorrow morning."

Everyone was finishing their gnocchi when a chirping sound got their attention. Pilar pulled open the purse that hung from her chair back, pulled out her phone, and checked the number. "Excuse me," she said. "I have to take this." She got to her feet and walked toward the door of the restaurant while putting the phone to her ear. Rick and DiMaio, who had stood up when she did, sat back in their chairs.

"Alfredo," said Betta, "we were a bit surprised to see Pilar with you when we arrived here tonight."

"You thought she would be in mourning and not want to come out?"

"No, no. Not that…"

"You think she's a suspect, Betta? If I'm not mistaken, Pilar was in Spain when her father was killed."

Rick noticed the edge in the policeman's words. "Alfredo, it makes perfect sense to talk with Pilar in an informal setting rather than at the *commissariato*. She has already given us some insights into her father and his relationship with the others.

You were right to include her this evening. And I'm certain the fact that she is a beautiful woman had nothing to do with inviting her."

DiMaio smiled. "Of course it didn't." Rick was successful in breaking the tension. He and DiMaio rose to their feet as Pilar approached the table.

"Please excuse me," she said as DiMaio helped her with the chair. "It was my chief designer. She had an issue about dealing with one of our customers who can be very demanding." She replaced her napkin in her lap. "What do you recommend for a *secondo* here, Alfredo?"

—

Later, Rick and Betta emerged from a small street into the square in front of the duomo and the Palazzo Ducale. The cool night air felt good on their faces after the food and wine, and they were purposely taking a circuitous route back to their hotel. Arrow-shaped tourist signs for the city's landmarks got them through the maze of alleys and passageways outside the restaurant to reach the heart of the city. They stood before the two buildings Rick had seen from their hotel room window, a rectangular *piazza* separating them. A long banner for the upcoming exhibit hung horizontally from the plain facade of the palace, lit by a spotlight. In contrast, the portico on the side of the church held only shadows and darkness. They stopped to take in the scene and enjoy the light breeze coming up from the streets below.

"You said you've been to the museum, Rick?"

"Yes, but a long time ago. In my youth."

"You'll enjoy it more now that you're an old man." She took his hand and after some silence spoke again. "Alfredo was somewhat defensive about having Pilar there tonight."

"It was a bit strange to see her there, but I think he knows what he's doing."

She chuckled. "Oh, I'm sure."

"I didn't mean that, but you're right, of course." He put his arm over her shoulder. "I certainly can't criticize Alfredo for wanting to be with a beautiful woman; that would be very hypocritical."

Betta gave him a peck on the cheek. "You have a way with words."

"It's my job."

"Did you also find it strange, Rick, that Pilar had to take that call during dinner? Why wouldn't her assistant have called during the day? I think someone else was calling, and she didn't want us to know who it was."

"That never occurred to me. Perhaps you've been in the police so long that you suspect everyone."

"Or I've been an Italian too long."

An elderly couple dressed in wool coats walked slowly past them, speaking so that only they could hear each other's words. Rick and Betta watched them shuffle along cobblestones made smooth by countless other pedestrians over decades and centuries.

"I am worried that this drawing will never be found."

"It's been barely twenty-four hours since it went missing, Betta. You're the art cop; don't these things take time?"

"I'm afraid that the theft and the murder are connected, and every hour that passes makes it more likely that neither crime will ever be solved. So I hope we learn something tomorrow. This man Morelli, the art dealer, seems the most likely to have committed both crimes. He gets revenge on Somonte for having outbid him for the drawing and has it in his hands as well. We encounter this kind of collector frequently, one who doesn't care if the artwork is stolen but gets pleasure from simply having it in his possession. It doesn't matter that he can't show it to anyone else."

"Couldn't you say the same thing about Vitellozzi, the museum guy?" Rick inclined his head toward the Galleria Nazionale delle Marche. "He files it in some drawer in the museum archives and it magically turns up somewhere in town a few years from now. Then he convinces Somonte's heirs that it really should stay in the collection in Urbino."

Betta shook her head. "That's a bit of a stretch, but I guess it's possible. We'll be meeting both Morelli and Vitellozzi tomorrow, so let's hope we have a better idea about them after that." She tugged on his arm. "Let's go. You have to get up early for your run, and it's already been a long day."

"I was thinking we could extend it a bit longer."

"What a coincidence...I was thinking the same thing."

# CHAPTER FIVE

Rick's morning run had been a trip through a cloud. Urbino's fog was not the heavy, wet kind common to Mantova, where he had worked a few months earlier, but rather a fine mist that barely clung to his T-shirt and shorts. When he finished, the moisture on his body was mostly sweat. The route had taken him up the hill to the duomo and palace, a loop around the obelisk, and back down the steep Via Veneto before climbing the even steeper Via Raffaello. He passed Bruzzone's art gallery but did not notice it since his eyes were squinting through the fog at the plain facade of the house of Raphael on the other side of the street. The top of the hill offered some respite, thanks to a flat, grassy area around the battlements of the Fortezza Albornoz. He stopped, panting, at the edge of the park where he knew there had to be an excellent view of the city, now obscured by the mist. He turned and started the easy descent that would take him back to the Hotel Botticelli for a hot shower and breakfast with Betta.

The coffee was hot and waiting for him as he entered the breakfast room. Like the hotel itself, the room was small or, as the hotel described it on their website, cozy. Betta sat at a table against the wall talking with Pilar Somonte. He should have realized that Alfredo would have found her a room at the same hotel. She was dressed more casually than the night before, in well-cut jeans with a sweater. It appeared that her wardrobe always included something in wool, which would make perfect sense. She was a walking advertisement for the family business. Betta was back to her police business attire, a dark blue pantsuit and white blouse. He pulled out his chair and stood behind it.

"*Buon giorno*, Pilar."

"*Buon giorno*, Rick," she answered with a small wave.

"Pilar was just telling me about the women's fashion business. There's juice and coffee here for you." Betta pointed at the buffet table. "I recommend the almond *cornetto*."

Rick took the advice, not needed since he was starved after his morning run. It was interesting that Betta had adopted the Roman word for the crescent roll that was called a *brioche* in much of her native north. Besides the *cornetto,* he loaded his plate with cheese, yogurt, and a banana before returning to the table. Betta had poured his coffee and added hot milk. He sat and stirred in sugar to his coffee before downing the orange juice.

"Keeps me from getting scurvy," he said, putting down the empty glass and lifting the cup of coffee for his first shot of caffeine. "What are your plans for the day, Pilar?"

"I was going to work on transporting my father's remains back to Spain, but Alfredo told me this morning that the Spanish consul is in contact with Isabella on that, since she is considered the next of kin by both the Italian and Spanish authorities. That's fine with me." She looked at her empty coffee cup, considering whether to pour a refill. "I think I'll go out and see Urbino this morning, since I've never been here before. I need to clear my mind. The reality of my father's death is starting to sink in, and I think walking around in one of his favorite cities would help. Does that make sense?"

"Absolutely," said Betta.

"And what about you two?"

"I'm interviewing Morelli, the art collector, with Alfredo. Then Rick and I will be going to the museum to talk to a man named Annibale Vitellozzi."

"Someone my father knew?"

"He knew both of them and probably saw them on this trip."

Pilar held up her hands. "I don't think I want to know the details, but I hope it helps find whoever did this to my father. And helps you find that drawing." She started to get up and then sat down. "Do you think this could have just been a mugging that went wrong? I asked Alfredo that yesterday when he brought me here to the hotel. He didn't rule it out but thought it unlikely that a mugger would be carrying a gun and would know that my father had that valuable drawing."

"I leave the murder investigation to Alfredo," said Betta. "Either way, the drawing will turn up eventually and be returned to you."

"I'll have to fight that woman for it." She got up, said her goodbyes, and left the room.

Rick finished what was left of his *cornetto* and started peeling the banana. "You're going to interview Morelli?"

"Alfredo called just before you got here and asked me to sit in since I'm the art cop and Morelli is the art collector. He said it will be recorded, and you can listen in while it's going on."

Like a good Italian, Rick used a knife and fork to eat the banana. "I will enjoy that. Too bad he doesn't have one-way glass so I could also watch, like on the TV police shows." He ate the last slice of banana and started to open the container of yogurt. "Were you really talking about fashion when I got here?"

"Of course," Betta answered before picking up her cup and taking a sip.

—

The same sergeant was at the desk at the *commissariato* as the previous day, but this morning he waved them in without making eye contact with Betta. DiMaio was talking when they got to the door to his office, and Betta pushed it open, thinking he was on the phone. Instead, a tall man with uncontrolled hair was sitting in the chair facing DiMaio's desk.

"I'm sorry, Inspector," said Betta with a formal tone of voice. "We didn't realize you had someone with you."

DiMaio looked relieved. "No, no, we were just finishing. Were we not, Professor?"

The man nodded but did not appear convinced.

"Professor, this is Signora Innocenti and Signor Montoya, visiting from Rome." He looked at Rick and Betta. "This is Professor Florio, the director of the botanical gardens."

Florio's eyes widened. "Are you here because of the murder of Signor Somonte?"

"I am with the art police," said Betta. "We don't investigate homicides."

Florio turned his head quickly, making his long hair flop over one eye. "Inspector, didn't you mention a missing work of art belonging to Signor Somonte?"

The look on DiMaio's face indicated he had indeed mentioned that, and was now regretting it. "Professor, thank you for coming by and offering advice. I really must speak with these people."

"Yes, of course, Inspector. I understand the importance of the first days of an investigation. Montalbano always drummed that into his lieutenants. Keep in mind what I told you, and if I think of anything else, I'll be sure to let you know immediately." Florio turned to Rick and Betta and gave them a short bow. "It was my pleasure. I hope you will find time to visit the botanical gardens while you are in our city." He left.

Rick and Betta took their previous day's seats, and DiMaio settled into his chair behind the desk.

"Did the professor break the case wide open for you, Alfredo?"

"Riccardo, the man is *pazzo*. I would like to tell him in very strong terms to go tend to his plants, but he might complain to the rector, who would talk to the mayor, and then I'd be in trouble. His latest theory is that Somonte was in the gardens to bury an important document."

"The Piero drawing?" Betta said.

"That's probably what he's thinking, now that he knows the art police have arrived." He slapped his hands on the desk. "Let's forget Florio; we have someone important to the investigation coming here in ten minutes, if he arrives on time. Betta, let's go over how we want to handle the interview."

DiMaio was interrupted by the strains of the Lobo Fight Song coming from Rick's pocket. Rick pulled out the phone and checked the number. "I'll take this outside, and you two can conspire." He got to his feet and walked into the hallway.

"Commissario Fontana, it is an honor to speak with you." It was the standard greeting he always gave his police commissioner uncle.

"The honor is all mine, dear nephew. I was calling to see how you and Betta are enjoying Sansepolcro. I've never been, but I hear it is a lovely town."

Rick looked out of the window at the end of the hall, which gave him a view of the parking lot behind the building. "We saw very little of Sansepolcro. There was a problem, and we are now in Urbino."

"Problem?"

Rick described the events of the previous twenty-four hours. Partway into the explanation he could hear his uncle clicking away on the keyboard of his office computer and knew the policeman was looking up the case.

"I've got DiMaio's initial reports on my screen now, but they are mostly about the crime scene and autopsy findings. Nothing here on suspects. He does mention the missing artwork, some kind of drawing?"

"The Piero della Francesca drawing that was going to be donated to the museum in Sansepolcro."

"Of course, you told me about that, and that would be why they wanted Betta in Urbino. Are you making yourself useful or just getting in her and DiMaio's way?"

"I've been translating since the widow doesn't speak Italian. In fact, she doesn't speak much at all. I can't say she's been very cooperative."

"Too shaken by the death of her husband?"

"Hard to tell. It may just be her personality."

"You'll have a lot to tell me when you get back to Rome. They're calling me into a meeting so I have to cut this short. Give my best to Betta, and regards to DiMaio."

Rick said he would, turned off his cell phone, and walked back to the office. "Commissario Fontana sends *saluti* to you both. Are you ready to interview Morelli?"

"I think so," answered DiMaio. "Betta has found out from her office that Morelli is in their files for questionable dealings, but there's never been enough on him to investigate."

"Interesting," said Rick as he returned to his chair. "What was he doing?"

"He may have been buying from disreputable individuals," said Betta. "Mostly ancient art, like Greek vases. Morelli makes his money in olive oil he exports all over Europe and, from what we know, is totally reputable. But when he leaves business and gets into art collecting, he sometimes deals with shady characters. When he was spotted with a couple of them, he got on our radar."

The uniformed policeman from the front desk tapped on the door. "Inspector, Signor Morelli is here."

"Tell him to wait, Sergeant. I'll be right there." DiMaio stood up and took a set of earphones from among the papers on the desk. "Riccardo, you can come and sit in this chair. Just put these on; they're connected to the recorder in the next room where we'll be questioning Morelli. Shall we go, Betta?" They left Rick sitting at the desk. He picked up the earphones, tried them on, and put them down. For a moment he thought about putting his feet up on the desk, but the thought passed quickly.

DiMaio and Betta walked to the waiting area where Cosimo Morelli was standing in one corner talking on his cell phone. He noticed Betta first, his eyes moving up and down her body, before glancing at DiMaio. He said something into the phone before stuffing it into the pocket of his brown suede jacket. The rest of his outfit was equally casual and expensive: a silk turtleneck, well-pressed blue jeans, and loafers. His hair was long, too long for someone Betta estimated to be in his midforties, giving the impression he was clinging to a younger image. The tanned face said the same, as did his physique. The man worked out.

"Signor Morelli? I am Inspector DiMaio." They shook hands. "This is Dottoressa Innocenti, who is assisting in the investigation of Somonte's murder."

"It is my pleasure," said Morelli as he took Betta's hand.

"She is with the art police in Rome."

Morelli stiffened but quickly composed himself. "I welcome you to Urbino, though I don't understand why your office needs to be present. This is a murder investigation, isn't it, Inspector?"

"We can get into that inside," said DiMaio. "Let me lead the way."

The room was without windows but otherwise not as intimidating as Betta had hoped it would be. The table in the middle looked almost new, as did the four comfortable chairs around it. In front of each chair sat a microphone, its wires joining with the others at one end before running into a plug in the wall. On one side of the room was a credenza with bottled water and glasses on a plastic tray. The walls were bare except for two tourism posters of the city, one a view of the palace, the other a famous self-portrait of Urbino's favorite son, Raffaello.

DiMaio pointed toward one of the chairs. "Please sit down, Signor Morelli. We will be recording our conversation, which is purely routine, I can assure you. Would you like some water?"

Morelli looked at the microphone. Its red light had come on when DiMaio flipped a switch under the table. "Thank you, no. I'd just as soon get this over with. I have business to attend to." He sat and focused his attention on Betta, even when DiMaio began to speak.

After noting the day, time, and their three names, he turned his attention to the man sitting opposite him. "How long had you known Manuel Somonte?"

Morelli reluctantly took his eyes off Betta. "Several years. We became acquainted through Ettore Bruzzone, who runs an art gallery here. Ettore had an opening for an artist from Milan, if I remember correctly, and Somonte was in town. We struck up a friendship since we shared an interest in art. Owning art, that is. Whenever he came to Urbino we had dinner together."

"But in the case of the Piero drawing, you were rivals, were you not?"

Morelli smiled, pleased that he could speak directly to Betta. "You are well informed, but I would expect that from the art police. We both were trying to buy the drawing, if that's what you mean."

"You were disappointed to lose out to him, I suppose."

"Let's just say that I am accustomed to getting what I want, Dottoressa."

Betta returned his stare. "Was this the only instance when you were bidding against Somonte?"

"You would have to ask Bruzzone. If there were others, it would have been Somonte who ended up not getting the artwork." His fingers drummed on the tabletop.

"Did you see Somonte after he arrived in Urbino this time?" DiMaio asked.

"I was expecting that question, Inspector. I did see him the day he was killed, in the afternoon. We met for coffee, had a short chat, and arranged to have dinner tonight."

"Did he mention the donation of the drawing?"

He smiled. "Oh, yes. In fact, he had the drawing with him in this ornate case, which he opened with great care to show me what was inside."

"But you had seen it when it was on sale."

"Of course. But it was Manuel's none-too-subtle way to remind me who had won the bidding war on it." He shrugged. "I might have done the same thing if our roles were reversed, though of course I would not be donating the drawing to a museum."

"Did he say what he was going to do the rest of the day?"

Morelli shook his head. "He didn't, and I didn't ask."

"Where were you that evening?"

"My alibi? That's what you mean, isn't it? I was at home."

"Alone?"

"I am not married, Inspector. But, yes, I was alone."

It was Betta's turn to speak. "You were surprised that Somonte decided to donate the Piero drawing to the museum in Sansepolcro?"

He shrugged. "The donation was of no consequence to me. Somonte was free to do whatever he wished with the drawing. It was his. The one who was most agitated about the donation was Vitellozzi, the director of the museum here. He told me, just after the news came out about Sansepolcro getting it, that it was like a slap in the face. I'm sure he's over it by now, and it isn't as if his collection is lacking in works by Piero." Morelli cracked a thin smile. "Donating is not something I would do with my collection unless I were about to die. Perhaps, somehow, Somonte knew that his time was almost up. Now he's dead and the drawing is missing, isn't it? That's why you are here, is it not, Dottoressa?"

The reply came from DiMaio. "It would seem logical that the death of Somonte is connected to the missing work of art."

"Indeed it would," Morelli said, shifting in the chair.

"Did you ever meet Signora Somonte?"

"She doesn't speak Italian, so she didn't always accompany him on his trips to Italy. At least that's the reason he gave. I think I saw her at one of the openings here, but we never spoke. He told me the other day that she came with him this time because of the ceremony in Sansepolcro."

A pause followed his reply, and DiMaio turned aside to Betta. "I have nothing else," she said.

Morelli rose to his feet. "I hope that has been helpful," he said, putting an emphasis on the last word. "And I trust you will bring the murderer to justice quickly, Inspector. There is no telling when he might decide to murder another art collector."

"What kind of art do you collect, Signor Morelli?" Betta was still seated.

"A bit of this and a bit of that." He pulled a card and pen from his pocket, wrote something on the card, and passed it to her. "Given your position, you must be an expert, and I would be pleased to show it to you. I am having a few friends over this evening—perhaps you could come by then. Let's say seven?"

"I just might," she said, slipping the card into her pocket.

"Let me see you out, Signor Morelli." DiMaio opened the door and walked with him in silence to the reception area. They were shaking hands when Morelli noticed someone standing nearby.

"Ettore, are you a suspect in this as well?"

"Just helping the authorities, as any good citizen would," answered Bruzzone.

DiMaio checked his watch. "Thank you, Signor Morelli. Signor Bruzzone, if you could wait here, I'll be with you shortly." The two men resumed their conversation as DiMaio walked quickly to his office, where Rick had vacated his desk chair and was standing with Betta.

"Bruzzone is here, but before I bring him in, what are your impressions of our friend Morelli?" He took his chair behind the desk and motioned for Rick and Betta to sit.

"Since I could only hear him, I'm not the one to ask," said Rick. "You two could gauge his expressions and body language."

"It's just as well you weren't there, Rick. The way he looked at me made me very uncomfortable and would have annoyed you. Clearly, he considers himself God's gift to women."

"I heard him invite you to see his etchings, but I couldn't hear what you answered. You put him in his place, I assume?"

Betta's smile was more sly than playful. "Actually, I thought it might be interesting to see his art, since my office has some questions about him. I didn't tell him that if I came I would bring a friend."

DiMaio rapped on his desk like a schoolteacher. "Can we get this back to the murder investigation? All right, Morelli has no alibi for when Somonte was killed—that is worth noting. He also claimed indifference to the drawing being donated, after he missed buying it himself, but that may just be a front. His motive would be more anger that he lost the bid in the first place, since he admits he likes to get his way on such sales. As you noted, Betta, he does not come across as a very *simpatico* person, not that that matters. The real question is if he's capable of violence, and if being on the wrong side of a bidding war bruised his ego enough to lash out."

Rick rose from his chair. "You've summed it up perfectly, Alfredo. We will leave you to talk to this man Bruzzone."

Betta got up as well, followed by DiMaio.

"Don't you want to stay, Betta?"

"No, Alfredo. I already talked to him about the drawing, which is my main concern. And Rick and I have that appointment at the Galleria Nazionale delle Marche to talk to Vitellozzi. After that, we're going to drive down to Monterchi to find out more about the drawing's provenance."

"Give us a call if Bruzzone confesses to the murder," said Rick as he started toward the door.

"You'll be the first to know," said DiMaio, with a disgusted wave of his hand.

Five minutes later, Bruzzone sat in the chair vacated by Rick.

"I may appear a bit nervous, Inspector. I've never been in a police station before, and since it's in connection with a murder, well…"

"Perfectly understandable. I appreciate you coming in. I know you spoke with Signora Innocenti yesterday, but I have some other questions. How long had you known Signor Somonte?"

Bruzzone was relieved at the calming tone from the policeman, easing himself back off the edge of the chair. "It's been several years. I can certainly look back at my records to see when he made his first purchase."

"That won't be necessary. He simply appeared at your gallery?"

"He did. There aren't that many art dealers here in Urbino, as you may have noticed, so it would be natural that a collector would come in to see what I had to offer. We struck up a friendship, you could say, and I got to know where his interests lay so that I could alert him when I came into possession of some work he might want to acquire."

"As with this drawing by Piero della Francesca."

"Precisely."

"But there were others who wanted it."

"My goodness, yes. One was Cosimo, Signor Morelli, whom you saw earlier. He is another of my regular clients, so naturally I made him aware of the drawing as well."

"He was disappointed not to get it."

"That would be an understatement. He refused to come into my shop for six months. I haven't talked to him about it, but I'm sure the decision by Somonte to donate the drawing annoyed him as well."

"Was there anyone else who was equally disappointed?"

Bruzzone looked at the ceiling, gathering his thoughts. "No one in the same category as Morelli. There was a buyer from Milan, but he dropped out early." He paused for more thought. "Of course the museum here was very interested when they found out about it, but they couldn't afford the price. Vitellozzi, the director, asked me to hold off while he looked for some donor to cover it, but I couldn't wait. Both Morelli and Somonte were pressuring me to make a decision."

DiMaio had a pen in his hand that he tapped on the desk. "Did you see Somonte before he was killed?"

"I did. He came by my shop in the morning. He had the drawing with him in a leather case he'd had made for it. He said he was showing it to people for the last time before it went into the museum in Sansepolcro, which I thought was a bit of *bruta figura*. 'Look how generous I am,' he was saying." Bruzzone frowned and shook his head.

DiMaio recalled what Morelli had told him about their meeting for coffee, when Somonte had brought out the drawing to remind his adversary who had won the bidding war. Apparently, he did something similarly petty with Bruzzone. The image DiMaio was forming of the murdered man was less than positive. It was not mentioned in the interview room earlier, but perhaps Morelli didn't think it important. Or the drawing was so much of a sore point that he didn't want to bring up again.

"You didn't see Somonte again?"

"I did not. That evening I was at home since my wife was not feeling well."

A contrast with Morelli the bachelor, thought DiMaio. And unlike Morelli, Bruzzone had answered the inevitable question about his whereabouts at the time of the murder without being asked. Like everyone else in Italy, Bruzzone must watch too many TV crime shows. At least he wasn't obsessed with crime novels.

# CHAPTER SIX

The term Renaissance Man may well have been coined to describe the most renowned former resident of Urbino's Palazzo Ducale. Federico, Duke of Montefeltro, practiced the ruthless art of mercenary warfare, building a fortune by fighting for whichever city-state would pay him the most. Yet he wanted history to remember him not as a warrior but as an intellectual who brought the most famous artists of the day to his court and built a library rivaled only by that of the pope. A famous portrait showed a seated Federico in full armor, his infant son, Guidobaldo, leaning on his father's knee. The duke's sword remained sheathed on his belt, allowing him to use both his hands to hold a book that he read intently while the boy stared into the future. It was appropriate, then, that in later centuries when city-states joined into a single modern Italy, Federico's palace would again be a center for culture. The Galleria Nazionale delle Marche was not just the finest museum in the region but one of the most distinguished in Italy.

Viewed from the street outside, the Palazzo Ducale was not impressive. *Austere* was the word that came to Rick's mind when he looked at the facade, part of which looked out on the small square between it and the cathedral. Except for some lightly decorative stone between the doors, and stonework around the windows of the second floor, the building displayed its original brick. A frieze that began at the corner of the building ran for only a few yards, adding to the sense that the palace was a yet unfinished work of medieval architecture.

They were expected. The guard at the entrance handed them a floor plan and indicated on it where to find Vitellozzi on the *secondo piano*. Betta thanked her and they walked inside.

"Aren't the stairs that way?"

"They are, Rick, but let's take a quick look at the courtyard; it's one of the finest in Italy."

She was right. Open to the sky and the size of a basketball court, it was surrounded by Corinthian columns and looping arches, creating a continuous portico on all four sides. Above the columns Latin inscriptions ran below and above the windows of the *piano nobile*, the second-floor apartments and reception rooms.

"I can picture Federico receiving distinguished visitors here, and knowing that they were duly impressed."

"That was the idea," said Betta. "But he also used this court-yard to stage concerts and theater for invited guests. They still do concerts here in the summer, but now you have to buy a ticket." She touched his arm. "Let's go find Vitellozzi."

After climbing an elegant flight of low stairs, they found themselves in the rooms of the museum, and using the floor plan, they made their way to the spot where Vitellozzi was said to be found. Like the walls in the other rooms they passed through, this room's walls were white and plain, making the colors of their paintings more vivid by contrast. The art was spaced at wide intervals, but with so much space there was no need to crowd. A fireplace centered in one wall was large enough that

Rick could have stood up inside it. He concluded that if that was the only heating in the chamber, even with a roaring fire, the duke would have needed his long underwear on a winter night. A uniformed guard sat in a folding chair near the door, and two people who were clearly tourists stood before one of the paintings. No sign of anyone who might be Vitellozzi.

Betta walked quickly to the guard, who looked like he was nodding off. "We were told to find Dottor Vitellozzi here."

He looked up, startled. "What? Oh, yes, Vitellozzi. He was expecting someone. Through that door." The guard pointed to the far end of the room where a sign reading "Closed to the Public" guarded the tall wood door. The heels of Rick's cowboy boots clicked on the floor as they crossed the room to reach it.

The room on the other side of the door was the same size as the one they'd just left and had a similar massive fireplace, but in contrast this one was a hive of activity. Sets of panels, connected by hinges, were being positioned by two workers in white overalls. Another set of workers pushed together risers to make a small stage at one side of the room. Two young women were removing artwork from wooden crates, unwrapping each piece with great care and leaning them at intervals against the wall. At the opposite end of the room from the stage, two men were setting up a bar, unpacking wineglasses and arranging them on a long table covered by a white cloth. Standing in the middle of the activity was a man wearing sneakers, blue jeans, and a sweatshirt bearing the words "Keep Calm and Enjoy Art," in English.

"That has to be Vitellozzi," said Rick.

The man noticed the new arrivals and walked swiftly toward them. Rick estimated him to be in his late fifties, though the slight paunch could have made him look older than his years. Graying temples added to the aging, along with a hairline that years earlier had begun its retreat toward the top of his head. He smiled and moved his hands like a juggler, which Rick took as a reference to the work of setting up an exhibit.

"I assume you are Dottoressa Innocenti from the art police."

Betta acknowledged that she was, shook his hand, and introduced Rick as an American working for the police as an interpreter. Vitellozzi showed no surprise, making Rick wonder if he already knew about the investigation. Wouldn't he be curious as to why an interpreter was needed?

"You must excuse my informality of dress in greeting someone from the Cultural Ministry, but, as you can see, we are hard at work in preparing for the opening tomorrow night. I was speaking this morning to the ministry undersecretary about the exhibit, and he mentioned that someone from his art police was here. Then I got the call from Inspector DiMaio, and here you are." He held up a hand for Rick and Betta before turning quickly to the workers. "Not there! Center it against the wall!" His attention returned to Betta. "Sorry about that. It never fails that we are working at the last minute on arrangements that should have been taken care of days ago. But it's also very exciting. For most temporary exhibits I let my assistant curator do the setup, but for one of such importance I decided to get directly involved."

"All I know," said Betta, "is that it is about Raffaello, to commemorate the five-hundredth anniversary of his death."

Vitellozzi's delivery was rapid-fire. "Yes, Raffaello di Urbino, or as you Americans would say, Signor Montoya, Raphael of Urbino. The city's most famous native son, who unfortunately is buried in Rome. I am Roman myself, but I've come to believe that the master should someday be brought home. I'm sure an appropriate resting place would be found for him here. Fortunately, we were able to schedule this exhibit years ago, making this one of the first of the museums to honor him for the quincentenary. Which seems only right, since he was born in Urbino."

"What will be in the exhibit?" Betta asked.

"Well, as you probably know, the great scandal of Raffaello's work is that almost nothing of it is here in Urbino except for *La Muta*, and another smaller piece, here in our collection." He gestured toward a female portrait that had already been hung. "There is a painting on the wall of his birthplace that is attributed to him, but except for *La Muta*, virtually all of his masterpieces are in other cities. This is a disappointment to the wonderful people of Urbino, but what can be done? Well, one thing is to mount exhibits like this one. For it, we have brought in several of his most important works, on loan from museums in Italy. We made some attempts with other countries in Europe, but to no avail. You may know that the Louvre and the National Gallery in London both have numerous works by Raffaello. Fortunately, our sister Italian institutions were more forthcoming, though almost always with a catch, spoken or unspoken."

"I don't understand," said Rick.

"Reciprocity," Vitellozzi said. "We have paintings in our collection, most importantly those by Piero della Francesca, that they will certainly request on loan at some point in the future. The director of the Pitti Palace, when he agreed to send us the *Madonna della Seggiola*, as much as said so. The negotiations with the various institutions began years ago. We asked the Pinacoteca Ambrosiana in Milan for the cartoon of the *School of Athens*, almost sure that they wouldn't part with it, and we were correct. Raffaello's self-portrait was easier to get from the Uffizi. They understood that it was virtually a requirement for an exhibit of this type, but there's no doubt we'll hear from them sometime to cash in the IOU. Also, they have such a treasure trove there that it will barely be missed." He clasped his hands together. "I could go on, but you aren't here to talk about this exhibit but poor Somonte. If you don't mind, we can talk here so I can keep an eye on the progress. There are some chairs over in that corner with a bit less chaos."

The chairs were stacked, and he and Rick pulled them off and arranged them in a triangle. Vitellozzi took the one that put his back to the wall, making Rick think of a mafia don in a restaurant.

"You knew Signor Somonte well?" asked Betta.

"I would not say well, but since he always visited the museum when he was in town, I came to know him. His wealth and connection to Italy were not a secret, so any museum director would want to cultivate such an individual."

"Did he support the museum financially?"

"We are, of course, a government institution, but there is private support for specific events, such as this one. To antici-pate your next question, yes, Somonte gave us some financial assistance for this opening. As you no doubt saw on the poster outside, we have corporate sponsorship for the exhibit itself, but Somonte helped to defray the costs of this opening event. So it is all the more tragic that he will not be with us tomorrow night to receive our thanks."

"Then you didn't talk to him after he got to Urbino four days ago," said Rick.

"I was referring to public recognition of his support. I did see Signor Somonte the day after he arrived. I had just read in the paper about the donation of the drawing when he appeared in my office, which I found somewhat ironic. We had a short conversation."

"That was the day before he was to go to Sansepolcro."

Vitellozzi nodded. "Yes. He talked about the donation of the drawing to the museum there, reminding me that his mother was born near that town. He brought up the subject, not me. Perhaps he was feeling some guilt that he hadn't given it to us."

"What did you say to him?" asked Betta.

He thought for a few moments before answering. "I could have reassured him that he made the right decision, but I couldn't bring myself to do it. We were not able to purchase it when it went up for sale—that was expected. But when we heard a few months ago that he was donating it to such a small museum rather than this one, well…" He shook his head. "So I changed the subject."

Rick recalled Morelli using the phrase "a slap in the face" when describing the museum director's reaction to the dona-tion. Vitellozzi was clearly uncomfortable talking about it now, but he didn't appear to hold much of a grudge. If he was still greatly annoyed, he was good at not showing it. Or he was never that upset about not getting the drawing, and Morelli had been exaggerating to deflect suspicion from himself.

"I understand," continued Vitellozzi, "that the drawing has gone missing. It is certainly a very valuable piece of art, but acquiring it doesn't appear to be reason enough for murder."

"Our experience," said Betta, "is that art thieves can get violent."

Something caught Vitellozzi's eye and he jumped to his feet. "Excuse me—I'll be right back." He rushed over to where work-ers were lifting a frame from one of the crates. The picture was the portrait of a young man with long reddish hair, dressed in a black shirt and cap. The features were soft, the neck long, the skin pale. The sitter had turned his face to stare at the viewer with a bored look, giving the impression he was unsure about having his portrait painted.

"That's the Raffaello self-portrait from the Uffizi," Betta said as they watched Vitellozzi hovering over the workers. "If he's going to run over each time one of these masterpieces comes out of its box, we could be here forever." She turned back to Rick. "What do you think of what he said about the drawing?"

"He admitted that he was unhappy not to have the donation. If he'd told us it meant nothing to him that Somonte snubbed his museum, that would have been hard to believe."

Vitellozzi's eyes moved around the room as he walked back. "Sorry about that." He settled back in his chair but kept his eyes on the portrait that was now being raised to the wall. "We were talking about Piero's drawing. I hope it turns up soon; it would be a great loss to the art world if it isn't found. My fear is that whoever did this to Somonte didn't know its value and simply threw it in the trash." He frowned at the thought. "But artwork has a way of reappearing. Remember that Somonte's drawing was found hundreds of years after Piero sketched it."

"I hope you're right," said Betta. "Inspector DiMaio requested that I ask you where you were the evening before last. Purely for the record, you understand."

Vitellozzi had been looking at the portrait of Raphael, but the question got his attention. "Being routine doesn't detract from the fact that I may be a suspect. To be frank, it hadn't crossed my mind, but I suppose there might be some suspicion, since I knew the man and saw him that day."

If he was waiting for reassurances from Betta about her question being a routine requirement, they were not forthcoming.

"Well, like most of the evenings for the past week I've been here preparing for this exhibit. In my office, that is, which is one floor down. Since I come and go through a back door to the *palazzo*, I'm afraid the guards won't be able to vouch for me. Their concern is the safety of the art collection, not the movements of the director."

"I understand," said Betta. "Tell me something, Dottore. In your opinion, if someone had the drawing in their possession, where would be a logical place to sell it?"

"Well, really now, isn't that the kind of thing you art police are supposed to know?"

"We often find that local sources are the most reliable."

"You should ask that question to someone like Bruzzone, the man who sold Somonte the drawing in the first place. I don't follow the black market in art." A glance at his wristwatch was more of an unspoken comment than a need to find out the time.

Betta got up from the chair. "Dottor Vitellozzi, I appreciate your time, especially with what is happening now."

Vitellozzi's smile showed more relief than friendliness. "I hope I was of some help, though for the life of me I can't think what it might be. We will see you two tomorrow night, I trust?"

"We would love to," Rick replied quickly.

After thanking the museum director, Rick and Betta went back through the same door, leaving the hubbub of the exhibit preparation. The guard looked up for a moment but then resumed his vigil. He concentrated his attention on a group of young tourists, thinking these two visitors might report back to Vitellozzi.

"We have time, Rick—let's see a few of the masterpieces. The two by Piero should be along here somewhere. I'd ask the guard, but he's busy keeping an eye on those kids." They walked through a set of open doors into another chamber that was smaller but kept the vaulted ceilings. Only an occasional tall window distracted from the paintings, since the walls kept their somber white. "I think that's the *Madonna di Senigallia* over there."

They walked to the middle of the rectangular room, passing works of art that in lesser museums would have drawn crowds. Piero's work had an audience of three when they reached it. An elderly couple studied the small painting, speaking German to each other in low voices. Next to them was a man whose nationality was not apparent, since he was dressed in clerical black and his silence could betray no accent. The priest, too, looked deeply into the eyes of the four figures in the painting, but unlike the Germans, he was more interested in the spiritual than the artistic.

Rick saw the hand of Piero immediately in the faces of all four figures. They had the drooping eyes and wide forehead, just like the painting in Sansepolcro, and they stood stiffly, as if the artist had placed them in a pose and asked them not to move. Only the angel on Mary's right looked straight at the viewer; the other angel stared at the head of the Madonna, and the eyes of the Virgin herself were cast downward. The infant Jesus held up his hand in a gesture of blessing while looking into the distance, perhaps considering his future. Even the small piece of doorway and ceiling in the background showed Piero's mastery of perspective, as did his subtle use of light that washed over the four from an unseen window to the left. Every detail of a Renaissance painting had a message, and Rick wished he had his book of signs and symbols to decode these. Why the piece of coral around the baby's neck, and what was the flower he was holding? The colors on the Virgin's dress—what did they represent? The basket on the shelf was most puzzling.

He was about to ask Betta when his concentration was broken by familiar voices coming from three paintings away. They were spoken by a man and a woman, and the language was Spanish. He leaned toward Betta's ear. "I believe it's Signora Somonte and Lucho Garcia, and they appear to be having some sort of disagreement. Stay here and I'll say hello."

"I was not expecting her meddling—you should have fore-seen it," said the widow to Garcia. The sharpness in her tone was the same as when she had met with Rick and DiMaio in the hotel, but without the nasal flatness. Her cold had abated.

"Do you think I saw it coming?" Unlike on the previous day, Garcia was less than deferential to his boss's widow.

When the two Spaniards noticed Rick walking toward them, the conversation stopped and their faces assumed stiff smiles. Signora Somonte was dressed more sedately than yesterday, but only slightly. Today it was a dark pantsuit with low boots, and her blond hair was more in order. In contrast Garcia wore the same jacket and pants, perhaps the same shirt, but a different tie than Rick remembered.

"Señor. . . ?" she began and stopped. Garcia whispered in her ear. She went on. "Montoya. Of course I remember you, Señor. I just did not expect to see you here."

"Nor did I expect to see you, Señora, but it is good that you are out and about. Your cold seems to be better."

"It is." She was searching for something to say. "This museum was one of Manuel's favorite places in Italy. I thought it would be right for me to visit it before returning to Spain."

"I understand completely. When are you planning to fly home?"

"It will depend on the police. Your police."

"It may take some time to find who killed your husband, Señora."

"I know that, but I was hoping that the drawing would turn up. That *maldito* drawing that is the cause of all this." Her voice betrayed frustration mixed with anger.

"You will take it back to Spain?"

She glanced at Garcia. "I haven't decided. It's mine now that Manuel is gone."

"Of course," said Rick. He had assumed the donation would

go forward once the drawing was found, but this was not the time to discuss the commitment Somonte had made to the museum in Sansepolcro. Did her indecision—if that's what it was—add a new twist to the murder investigation? "I know Inspector DiMaio is working hard to find it." He could have added that finding the drawing was likely the same as finding the murderer. "I will call you immediately if he has any news, but if I can be of any assistance in the meantime, as an interpreter, you can call me. I gave Señor Garcia my hotel phone number yesterday."

"Thank you," she said, her voice indicating that the conversation was over.

Rick took the hint, said goodbye, and returned to Betta's side. The three other people who had been studying the painting had been replaced by two others who spoke Italian with a northern accent.

"I was watching as you talked to them. Signora Somonte doesn't appear to have settled well into her role as the grieving widow, and I can't help but speculate on the relationship between her and Garcia."

"My thoughts exactly, Betta. Shall we be on our way?"

—

Most of the route from Urbino to Monterchi was on the road they had driven the day before. The car made the same bends and cutbacks, and the views were the same, but the difference was that now they were going downhill. Fortunately they didn't find themselves behind a truck or other slow-moving vehicle this time. After an especially serpentine series of cutbacks they reached the Tiber River valley where the terrain became boringly flat, but Rick was not about to complain.

Instead of retracing their route exactly by turning north toward Sansepolcro, Betta continued straight, following the signs for Monterchi and crossing under the expressway that connected Rimini on the coast with Perugia.

The fertility of the soil in the valley was evident, not just from the vast fields starting to sprout crops but in the agro-business buildings and warehouses that appeared regularly along the straight road. Betta slowed as they entered the town of Petrino. Change the sign at the edge of town, Rick thought, and it could be any of a hundred small agriculture-based cities in northern Italy. Two-story residences appeared as soon as the fields ended, along with the occasional gas station. Then, once into the center, a church, shops, a park, a school, and the inevitable pizzeria. The sequence reversed and they were out into the fields again. For a brief few kilometers they drove through the northern bump of Umbria that pushed against Tuscany, before the car crossed the border. The people of Monterchi were Tuscan rather than Umbrian by a scant kilometer.

Like so many other towns in Italy, Monterchi was built on a hill, the better to fortify and protect its inhabitants when danger threatened. As hills went in Tuscany, this was a small one, but high enough to offer a view of the valley and spot anyone approaching, be it friend or foe. A large parking area lay between the town and the road, set up for tourists who were prohibited from driving up the narrow streets to the old part of town. Along with cars, a few buses sat waiting for the people who had walked the final few meters up to the *centro storico*. Betta spotted a traffic policeman, pulled in, and rolled down her window. The cop, who had been issuing tickets, noticed and walked a few steps to the car.

"We're looking for Via San Frediano," she said.

"Right there," he answered, pointing with his pen to a street directly on the other side of the parking area. "You could leave your car here and walk, if you'd like. Just get a ticket from the machine and put in on your dashboard where I can see it."

She thanked him and pushed the button to roll up the window. "He probably gets paid from the fines he writes." They pulled to the edge of the lot, waited for a break in the traffic, and crossed over the road to enter Via San Frediano. After only twenty meters she slowed, checked out the number on one of the buildings, and pulled over to park. "This should be it."

The house looked like the one next to it and the two across the street, as if they had all been projects of the same *geometra* and put up at the same time, which Rick estimated to be at least a half century earlier. It was two stories and essentially a single long box with shuttered windows, all the same size. Stucco had chipped off in a few places, exposing the cement block underneath, but the overall impression was neatness. Washing hung from a wire running between two of the second-floor windows, and two satellite dishes aimed skyward from positions on the slightly pitched roof. Set precisely between the bottom windows was the plain, wood door. Rick and Betta got out of the car and walked to it.

Two doorbells were lined up at eye level on one side of the door, neither of which had the name that Betta expected to see. She looked above the door at the number.

"This is the address Bruzzone gave me, but I don't see a Spadini. Well, we've come this far—let's see what we can find out. Pick one, Rick."

"*Sinistra.*"

Betta rang the left bell for a few seconds and they waited. "I think I hear some movement."

A few moments later fumbling was heard inside, and the door creaked open. From down near the floor a small head peeked out. Betta smiled down at it. "Hi. We would like to speak with Signora Spadini. Is she here?"

The face belonged to a boy of about five. He looked up at Betta with wide eyes, then switched them to Rick, who smiled and waved. The boy was still staring at the two visitors when a female voice came from deep in the house.

"Who is it, Giorgio?"

Giorgio looked behind him toward the voice, then back at Betta, before slowly closing the door.

"The lad needs to work on his greeting routine," Rick said. "He's got the door opening part down pretty well, but after that, it's definitely lacking."

They could hear the sound of footsteps approaching quickly from inside, and the door was opened by a woman wearing an apron over slacks and a baggy sweatshirt. She gave them a puzzled look. "May I help you?" Giorgio was wrapped around one leg, staring up at Betta.

"Signora Spadini?" said Betta. "We're with the police. Can we speak with you a moment?"

The woman's face froze. "I…I am not Signora Spadini. She lived here until she died, but that was six months ago." She made no move to open the door more than half way. "I am her daughter, Egle Camozzo."

"Our condolences, Signora. Obviously we were not aware of your mother's passing. I am with the art police in Rome, and we are investigating a missing drawing that your mother first discovered."

The words had the effect of calming the woman, and she opened the door fully. "I saw something on the news about that. The Spanish man who was murdered? Please come in. Giorgio, let go of my leg."

They were in a small hallway with two doors. The boy

released his grip on his mother and pressed himself against the wall, still keeping his eye on Betta. She and Rick followed the woman through one of the doors into a sitting room, its floor strewn with plastic blocks. A flat-screen TV was propped on a side table, faced by chairs where the three adults sat after maneuvering through the minefield of blocks. Giorgio hung back in the doorway. After Betta introduced herself and Rick, they were offered and politely declined something to drink.

"I saw the story on TV but didn't know that it was my mother's drawing. That's what you're saying, that it was her drawing that's missing?"

"It was," answered Betta. "We got her address, this address, from the man who bought it from her. Had you met Signor Bruzzone?"

"Bruzzone? No, this is the first I've heard the name. You see, my mother didn't tell me about finding the drawing until after it was sold. My husband and I were living in Città di Castello at the time, and my mother was renting this house. I should say this half of the house since it's a duplex and there's another family on the other side. With the money from the drawing she was able to buy it, and when she died it was bequeathed to me. We were paying rent in Città di Castello so it made sense to move here, since my husband can easily drive back to his work. It was also larger, so Giorgio has more room to play, and his sister loves the school here."

The boy took the mention of his name as a cue and walked over to pick up a pair of the plastic blocks. He looked at the two visitors before walking to Rick. "My blocks."

"Those are nice blocks," said Rick. "Can I see them?"

Giorgio put the two blocks in Rick's hand and bent down for more.

"You have made a friend, Signor Montoya," said Signora Camozzo.

"I am honored." Rick put the blocks on the coffee table in front of him and started to arrange them into walls, while Giorgio picked more off the floor and brought them to him. "Don't let us interrupt the conversation."

Betta looked at Rick and the boy for a moment before turning back to Giorgio's mother. "Did your mother tell you where she found the drawing?"

"Not exactly. She mentioned an old trunk. But for several years, even before that, she had been starting to show her age. I was never sure if what she was saying was something that had really happened or if it had been remembered from years before. It wasn't dementia; she was still very sharp, but there were occasional lapses. I'm sure she simply didn't want to share the details with me."

"Why would that be?" Betta asked.

Signora Camozzo took a deep breath and let it out slowly as she decided how to answer. "She resented that we lived so far away and she couldn't see her grandchildren every day."

"Città di Castello couldn't be more than a dozen kilometers from here," said Betta.

"That's true, but my mother didn't have a car—not that she knew how to drive if she'd had one—and she hated getting on the bus since it stopped several blocks from our house. Because of that she only saw us on weekends when we would come here for lunch, or pick her up to drive her back to our house." She shook her head with the memory. "In her mind we might as well have been living in Perugia or Florence, and my husband was to blame. Because of that she never wanted to tell me things because she didn't want him to know anything. It was spiteful and childish, but that's the way she was."

Rick listened to the exchange while stacking blocks.

"Fortunately," the woman continued, "the children didn't know what was going on between their grandmother and their parents, and Mamma was very good with them. Perhaps I'm making too much of it all. Are you sure you won't have some coffee? It won't take me but a minute to prepare it."

Betta assured her that they were fine. Rick and Giorgio had built a foundation and were leaving spaces for the windows, so that it was starting to look like the house where they all were sitting.

"How did your mother die?" Betta asked. "If you don't mind me asking."

"The doctor said her heart gave out. She had been ill for several years with heart problems, so it wasn't a shock. I'm an only child, and since my father died years ago, I was the one to look after her. During the week I would drop my husband at his office, our daughter at school, and Giorgio and I would come here to Monterchi. After lunch we'd drive back to Città di Castello in time for school letting out."

"I'm sure your mother appreciated your efforts."

Signora Camozzo shrugged and looked at her son. "She enjoyed seeing Giorgio."

Later Rick and Betta stood on the street outside. It was warmer than when they had entered the Camozzo residence thanks to the rays of late-morning sun that struck the front of the building and bounced onto the street. A brown tabby cat, oblivious to their presence, apricated on one of the stone windowsills, his tail hanging limply over the edge.

"You and Giorgio were bonding well in there. I was not aware that you have such a way with children."

"I've had plenty of experience working on Legos with my two nephews, Betta. They had a huge bin of the things, and along with my brother-in-law we would spend hours constructing stuff. It's something I miss about not living in Albuquerque. That and green chile cheeseburgers. Speaking of which, where are we going to have lunch?"

"It's only noon, Rick. I thought we would first stop in to see the *Madonna del Parto* while we're here. It's the most famous work of art in the town."

"The only work of art in the town."

"You could say that."

They walked to the car and Rick opened the driver's side door. "Did you get anything useful from Signora Camozzo?"

She got in and waited for him to come around to the passenger seat. "As much as anything I was curious about how and where her mother found the drawing. Provenance is something my office is always interested in, especially with stolen pieces." She turned the key and started the engine. "In this case it likely has no real bearing, now that it's been stolen. That is, if it really was stolen, and if Somonte was in fact murdered to get it. If we're lucky it will turn up intact, and my involvement in this case will be ended. Then it will be nothing other than a murder investigation." She pulled into the street.

Rick adjusted his seat belt. With Betta driving even a short distance, he always prepared for speed. "I wonder if Alfredo has made any breakthroughs."

———

DiMaio looked deep into Pilar's eyes and hoped he was seeing a spark, even a small one. They sat in the sterile break room of the *commissariato*, not an ideal place for a tryst, but the best he could manage at the moment. Two people occupied one of the other tables: the switchboard operator on an early lunch break, eating pasta she'd heated in the microwave, and a traffic policeman sipping coffee from the machine. With DiMaio and Pilar also drinking from tiny plastic cups, the coffee maker was getting an unusual workout, considering its ignominious but well-earned reputation among the *polizia* of Urbino.

"I'm sorry we can't have lunch today, Pilar."

"Perfectly understandable, Alfredo. I'm sure your regular duties keep you busy enough without having to investigate a homicide. But I look forward to dinner this evening."

Her words comforted the policeman. "As do I. You'll enjoy the restaurant. Intimate. Good food. We'll have a chance to talk, just the two of us. Not that it wasn't fun last night with Riccardo and Betta."

"It was just what I needed to keep my mind off other things." She stirred the coffee with a plastic stick, a gold bracelet dangling out from the sleeve of her wool sweater. A cross between a long cardigan sweater and a jacket hung over the chair next to her. "Is there any news on the investigation?"

DiMaio could not but wonder how innocently the question had been posed. Was she probing? In the back of his mind all morning had been the realization that he was treading a fine line between a personal interest in Pilar and his duties as the lead investigator of her father's death. He'd admitted to himself that Betta and Riccardo may have been right in bringing it up at dinner. Now his guard was up.

He shook his head. "Not much. Betta and I interviewed Morelli this morning."

"The art collector who knew my father."

"Exactly. He was also the one your father outbid to get the drawing that has gone missing. He is not the most simpatico person I've ever encountered, and he fancies himself to be a ladies' man, much to Betta's annoyance. He has no alibi for that evening, so he has to be considered a suspect, but somehow losing out on the drawing does not appear to be motive enough for homicide."

"Maybe he saw this as the last chance to get the drawing before it gets put in a museum."

"It's possible, I suppose, which edges us into the expertise of Betta and her art police. She's said that there are people who steal works of art simply for the pleasure of ownership, and it doesn't bother them that they can never show it to anyone. But after interviewing him I would doubt that Morelli is that kind of collector. My guess is that he wants everyone to know it when he has a valuable work of art, but who knows? Perhaps Betta will find out this evening, since he invited her to see his collection."

Pilar tilted her head. "Really? Inviting a beautiful woman up to see his art collection? What would Rick think of that?"

"Rick will be with her, though Morelli doesn't know that."

She laughed, then turned thoughtful. "Perhaps Morelli tried to convince my father to sell him the drawing instead of donating it and they got into an argument. I can recall vividly my father's temper when anyone attempted to change his mind once he'd made a decision. I stopped trying years ago."

"An argument that turned violent. That's a possibility." He looked up and groaned.

At the door to the room stood a uniformed policeman, and next to him Professor Florio. When the cop spotted DiMaio he said something to the botanist and walked alone to the table. "I'm sorry, sir—I didn't realize you were with someone. This man says that he needs to see you urgently. If you'd like I can ask him to wait."

"That's all right, Sergeant." He gave a nod to the professor, who smiled and scuttled quickly to the table as the policeman left the room. DiMaio stood. "You wanted to see me, Professor?"

"Well, yes, but I—"

"It's all right. Let me introduce Signora Somonte, the daughter of your benefactor. Pilar, Professor Florio is the director of the botanical gardens."

"I am mortified that I am interrupting, Signora, but at least it allows me to extend my deepest condolences on the loss of your father." His face froze and he turned to DiMaio. "Oh, dear, does the Signora speak—"

"Yes, I do, Professor, and thank you for your kind words. I know that my father thought very highly of your institution."

"And we held him in high esteem as well."

The two men were still standing, and DiMaio did not show any eagerness to have Florio join him and Pilar at the table. "Is there something urgent, Professor?"

"No, no. Well, maybe. It's just that I had another theory on the crime and wanted to get your reaction. I recalled that in one of the novels I read last year the body is found in a garden and the police eventually track down the murderer through leaves. That is, leaves that they find. On the street. But please finish with what you were dealing with. I'll be out in the waiting room." He turned and hurried out.

DiMaio watched Florio leave and took his seat.

"What a strange man," Pilar observed. "Does he really think he can break open the case using the plot of a crime novel?"

"Apparently. I'd like to say that we get such eccentrics showing up all the time, but I can't. He's the first one I've encountered. The strange thing is that otherwise he seems quite rational. He is, after all, a professor of botany, so he couldn't be a complete *pazzo*."

A different uniformed policeman came into the room carrying a newspaper. "You'll want to see this, Inspector." He handed over the paper, looked at Pilar, and made his exit.

"Now what?" DiMaio spread the front page out on the table and began to read the story under a picture of the metal gate at the entrance to the botanical gardens. After a minute he slapped his hand down. "The same journalist who came to see me yesterday. Her story tells how your father's body was found, including a description of the plant that he donated to the gardens. How did she get this information? I gave specific orders to my officers not to give out any details to the press. Somebody is in trouble."

"Perhaps it wasn't someone from the *commissariato*, Alfredo."

"What do you mean?"

She stirred her coffee. "It could have been someone who wants to increase the number of visitors to the botanical gardens."

# CHAPTER SEVEN

Betta drove back to the main road and waited for a break in what was mostly commercial traffic going between Arezzo and Città di Castello. She went west for a few kilometers before turning toward the old section of Monterchi that rose on its hill just ahead. Signs for the Museo Civico took the car around the base of the town, which was just as well since the steep streets leading up to the center had originally been laid out for foot traffic, not cars. Fields spread out to the right as the street bent along the side of the hill. Two minutes later they found themselves in front of the building that housed one of Piero della Francesca's masterpieces. It looked more like a school than a museum, since that's exactly what it had been for the first part of its life. Had it not been for the signs, Betta might have driven right past. Instead she pulled over and parked.

Once again Betta's Cultural Ministry identification worked its magic, and they were waved in by the man at the counter. The first few rooms dealt with the history of the *Madonna del Parto*, which Piero had painted on the wall above the altar in a small church at the edge of Monterchi. The building was destroyed by an earthquake in 1785, but miraculously the fresco remained intact. It was carefully removed and put in a small chapel nearby. Only in the late nineteenth century was it identified as being from the hand of the great master, and the people of the town realized what they had. Restorations followed, and it eventually ended up in the former middle school, becoming a required stop—along with Arezzo, Sansepolcro, and Urbino—on what could be called the Piero della Francesca Art Loop.

As Betta and Rick studied the panels explaining the history of the Madonna, a woman came to the doorway with the guard who had checked Betta's credentials at the entrance. He spoke something into the woman's ear, and she walked quickly toward Betta. She wore a white silk blouse over a blue skirt, which could have been a uniform except for the string of pearls around her neck and shoes that were not made for someone who needed to spend time on her feet. Reading glasses held by a gold chain hung over a hint of cleavage. She wore no wedding ring.

"Excuse me—I was told you are from the ministry." Her face was friendly but curious. "I am Loretta Tucci, the director of the museum."

Betta shook the extended hand. "*Piacere*, Betta Innocenti. This is Riccardo Montoya. Ours is not an official visit to your museum; we were in Monterchi on other business but of course had to come by to see the Madonna."

"Other business? Dottoressa Innocenti, this is a very small town. What could you be doing in Monterchi that would be of interest to the Cultural Ministry?"

"I work in the office that looks into stolen art, and we're investigating a missing drawing by Piero della Francesca."

The woman flinched. "It couldn't be the sketch of the sleeping soldier, I hope. I am very familiar with it. But I thought it was going to be donated to the museum in Sansepolcro yesterday. Are you telling me it's been stolen?"

Betta looked at Rick, deciding how to reply. "We're not sure," she said. "The man who was donating it died in Urbino two nights ago, and the drawing hasn't been located."

"I got back into Monterchi this morning after visiting my mother in Milan, so I haven't heard any of this. I was invited to the ceremony in Sansepolcro, but because of my mother's illness I wasn't able to attend."

"It was canceled," Rick said.

"How did the man die?"

"The police are certain that he was murdered," said Betta. "Riccardo has been assisting the investigation in Urbino."

Tucci gripped her hands together. "That's terrible. Someone killed him to get the drawing? It is a beautiful piece, and valuable, certainly, but enough to kill for?"

"Had you seen it?" asked Betta.

"Certainly. I was the person who certified its authenticity. I have studied Piero's work extensively, which is how I came to be the director here." She looked at her watch. "I would appreciate if you could tell me more about the investigation. Are you returning to Urbino immediately? I feel an attachment to that drawing after spending so much time studying it."

"And I would like to hear about your work with it," said Betta. "We were going to have lunch before driving back. Perhaps you could join us."

"That would be perfect." She managed a stiff smile. "This comes as quite a shock. If someone killed that man to get the drawing, could I have been in danger during the time I had it?"

"That's highly unlikely," Rick replied. "When you had the drawing nobody knew it had any value."

Rick's logic had a calming effect. "Yes, you're right; that makes perfect sense." She took a deep breath. "You haven't seen our masterpiece yet. Let me show it to you."

They went from a bright room to one that was almost completely darkened. The only lights were those illuminating the Madonna on the far wall, giving the impression that the fresco floated without means of support. The composition was uncomplicated: the pregnant Mary stood in the center flanked by two identical angels holding back the folds of a tent-like pavilion. Her plain blue gown, which extended to the ground, opened slightly where her hand touched the top of her belly. Rick noticed the same haunting features on the Madonna that he'd seen in Piero's other works. Her eyes were cast downward, in contrast with the two angels, who looked directly at the three people staring back at them through the darkness. After several minutes the museum director broke the silence.

"It is believed that Piero completed the work in seven days, though we don't know for sure. What is certain is that he was in Monterchi for the funeral of his mother, who was from here. It is not illogical, given the subject and the reason he was here, that he painted it in homage to his mother. There are features of the fresco that indicate that it was done quickly. Or the lack of features, one could say. The subject of the pregnant Mary had been used by other painters of the time, and most of those included religious symbols such as Mary with a book, pendants, or other items that added biblical allusions. Piero's work has very little of that." She was standing between Betta and Rick and turned to him. "Also, do you notice anything about the two angels? Besides their being shorter than the Madonna, which you would expect."

"I imagine you're asking me because you know Betta has the answer." He leaned toward the wall. "They look like twins."

"*Bravo*, Rick," said Betta. "Piero used the same paper cartoon for both angels. The technique at the time involved making the drawing and then punching tiny holes along its lines. He attached the paper to the wall and poked the holes to make marks in the surface, then used the dotted image it produced to paint the figure. But in this case he simply flipped over the cartoon and used the holes again on the other side of the Madonna to create a mirror-image angel. Because of that, not only are the faces the same but also the folds in their clothing as well as the position of their arms. Everything."

Rick's eyes moved from one angel to the other and back. "Very clever. And he used different colors on the clothing so the trick wouldn't be as obvious. But that would have certainly allowed him to work quickly."

"I didn't mean to give the impression that the work is void of religious symbolism." The museum director went on to point out other aspects of the fresco and how they fit in with or expanded the iconography of Piero's time. By the time she finished, Rick knew enough to take over tour guide duties, and the three of them were on a first-name basis. As they stood on the steps just outside the door of the museum, Tucci asked Betta how she got into the art theft squad.

"My father, who owns an art gallery, had cooperated with the office on occasion, so I knew about their work. Thanks to Rick, I became acquainted with the office more directly, and they were recruiting women with an arts background. My degree in art history finally paid off. What about you?"

"I started off as an artist, working in Milan and thinking I could make a living from my work. I did for a while, but soon it became apparent that I needed the stability of a regular salary. I went to the university, got a degree like you in art history, and started working my way through the bureaucracy." Where they stood offered a view of the green fields that squeezed against the edge of the town. "Sometimes I wonder if I made the right decision. I still miss the Milanese art scene, the excitement when a new artist appears, gossiping over a coffee at a bar near the Brera." Her eyes looked over the flat land to the northwest, as if straining to see the spires of the duomo. "Shall we be off?"

Tucci had suggested a restaurant just to the north of town, and they followed her black, late-model BMW. It was a car Rick had long coveted but out of his price range even if he ever decided to have a car in Rome. She led them back down the hill, across a small bridge, to the east–west road. They started west toward Arezzo but at the edge of Monterchi turned north in the direction of Sansepolcro. The residential buildings soon disappeared, replaced by the occasional agriculture structure or farmhouse, including a long, low food-processing operation. The passing fields sprouted with sunflowers, corn, and waving plants, most of which Rick was unable to identify. Clumps of trees bordered the cultivated land, some dense enough to be called small forests, but mostly the terrain was open, providing views of distant hills.

Ten minutes into the ride, Tucci signaled for a turn onto a narrow dirt road. Moments later the cars drove up to a three-story brick building that centuries earlier had been built to store crops and livestock on the lower floor and house the family above. They parked and climbed the steps to a porch and the entrance. A waiter spotted them as they came in and pointed to a table near a window overlooking the fields. The large room was half full with a mixture of ages and genders. It was the kind of place that would be packed with families on Sundays, but today the din was benignly low despite cement floors which amplified the smallest sound.

"I hope you enjoy this," said Tucci while spreading a napkin over her lap. "And that you have an appetite. Their portions can be quite generous."

"I'm ready," said Rick.

The rustic setting—brick, dark wood beams, farm imple-
ments decorating the walls—called for an appropriately rustic
start to the meal. They decided to share an antipasto platter
with a bottle of the house red.

"Loretta, how did you come to evaluate the drawing?" Betta
asked. "Did the woman who found it come to see you at the
museum?"

"No, it wasn't that way at all. She had no idea that it was
by Piero, nor even knew who Piero was. She knew about
our Madonna, of course, like everyone in town, but it hadn't
occurred to her that it was by the same artist. No, when she
found the sketch she called an art dealer in Urbino."

"Bruzzone."

"Yes, Bruzzone." The wine arrived and was poured. After
a quick toast she took a sip and returned to the story. "It was
Bruzzone who contacted me when he came down here himself
after the woman had called him. He recognized the face immediately as the sleeping soldier, but he wanted to be sure it was
authentic. I was the nearest Piero specialist."

The waiter set a platter in the center of the table. Arranged
on it was an assortment of sliced prosciutto, salami, and bre-
saola, next to a row of toasts covered with a meaty spread. Rick
nodded to the two women, who picked up forks and transferred some of it to their plates. When they finished serving
themselves he took his portion.

"Was there any doubt about its authenticity?" Betta asked
before taking a bite of the toast.

"At first I didn't want to get my hopes up. As you can imagine
it was very exciting when Bruzzone pulled it out of the enve-
lope. But it didn't take long to confirm it. The composition, the
lines, everything about it pointed to Piero. I did tell Bruzzone
he should have the paper and charcoal tested and dated, just

to be sure, and he did that. I think he took it to a specialist in Milan after I had studied it for a few days in my museum office and called him to confirm my evaluation."

"Did it have the little holes?" Rick asked.

Tucci gave him a blank look and then understood. "Oh, you mean what is called pouncing, like the angels you saw. No, it was a study he did before coming up with the final idea for how the figure would look. In fact there are some subtle, minor differences between the drawing and the finished work in Sansepolcro. It looked like it was out of a sketchbook, so there may have been others. Maybe they'll turn up sometime as well."

"It's unfortunate that the drawing could not have been put in your museum, having been found in Monterchi."

"I agree, Betta. We could have put it in a place of honor. But the city didn't have the funds to buy it, and the woman was not in a position to donate it. Signor Bruzzone told me she was of very modest means, so it is good that she was able to benefit from the discovery. If it was going to be put in a museum, Sansepolcro was where it belonged, next to the painting it was drawn for."

"Let's hope it is eventually found and put there, as the donor intended," Rick said. "These toasts are excellent. What's on them?"

"It's usually game of some sort. Possibly pheasant." She took a bite. "Maybe duck. Have you been able to see some of Urbino's art while working on the case?"

Betta cut a slice of prosciutto and put it on a piece of crusty bread. "We were at the Galleria Nazionale this morning to interview the director and saw a few works."

"Vitellozzi? He's getting ready for that big exhibit."

"He was doing just that when we talked to him," said Rick.

He'd finished his share of the antipasto and was thinking of the pasta course. The waiter was on his wave length, appearing to ask what they would like next. Perhaps some freshly rolled *pici* in the sauce of their choice?

"This is filling me up," said Betta. "I think I'll skip the pasta and go directly to a *secondo*."

"I agree with that," said Tucci. "But Riccardo, you go ahead and order some *pici*. They're very good here."

"No, no," Rick answered with a sigh, "I'll also pass on the pasta."

"He loves playing the martyr," Betta said before turning to the waiter. "What do you suggest?"

"The chef made an excellent *cosciotto di maiale al chianti* this morning." Perhaps for Rick's benefit, he added, "It comes with roasted potatoes."

The order went to the kitchen.

"If you've been to the Galleria Nazionale you've seen the best that Urbino has to offer," Tucci said. "The house of Rafaello is interesting from a historic point of view, but there's not much to see there as far as art."

"We'll be seeing some privately-owned art this evening," said Betta.

"Oh, really? Whose collection?"

"A man named Morelli."

Tucci looked past Betta and then back. "Sorry, I thought it was someone I knew from Sansepolcro. Did you say Morelli? I think I've heard of him. What does he collect?"

Rick wondered if Betta would say "women," but instead she answered: "I'm not sure, but he apparently is one of the largest private collectors in Urbino. I met him this morning, and when he found out I worked for the ministry he extended the invitation."

There was no response from Tucci. She took her wine-glass in hand and brought it to her lips just as the plates of their next course were brought to the table. Each had thin slices of pork lightly spread with the dark red sauce from the wine in which it had been roasted. Crisp squares of roasted potatoes completed the dish. That the pork leg was cooked in Chianti—almost the official wine of Tuscany—reminded Rick they were in that region, albeit on its most eastern edge. He tried to identify the spices wafting from his plate, but they had merged too well in the cooking process. Cinnamon? Cloves? It didn't matter; the combination was perfect. Conversation turned naturally to food and the specialties of the area, which, according to Tucci, were quite different from those of Urbino despite its proximity. Betta talked about the cooking in her native Veneto, and Tucci that of Turin, where she had been born and raised. By the time they returned to art, the plates were empty. They turned down the waiter's suggestion of dessert and ordered coffee.

"I hope you are successful in finding the drawing," said Tucci as they stood by their cars later outside the restaurant. "And Riccardo, good luck in finding the murderer. The man was Spanish, I understand. I saw his name on the invitation to the donation ceremony."

"Yes, he was. We assume that if the drawing is found his widow will honor the donation and it will be given to Sansepolcro."

Tucci laughed. "Perhaps she'll decide to give it to my museum. Wouldn't that be an interesting turn of events."

They said their goodbyes and drove off to different destinations. They were barely out of the parking lot when Betta said, "That last comment was curious, don't you think, Rick?"

"What was more curious was her reaction when you mentioned your invitation to see Morelli's art collection this evening."

———

It was late afternoon when Betta pulled the car into a space in front of the *commissariato*. They considered going in to brief DiMaio on meeting the two women in Monterchi, but Betta felt the need to call her office, and Rick wanted to check his emails. As they opened the doors, a dark blue car driven by a man in a suit and tie pulled up two spaces away. In back sat a lone passenger.

"Betta, go ahead to the hotel and make your calls. I may be needed here."

The driver of the car had emerged from his seat and was coming around to open the door for his passenger. Betta noticed who it was, nodded to Rick, and started to trudge up the hill, glad to stretch her legs after spending so much time in the car. Rick walked a few steps to where a woman was getting out of the back seat and switched his brain to Spanish.

"Señora Somonte, can I be of assistance?"

She tried to conceal her surprise at seeing him, quickly replacing the initial startled look on her face with a smug smile. Her dress clung to her hips, and she smoothed it down, perhaps without realizing she was doing it. "Señor Montoya, your appearance at this moment is perfect. Now I won't have to deal in two languages with that unpleasant policeman. I was going to express to him my annoyance that nothing has been done to find my husband's murderer. Or if it has, I've been kept in the dark about it." She folded her arms across her chest and leaned back against the car. Her driver had discreetly moved out of earshot.

"I just came back to town myself, Señora. If there is news about the case I'm not aware of it. I will be glad to express your concerns to Inspector DiMaio if you don't wish to speak to him directly." He could see that her mind was working and waited for a reply, likely something sharp and nasty to match the other two encounters he'd had with her.

She stared at him for a full minute before speaking. Her words were not what he expected.

"Señor Montoya, I loved my husband. People have always assumed otherwise, and that is understandable, given the difference in our ages and his wealth. I could see that same skepticism in the eyes of your inspector when you both came to the hotel. I know that look well, since I've been dealing with it for years in Spain. But I am a good judge of character, and I sense that you just might believe me."

"I have no reason not to, Señora. But I can assure you that the police here are not judging you, and they're doing everything in their power to find the person who killed your husband."

She continued as if he had said nothing. "Manuel knew his health was not good and confided to me that this would likely be his last trip to Italy. The donation of the drawing was to be his tribute to his mother. That, along with paying for the opening of the Raphael exhibit, would be his final act of generosity to the art community here. He liked that people in Italy thought of him as a patron of fine art rather than just a wealthy factory owner, as he is known in Asturias. It was as if he had two separate lives." She looked up at the castle where the late-afternoon sunlight reflected off the windows of the upper floors. "He was a different man when he came here, and he was in a bad mood for days after he returned to Spain. I must confess that I resented that. Can you understand?"

Rick nodded but said nothing. Why was she telling him

this? It had to be that she had no one else to talk to about her feelings. Pilar wouldn't speak to her, and Garcia was still an underling, even if there was something between them. Rick was available and perhaps would be a sympathetic listener. But the cynic in him—or was it his Italian side?—said that she was simply trying to soften her image with the police, since she knew that what she said to him would get back to DiMaio.

"I was hoping," she continued, "that on this trip I would finally begin to see Italy the way he did, rather than as a rival for his affection. I was jealous and felt guilty for it. I was hoping that the jealousy would end." She put her hands together as if in prayer and touched her fingers to her lips. Her eyes were downcast. "And then all this happened, and now I hate this country even more than before."

"That's perfectly understandable, Señora."

She looked at Rick and appeared to be deciding what else to say. Or thinking she may have already said too much. "Thank you for being so understanding." She started to extend her hand but then let it fall to her side. Her eyes darted toward the police station and back to Rick. "I trust that your police inspector is not assuming this crime must have been committed by an Italian." She turned and jerked her chin to signal the driver.

Rick stepped to the car and opened the rear door. The driver hurried over and got in behind the wheel before starting the engine. Isabella Somonte stared straight ahead as the car pulled out into the street and drove off. Rick watched it go and walked toward the police station to pass the widow's concerns on to DiMaio, including her final comment. What else he would tell him about their conversation he didn't know.

Meanwhile, Betta was walking into the lobby of the Hotel Botticelli. As she approached the desk to pick up the room key she noticed Pilar sitting in the far corner, holding tightly to her cell phone and staring at the floor. Betta walked over and sat in the chair next to hers.

"Pilar, are you all right?"

"What? Oh, it's you, Betta. I just got some news I wasn't expecting."

"Bad news?"

Pilar shook her head. "No, not really."

Given the look on Pilar's face, Betta was not convinced. "Do you want to talk about it?"

"It might help." She tucked her phone into a purse on the small table between them. "The call was from our family attorney about my father's will. Apparently my understanding of the will was essentially correct. I remember vividly when my father called me in just after he remarried and told me exactly what I was getting and what would go to that woman. It was a very cold, very short meeting. But the lawyer just told me that something in the will was changed—added, really—about six months ago. Either my father didn't want to tell me face to face, or he wanted it to be a surprise after he'd died. Or he may not have wanted Isabella to find out until he was gone." She looked at Betta. "I'm not making any sense, am I?"

"You're making perfect sense. Take your time."

Pilar took a tissue from the purse and held it at the ready. "When I was a child my father spent even more time at work than he did later, because he was building the business. I now understand how difficult that was, but at the time I resented it. Summers back then were especially busy for him, and he never took time off, even on weekends. He believed that vacations for him would come once the business had grown, and he was correct. While he worked during those summer months, my mother and I went off to a tiny rental cottage overlooking the Bay of Biscay, all we could afford at the time. It was very rustic, with no electricity, and water from a well, but I loved it. My most treasured memories of my mother are from those summers. She read to me by candlelight and told me stories of when she was growing up. Every day we walked down to the small, rocky beach and splashed in the water."

She pressed the tissue to her eyes. "When the business became more successful my father rented a villa for us on Minorca near the one he eventually bought. I was thirteen at the time. Mamma was happy with the villa, of course. But I felt betrayed, and at first I refused to go. Part of it was my resentment that my father was still spending so much time at the office instead of with me. But I also understood that those times with my mother were coming to an end, though I didn't want to admit it. My father couldn't understand why I would not be happy to spend the summer at a beautiful villa." She blew her nose in the tissue and pulled out another. "Betta, now I know that he did understand."

"That's what the call was about," said Betta.

"Yes. The lawyer told me that six months ago my father heard rumors that the property where we used to rent the cottage could be up for sale and that a conglomerate would likely buy it, tear down the cottage, and build a hotel. He moved quickly, making a generous offer to the owner that was accepted."

"And now it will be yours."

Pilar nodded but took a minute to answer. "Betta, I'll never be able to thank him."

"It was the way he wanted it, Pilar. From what you've told us, he was a private man, so you have to accept that. Just be thankful for a posthumous olive branch, and remember this gesture rather than the disagreements you may have had with him."

Pilar sniffed in a breath. "Yes. Yes, you're right. Thank you for listening to me run on." She rose to her feet. "I think it will help if I walk around, since my father loved this city so much. It will almost be like walking with him."

"Good idea," said Betta as she stood and gave Pilar a warm embrace.

Two minutes later Rick came through the door and spotted Betta in a chair in the corner. He walked over and sat down next to her.

"I passed Pilar on the street, but she just smiled and waved. Did you see her?"

"I certainly did." She recounted what she had just heard.

"Fascinating," said Rick, when she'd finished the story. He stretched out his legs and crossed one cowboy boot over the other. "It appears that old man Somonte was not as hard-hearted as we'd come to believe. I got a bit of that from his widow as well. She claims that they had a wonderful marriage, based on mutual affection."

"She was all sweetness?"

"Not exactly. She asked me to light a fire under Alfredo to find the murderer. And her last comment insinuated that he should not just be looking at Italians when making his suspects list."

"Meaning Pilar or Lucho."

Rick held up two fingers. "Or both of them. But it could just be the bitter and grieving widow talking, without any real basis for her suspicions."

"Or Pilar is, in fact, behind the murder, even if she didn't pull the trigger herself. And now, after this gesture from her father in his will, she's feeling remorse." They both thought about that possibility for a few moments before Betta asked, "Did you tell Alfredo what Signora Somonte said?"

"I was going to, but he wasn't there. We'll let him know about our meetings with the Somonte women next time we see him."

Once in the room, Betta sat at the small desk and dialed her cell phone. Rick turned on his laptop, kicked off his boots, and propped himself up on the bed. Getting his emails was worth the effort: a message confirming that a check was on the way for a translation he'd done, and a request for his interpreting services. The interpreting job sounded interesting—an international seminar at a think tank in Rome on the long-term consequences of Brexit for Italy. Well, it would be interesting if not dominated by economist-speak, which was not much fun for the interpreters.

Betta's phone call with her boss was less satisfying.

"He's not happy with the lack of progress," she said after pulling off her shoes. "I'm not pleased either, but they can't expect this to be resolved in twenty-four hours. I know what they're thinking, though. It's like the murder investigation is for Alfredo. Every day that goes by without finding the murderer, the chances of solving the case decrease exponentially. Same with finding the drawing. We need to catch a break."

Rick got off the bed and walked over to stand behind the chair. He placed his hands on her shoulders and kneaded them lightly. "You're too tense, Betta, and all that driving didn't help. You need to relax."

"That feels good. Don't stop."

"It's the way I always show appreciation to my chauffeur."

"I will have to drive you around more often." She closed her eyes and moved her head from one side to the other as his hands moved over her neck and shoulders. "This is wonderful, but with all the driving today, I think I should get more than a neck rub."

"Perhaps that can be arranged."

—

The temperature was cooling when they left the Botticelli for the home of Cosimo Morelli. While Betta was taking a phone call, Rick had asked directions at the front desk and was given a map with assurance that it was an easy walk. As expected, the route started with an uphill climb. Like so many other Italian cities, Urbino was crisscrossed by main arteries that offered enough width to accommodate large carts when they were laid out and now cars and small delivery trucks. Splaying off these wider streets was a matrix of smaller ones, in some cases virtual alleys barely wide enough for two people to walk side by side. Fortunately the map from the hotel was detailed enough to cover everything in the web that was Urbino's municipal grid. The desk clerk had drawn the route with his pen, like a line through the maze on the puzzle page in a newspaper. It was initially the same streets Betta had walked on her way to the art gallery of Signor Bruzzone, up Via Mazzini and then a steeper climb on Via Raffaello. Every Italian town of a certain size had a street named for Giuseppe Mazzini, who had helped create a united Italy, but very few honored Urbino's most beloved artist. The lights were on in Bruzzone's art gallery, and Betta toyed with the idea of dropping in to introduce Rick. Instead they continued up the hill past the house of Raphael.

"Morelli's name came up when I talked to my boss," said Betta. "I told him we were going to see his collection, and he asked me to observe closely and let him know if there's anything suspicious."

"How will you know?"

"Good question. If Morelli has anything questionable it will be the Greek vases, and I am hardly an expert on things Greek. Not to mention that the man is not going to show me anything questionable since he knows where I work. I told my boss I'd keep my eyes open."

"I will too, Betta. Two eyes are better than one."

"What?"

"Something my Tía Luz in New Mexico used to say. Now

all the Montoyas use the expression." They came to a corner, and Rick looked up before consulting his map. As in most Italian cities, the street name was inscribed on a stone plaque cemented to the corner building. "We turn here."

The new street was half the width of Via Raffaello, had no commercial activity, and had no incline as it followed the horizontal contour of the hill. The buildings were solid stone, two and three stories tall, with tiny windows and narrow, uninviting doors. The flat walk ended at the next corner when they turned once again up the incline. Rick stopped.

"We're almost there. Look at that." A metal arrow indicated that if they were to continue on that street, the botanical gardens were a hundred meters ahead. "Interesting. On the way to Morelli's house we pass close to the scene of the murder."

Betta took his arm. "In Italian hill towns, Rick, everything inside the walls is close to everything else."

"I suppose you're right." He checked the stone number on the first doorway. "This is the street—his place should be just ahead if the numbers run in the right sequence."

"Don't count on that."

The sequence was correct, and their destination appeared on their right. It looked like every other building on the block, except wider. The street had steepened so much that a massive window on the right side of Morelli's house looked out over the roof below it, even though both buildings were the same height. Morelli's door was at the lowest point, heavy wood set in the stone facade next to another opening less than half the size. The smaller door was older, its hinges rusted and covered with dirt. Betta noticed Rick looking at it.

"*La porta del morto,*" she said. "Haven't you ever seen one?"

"A door for dead people to enter the house?"

"To depart the house. It was considered bad luck in the

Middle Ages to use the main door when removing the casket of a family member. Something about the spirits staying inside when the body left the premises. It was a standard building feature during the plague years." She rang the doorbell. "Let's hope Morelli lets us use the big door when we're leaving tonight."

The big door was opened by a man in the gray uniform of a household servant. He wished them a good evening and stepped back to let them enter before closing the door and walking quickly ahead to lead the way. A few steps inside was the start of a stairway leading up to the second floor. Wrought-iron hand rails were attached to the stone walls, and tiny lights lit every step. On reaching the second floor the steps passed a closed door, turned back toward the street, and climbed to the third. At the end of the stairway they emerged into a room that appeared to take up most of the entire floor. The picture window they had seen from the street covered most of one side of the room, and a stone fireplace that must have been in the house from the beginning dominated the far wall. On either side of it, back-lit glass cases held a collection of Greek pottery. A set of comfortable chairs and a large sofa faced the window, and a smaller seating arrangement was set before the fireplace. Paintings filled every available wall space. Morelli, wearing a blue blazer and tie-less white shirt, stood in front of the fireplace talking on a cell phone. He looked up, smiled at Betta, but squinted when he noticed Rick behind her. Saying something into the phone, he pressed the screen and put it into the pocket of his jacket before walking to them and taking Betta's hand in both of his. His cologne and her perfume competed for air space.

"How nice of you to come. And you've brought a friend."

The two men eyed each other. Rick's smile was relaxed, Morelli's forced.

"This is Riccardo Montoya. Rick, Signor Cosimo Morelli."

They shook hands and Morelli turned to Betta. "I hope we can dispense with formalities. Please call me Cosimo. Riccardo, I don't recall seeing you around the city, so tell me what brings you to Urbino."

"I came with Betta from Rome, and I've been assisting the police in the murder investigation."

"So you're also with the art police?"

"Not exactly." Rick did not elaborate. He was enjoying Morelli's discomfort.

After an awkward silence Betta looked around the room. "Are we early?"

"My other friends unfortunately canceled at the last minute." He gestured toward a bar near the top of the stairwell. "Can Rino serve you something? I have an excellent prosecco open and chilled."

They accepted, and Morelli nodded to the man who was still standing at the top of the steps. Rino stepped behind the bar where a bottle sat in a silver ice bucket next to two flutes on a tray. He pulled a third glass from under the bar, filled the three with the bubbly, and carried the tray to Betta. After the two men claimed their glasses, Morelli offered a toast and they took their first sips while Rino disappeared down the stairs.

"Please make yourselves comfortable." Morelli motioned to the seating in front of the window. "The air is clear tonight, so the view is excellent."

Rick and Betta walked to the window. The roofs of Urbino formed an orange canopy pierced by chimneys and grooved with the lines of lamp-lit streets. The final rays of the afternoon sun painted the castle's western facade in the distance, and lights twinkled far off in the darkening valleys. The window glass was thick enough to keep out any street noise, though it wasn't needed. Later students and a few tourists might raise the noise level in some parts of the city, but now a tranquility had settled over everything. It was the Urbino of the Middle Ages.

The sound of a cell phone broke the mood. Morelli pulled it out and checked the number. "Please excuse me; I must take this." He walked quickly to the other side of the room and began talking in low tones so that his two guests could not catch even one word.

Betta leaned toward Rick's ear and spoke in equally low tones. "Did you see the look on his face when he saw you? Priceless. Listen, Rick, I want you to do something."

"For you, anything."

"You have your phone, don't you? At some point I'll distract him—"

"For you, that should be easy."

"I'll distract him, and I want you to use your phone to take a picture of that amphora."

Rick looked over her shoulder while she kept her eyes on the view. "The big one?"

"Yes, the big one."

"Leave it to me."

The phone call ended just as Rick and Betta sat on the wide leather sofa and placed their glasses on a low carved table in front of them. Morelli eased himself into one of the chairs and took a pull of his prosecco.

"I'm very sorry about that, Betta. You have been keeping occupied with this case, I trust?" Rick, it appeared, was to be ignored.

Betta crossed her legs under the attentive eye of the host. "Yes. My concern, of course, is the missing Piero drawing, and I'm trying to find out as much as I can about it. Today we drove down to Monterchi to interview the woman who found it in her attic, but we were able only to talk to her daughter."

"Was that revealing?"

"Not really. She didn't tell us anything we didn't already know."

"You don't think the woman who discovered the drawing could have anything to do with it going missing now, do you?"

"Likely not, but I had to check all the possibilities. We also spoke with the director of the Madonna del Parto Museum in Monterchi." She paused to take a sip of her wine, allowing Rick to observe Morelli's reaction. Was there something? He couldn't tell.

"It was she who authenticated the drawing at Bruzzone's request."

"Aha," said Morelli. "I knew someone had done the authentication but didn't realize it was the museum director. But that would make sense."

"Have you met her, Cosimo?"

The question forced him to recognize Rick. "The arts community in this part of Italy is not as small as you might think, Riccardo. I have not had the pleasure of meeting this Dottoressa...?"

"Tucci."

"Tucci. The name sounds familiar, but I meet a lot of people and immediately forget them."

Like me, Rick could not help thinking. "What business are you in, Cosimo? You must be very successful in it."

"Oil." He glanced at Rick's cowboy boots, and added, "Olive oil, that is, both domestic and imported." He waved his hand toward the display cases. "Which is how I became interested in Greek pieces, from my frequent visits to that country. It began with oil lamps, as would be expected given the places I go to buy it, and then moved to larger objects." He returned his attention to Betta. "Would you like to see them?"

She got to her feet. "Certainly. That's why you invited me up here, wasn't it?"

Morelli didn't answer but stood and walked with her to the display cases. Rick trailed behind them. Except for the one case that held the tall amphora, the others were all a smaller size. Unlike those found in museum collections, the pieces were not identified, as if their beauty was more important than date and location. Not a big fan of pottery, Rick found them to be interesting but nothing more. He was curious about the details but wasn't about to ask Morelli, assuming the man wouldn't need any prodding. He was correct.

"I see that the amphora has caught your eye, Betta. It is the prize of my collection, sixth century BC, found on the island of Mykonos. Given its decoration, size, and shape, most likely it was used for wine, and on festive occasions. But I would like to think it contained olive oil at some point in its life."

The pointed base of the pear-shaped vase sat on a wire stand. A mirror on the wall behind it allowed a total view of black figures painted on a light brown background. Women in flowing robes carried vases similar in shape and size, forming a circular parade around the widest part of the vessel.

"It is very beautiful," she said. "And these?" She pointed at a row of ceramic pieces somewhere in shape between a saucer and a cup. Some had handles, and all were decorated with figures, both male and female.

"Drinking cups, from different parts of Greece."

"Do you have one dealer you always use in Greece?"

Morelli could not conceal his annoyance. Was it Rick's question, or just his presence? "I have several who know my interests. They contact me when something comes on the market that I might wish to acquire."

"As with the Piero drawing? I assume Bruzzone called you."

"Had he not, Betta, I would have been very unhappy." He walked to the next case. "And these are the oil lamps. I have too many of them, perhaps, but can one really possess too many objects that have both function and beauty?"

Morelli did not see Rick squeezing Betta's arm, nor her poking back.

"This one is interesting," she said. "It's bronze rather than terra-cotta." She leaned forward to get a closer look at an oil lamp with a leaf-shaped handle and floral etching on the top and sides.

"Roman third century. It's not genuine, but I love its character."

"That de Chirico I'm certain is genuine." Betta was looking at the paintings on the opposite wall.

"And it would be my pleasure to show it to a member of the art police who should certainly be able to verify its authenticity."

The two walked across the room while Rick stayed where he was and slipped the phone from his pocket. Seeing that Morelli was giving all his attention to Betta and the painting, he took two pictures of the amphora and then, for good measure, several of the other display cases. After checking his work he put his phone away and returned to the table where he picked up his flute and had another drink. It was an excellent prosecco and somehow tasted even better after he had played undercover art cop. He walked to the window and saw that the sun was gone, bringing darkness to the highest parts of Urbino and causing a few stars to appear in the cloudless sky. Light pollution was a big issue in communities around New Mexico, he recalled, with regulations requiring outdoor lighting be directed downward. Could Urbino have the same rules? The streetlights he could see from the window fit the bill their rays went straight to the pavement.

Rick returned to the issues at hand. Did Morelli really have some hot art? If Betta could not track down the missing drawing, it would be helpful if she could at least snare some other malefactor, and Morelli just might be the one. But was he evil enough to be the murderer as well? Somehow Rick couldn't see him shooting *el viejo* Somonte. No, the oil merchant, as oily as he was, just didn't fit the bill. After reminding himself that he wasn't a specialist in criminal behavior, Rick walked to where Betta and Morelli were standing in front of the de Chirico.

Like most works by the artists, this one was without people, animals, or indeed anything that could be called living. The results of human activity were evident, however: an open plaza, the columns of a classical building, and a distant statue. Late-afternoon—or possibly early morning—sun cast long shadows. The position of the few objects and a clear vanishing point allowed for well-painted perspective, but somehow everything did not line up the way it should, adding another surreal aspect to a picture that was already unearthly enough.

"Do you like it, Rick?"

"Not really my style. I prefer the masters, like the Pieros we saw today."

Morelli said, "Piero's *Flagellation*, which is at the Galleria here in Urbino, has some aspects of this style: an open square, a few silent figures, a certain eerie quality. It could have influenced de Chirico."

"But look at the perspective here and compare it with Piero's works," said Rick as he continued to study the work. "I prefer the master of perspective."

"Often artists bend the rules just to show they can do it." Morelli's voice had assumed a tone of condescension. "That was the case with de Chirico. If you had ever studied—"

Betta stepped in. "Cosimo, it would be rude of us to get

into a heated discussion when we're guests in your home, even over such a fascinating topic as the qualities of surrealism. And unfortunately we can't stay; we have a dinner engagement with Inspector DiMaio."

The mention of the policeman took Morelli's attention away from the painting, but he quickly regained his composure. "I am sorry not to be able to enjoy your company longer, but it was a pleasure to see you nonetheless." His words were to Betta. Rick had once again become invisible.

They complimented him on his apartment and the art collection, and he accompanied them down the stairs to the street.

"You must be sure to give my warm regards to Inspector DiMaio."

Betta promised they would. The door closed and they started down the street.

"That was certainly enjoyable," said Rick as Betta took his arm.

"He does have a certain reptilian character, but his collection is impressive. Were you able to get a picture of the amphora? That was my main reason for going."

"He was so enthralled with you that I photographed not only the amphora but also several of the other items. I can send the photos to your phone."

"And I'll forward them to my office. It's a bit of a long shot, but who knows? It might be on the list of missing amphorae, but I doubt it. He's got a huge ego, but he's intelligent enough not to show a stolen item to someone from the art police."

"He knows Greek is not your specialty, and besides, his desire to get you alone must have clouded his thinking."

Betta smiled. "Did you notice that he claimed not to know Loretta Tucci?"

"At lunch today she gave the impression she didn't know him either." He glanced down at her face, which was still smiling.

"Betta, I may be just a naive American, but it occurs to me that perhaps they really don't know each other."

She shrugged.

Rick moved on. "I didn't know we were having dinner with Alfredo."

"He doesn't either. He thinks he's dining alone with Pilar. That was the call I took at the hotel."

"Dinner probably won't be a good time to tell him about my meeting with the widow."

"No, Rick, it won't."

# CHAPTER EIGHT

The restaurant was near the Palazzo Ducale, not exactly around the corner from Morelli's house but still within the city walls and therefore walking distance. They strolled down his street and retraced their route to get back to Via Raffaello. The shops on it were already shuttered or about to have their gates rolled down and padlocked. In only one could they see any customers, a *salumaio* with last-minute shoppers picking up something for dinner. At the bottom of the hill they passed the small square in front of the municipal building, and a theater across the street showing a French film that neither of them recognized.

The street name changed to Via Vittorio Veneto, but unlike its wide and tree-lined Roman namesake, this one was narrow and steep, barely wide enough for two cars. Which was likely why it was in a pedestrian area. And pedestrians there were, mostly young people whom Rick guessed to be students at the university, heading in the opposite direction, down the hill. Perhaps the cheaper restaurants were down there, away from the tourist area surrounding the duke's palace. As they got to the top of the hill, the street widened slightly and on the right were steps leading up to the cathedral. Betta looked at her watch.

"The restaurant is close and we're early. Do you want to walk down toward the university?"

Rick looked up at the cathedral facade, a clean white marble showing the required features of the classical style. He was certain there had been a church on the site for more than a millennium, given the age of Urbino, but he was equally sure that this was not the original structure. Two people emerged from the right door.

"The duomo is still open; why don't we check it out?"

"I recall you telling me that when you were a kid you dreaded being dragged into churches by your parents."

They started to climb the steps. "I also didn't like girls when I was in grade school. A guy can change, can't he? I am now grateful that my parents insisted on taking me into all those churches; it gave me my first appreciation of history, art, and architecture. This one, however, looks like the classic case of taking a wonderful ancient church and renovating it into the stylistic flavor of the moment."

They went through the door and immediately decided his assessment was correct. A panel just inside gave a short history of the building, which they read after dipping their fingers in the font and crossing themselves. The first cathedral on the site had been constructed in 1021, but it was rebuilt by Duke Federico da Montefeltro in the fifteenth century. A devastating earthquake in 1789 required another total renovation, and it was done in the neoclassical style popular at the time. The overriding impression of this renovation was mass rather than space, thanks to thick, square columns supplemented by Corinthian decoration and the same color—white—covering everything. Lighting was minimal, except for what illuminated the coffered cupola visible in the distance over the main altar. Rather than walk straight down the central nave, they started along the right aisle. Columns and arches ran along their left, the outer wall on their right. Opposite the arches were altars under tall paintings done in the style of the early nineteenth century, with dark figures and darker backgrounds. It was not Rick's favorite. He could not help wondering what the Duke of Montefeltro's church was like before the earthquake spelled its destruction.

As they stood before the first painting, raised voices echoed from the opposite side of the church. Rick squeezed Betta's hand and held up a finger over his lips. The conversation reached their ears in disjointed words, but one thing was clear: the two people were speaking in Spanish. Rick guided Betta behind the nearest column.

"That's Pilar's voice," whispered Betta after they had listened for a minute.

"And the man is Lucho Garcia, Somonte's assistant."

Rick held up his hand and strained to hear what they were saying, which was not easy since two rows of columns and the nave stood between them. The lack of ornamentation and the stone floor allowed sound to bounce off the surfaces, but it reached Rick's ears only intermittently. What was clear, however, was that the two Spaniards were not having a friendly chat. As the moments passed, Pilar's voice raised and Lucho's was edged with anger.

"Can you get anything they're saying?"

"Only a few words," Rick answered. "The factory, her father, the inheritance—"

He was interrupted by Pilar's raised voice, the unmistakable sound of a slap, and Pilar's heels clicking on the stone as she hurried toward the door.

"What did she just say?"

"That, I heard. She called him a rude name. Just before hitting him."

"You can't stage a more dramatic exit than that. Do you think he followed her out?"

Rick peeked around the pillar. "I see him. He's walking toward the door, very slowly, and rubbing his face. Let's amble down toward the altar and wait a while. We don't want to run into either of them outside."

"Rick, do you think she'll be at the restaurant?"

"I don't see why not. Thanks to the confrontation, she's probably worked up an appetite. But I doubt she'll bring Lucho."

They walked along the side aisle to the main altar, looking back to be sure the two Spaniards didn't return, though there seemed little chance of that. Under the dome the altar was a simple stone table draped with a white cloth, a gold cross in the middle. Above it on the wall hung another dark painting, but larger than the others. They took the other aisle for their return to the door, and on reaching it, Rick peeked out. No sign of either Pilar or Lucho.

"We should tell Alfredo about this, Rick." They stood outside at the top of the steps. In the small square between the church and the palace, three people studied the poster for the Raphael exhibit, then started down the hill.

"Let's think about it. If I recall correctly, Pilar said that she was likely to keep Lucho on at the family wool mill. So it would make sense that she would want to talk to him about his position there. She had only talked to him on the phone since her father's death and must have wanted a face-to-face meeting. I will admit that it did not appear they were exclusively discussing wool back there, but what do we really know, except that they were having an argument? It could have been about anything. Why don't we wait to see if she says something at dinner? And if she doesn't, to coax out what might be going on, I can ask her some seemingly innocent questions."

"Such as, 'Does your hand still hurt?'"

He laughed. "That would work."

"Rick, what you're really concerned about is Alfredo's disappointment if he finds out that his new flame is a possible suspect. Pilar and Lucho could have planned the murder together. It's even possible that the three of them could have done it. They all benefit from the old man's death, and the animosity between the widow and the daughter could be an act."

"If they were going to kill him, why do it in another country? It would have been less complicated if Somonte had met his fate in an accident at home, or at his wool mill. They could have simply pushed him into a vat of dye." He put his fingers to his forehead. "Wait, it just occurred to me that the words in English for die and dye are homophones."

"What?"

"Sorry. The musings of a professional translator. Why don't we see what she says at dinner, and if she's not there, we'll tell Alfredo what happened. We can also tell him about my meeting with Signora Somonte."

She took his arm and they started down the steps. "Agreed."

Ten minutes later they came to the Ristorante La Balestra. It would have taken them five minutes, but it was difficult to find among the winding alleys of Urbino. One person they asked for help turned out to be a tourist, so Rick ducked into a bar where he got detailed instructions. Adding to the search time, only a small and dimly lit sign marked the entrance, and when they finally spotted it they realized they'd walked by it twice. After they passed through the door it became clear that the hidden location wasn't an issue—the place was full and loud. The dining room was on a slightly lower level from the entrance, giving them a full view of the animated scene spread out below them. The decor went with the restaurant name: ancient crossbows decorated the walls, each mounted next to a collection of short, dart-like projectiles that the *balestre* shot. Two couples waiting for a table glanced at Betta and Rick before returning to their conversation. Betta looked down and saw DiMaio waving from a corner table with Pilar next to him. He was seated with his back to the wall, facing out, like he was expecting trouble.

They walked down the steps and worked their way through an obstacle course of tables and diners to where DiMaio was now standing. He kissed Betta on both cheeks, shook hands with Rick, and waited while they greeted the seated Pilar.

"I was so glad to hear that you two were going to join us," DiMaio said as he pulled out Betta's chair.

"I'm sure you were," answered Betta while smiling at Pilar.

"I ordered a bottle of Bianchello del Metauro," said DiMaio, "a good local white. I trust that will work for everyone." He was about to take his seat when a waiter hurried up to him.

"Can I bother you for a moment before you sit down, Inspector?"

"Of course." He turned to the others at the table. "It's impossible for a policeman to go incognito in a town this size. And what can I do for you?"

"Can you reach one of those bottles on the shelf behind you? No, the other one. The Chianti. Thank you; please excuse me." He hurried off with the bottle in hand.

DiMaio sat down and spread a napkin on his lap. "It took special police skills to remove that bottle."

"No doubt something you learned at the police academy," said Rick. "Like the skills needed to find this place."

"That's the way we like it," answered DiMaio as he poured water and wine into the glasses of the new arrivals. "We don't want any tourists wandering in here."

"I don't think there's much danger of that," said Betta while picking up her wineglass. "*Salute.*" The others tapped her glass and everyone took a drink.

When the glasses were back on the table Pilar began the conversation. "Alfredo was telling me about your friend Morelli, so we're anxious to hear how the visit to his art collection went."

"Both his home and his collection are impressive, but I can't say the same for him. As you would imagine, he was not overjoyed at seeing Rick, but since there was nothing he could do about it, he dutifully played the good host. Before I forget, Alfredo, he sends warm regards."

"Very kind of him. Were you able to spot some contraband?"

Betta shook her head. "I'm afraid not. He knows where I work, of course, so I didn't expect to make a seizure. There were no empty spaces in his display cabinets. If he put something away for the night, then he must have added another piece in its place."

"And that wouldn't surprise me," said Rick while looking at food on the tables nearby. "Alfredo, you must come here often. What's good?"

"They only make a few dishes each night, and there's no printed menu. Our waiter will be back in a minute, but he told us the specials today are the *maccheroncelli alla campofilone* for your *primo* and *petto di pollo trifolato* for the main course." He pointed at the bottle of white wine. "Keep in mind that I ordered this local *bianchello*, but our second bottle can be a red."

"Those both sound good to me. How about you, Betta?"

"I'm in. Pilar?"

"I am, as well. For some reason I have a large appetite. As I recall from my years in Italy, when they push you toward a daily special, it will be good. And we'll make it easier on them if we all order the same thing."

The waiter appeared and was pleased to hear the order.

He complimented their decision and assured them that they would not be disappointed. Like all good Italian waiters, he wrote down nothing.

"I haven't seen you two since this morning," DiMaio said. "What did you get from Vitellozzi?"

"Not much," said Betta. "He was busy setting up the big exhibit, so we talked with him among the crates. He said Manuel Somonte had visited him in his office the day after arriving in Urbino and talked about donating the drawing to the museum in Sansepolcro. Vitellozzi had the feeling he was apologizing for not giving it to him."

"I think my father supported the Galleria Nazionale delle Marche, so the man couldn't complain that much."

"That's true, Pilar. In fact he paid for part of the exhibit opening tomorrow night." Betta turned back to DiMaio. "Vitellozzi didn't have an alibi that could be corroborated; he said he was working late on the exhibit."

The waiter returned, laden with plates and a platter, which he put on a side table next to theirs. The platter was piled high with what looked like thin, flat spaghetti in a tomato meat sauce. With a fork and spoon between the fingers of his right hand, he deftly transferred portions of the pasta onto the four plates and whisked them in front of each of the diners. After wishing them a *buon appetito*, he took his cutlery and platter and headed back to the kitchen.

Everyone stared at their plates while breathing in the flavors.

"I thought *maccheroncelli* would be some local type of *maccheroni*," said Rick. "This looks suspiciously like tagliatelle or fettuccine. Not that I'm complaining—it smells wonderful."

"Riccardo," said DiMaio, "yesterday you wanted to call the *vincisgrassi* lasagna, so you are hardly the person to give them lessons on naming pasta." He picked up his fork. "*Buon appetito.*"

A collective analysis of the pasta sauce followed. It was a tomato base, with minced chicken and veal, flavored by nutmeg and onion. Bits of carrot and celery could also be detected. The combination of it all, they agreed, worked quite well. When most of the plates had emptied, talk went back to where it had left off, with Betta and Rick in the duke's palace.

"After we left Vitellozzi to his picture-hanging," Rick said, "I bumped into Signora Somonte and Lucho Garcia. They were looking at a painting by Piero." He watched for any reaction from Pilar and detected none. "She said something that surprised me." Still no reaction. "If the drawing is found, she is undecided about donating it to the museum in Sansepolcro. It would be hers to do with whatever she wishes, in her opinion."

"Is that true?"

Betta considered Pilar's question and shook her head. "I couldn't say. It would depend on what kind of agreement the man had with the museum, and if his heirs are bound by it. Do you have any interest in the drawing?"

Pilar waved a finger before taking a drink of wine. It was a very Italian gesture, and Rick wondered whether it was one common in Spain as well. "Tell me, Pilar, have you decided yet if you're going to retain Garcia at the mill? Last night you were leaning toward a yes." He looked at Betta, who was carefully placing her fork at the top of her empty dish, avoiding his eye.

At that moment the waiter arrived, and they paused while he removed their pasta dishes. DiMaio tapped on the almost empty wine bottle, and the waiter gave him a confirming nod.

"I'm not sure, Riccardo. I talked with some of my section managers back in Spain this morning, and their reaction was mixed. It made me think that it might be time for a complete change in personnel. My father's death was not something I was expecting, of course, so I hadn't put any thought into what

I would do differently if I became the owner. So as far as Lucho, I'm still leaning toward retaining him, but thinking about it."

"If I were in his shoes," said DiMaio, "I'd be worrying about my position and doing some lobbying with the new boss." He glanced up. "But we should be trying to keep your mind off such decisions and get back to the important business of enjoying this meal. Our chicken has arrived."

Like the first course, the second came on a large serving platter along with four plates. The chicken breasts, topped with thin slices of prosciutto and melted cheese, rested on pan drippings that had been swirled with cognac. The smells of the other flavors, rich as they were, played second fiddle to the shaved truffle sprinkled on the cheese. The waiter put a piece of chicken on each plate and spooned sauce over it before placing the plates in front of the four diners, who instinctively leaned forward and sniffed.

"Truffles can be overpowering," said DiMaio, "but here they add just the right amount of flavor so that it works." After initial tastes, they all agreed and became so engrossed in their enjoyment of the dish that they barely noticed the arrival of the second bottle of Bianchello del Metauro.

"When are you planning to return to Spain?"

Betta's question prompted an exchange of looks between Pilar and DiMaio.

"I'm in no rush, really. The mill is in good hands, and, despite the reason for this visit, I have to admit that I'm enjoying being back in Italy." She told them about her first experience, as a student in Florence, and how it had made her decide to pursue textile design as her life work. At the time she had considered staying in Italy, but her father had insisted she come home because of her mother's illness. It had been the right thing to do. By the time her mother died, Pilar was making all the design decisions at the company and thoughts of living in Italy had disappeared, or at least been suppressed. Now they flowed back. "I'll have to return to Spain. There is no alternative."

"But not immediately, I hope."

"No, Alfredo, not immediately."

An awkward silence was broken by Rick. "We also went to Monterchi. Don't you want to hear about that, Alfredo?"

"Oh, of course. How did that go?"

"The woman who found the drawing is no longer alive," Betta said, "but we talked to her daughter. The way she described the transaction is what I would have expected, since we've seen this kind of thing before. Work of art found in an attic, art dealer contacted, art authenticated, art sold for a lot of money. The daughter didn't know about it until the drawing was sold and her mother bought the house where the daughter is now living."

"End of story."

"Not exactly. We dropped in to see the *Madonna del Parto* and met the director. She turned out to be the Piero expert who verified the drawing as authentic. We had a pleasant lunch with her but didn't learn anything more of interest."

Pilar finished her last slice of truffled chicken. "What's next for you, Betta?"

"I don't know, Pilar. I need a break in the case. Something. Anything."

DiMaio nodded. "You could say the same about my case."

———

Rick and Betta looked up and down the street when the restaurant door closed behind them and took deep breaths of the cool evening air. It felt good on their faces after the wine and rich food.

"I should have dropped a trail of bread crumbs to find our way back," Rick said.

But they easily made it out to the main street, helped by the occasional sign for the Palazzo Ducale. The square in front of the palace was brightly lit, a single spotlight trained on the banner for the exhibit opening the next night. Only a few people were about at this hour, groups of university students and the odd worker on his or her way home from the late shift. Betta held Rick's arm as they looked at the massive outline of the building. She turned her face to the cathedral, also bathed in light.

"Rick, we'll have to say something to Alfredo about what happened there earlier. It may be nothing, but it could have some bearing on the case. Alfredo has to be the judge of that."

"Pilar certainly didn't appear upset at the restaurant. She is either very good at recovering from unpleasant incidents, or it may not have been anything serious. That could be the way factory owners normally treat their employees in Spain." He felt a pull on his arm. "Or perhaps not. It was interesting that she still is leaning toward keeping Lucho on the payroll."

"That's what she says. Who knows what she really intends to do." They began the walk down the hill to their hotel. Except for the last fifty meters, it would be all descent. "Have you ever wondered why Pilar came here at all?"

"What do you mean?"

"Well, she said she was estranged from her father and that she detests the second Signora Somonte. Why not just let the widow and Garcia take care of what needs to be done to bring the body back to Spain?"

"Come now, Betta. It's her father, and the man was murdered. She wants to find out what happened. You'll recall that it was Lucho who called her to give her the news, and I imagine he asked her to come."

"Yes, you're right. I'm trying to read too much into it. That slap has me inventing all kinds of scenarios, but that's the way we Italians think. There has to be something sinister behind everything, especially if it's as dramatic as what happened in the cathedral."

"One person's drama could be another's normal behavior."

"In that case, Alfredo had better behave himself."

Rick squinted toward the dimly lit square that ran along the side of the palace, where the obelisk planted in its center cast pointed shadows over the cobblestones. At the far end, a figure hurried into one of the narrow side streets and disappeared.

"Was that who I think it was?"

Betta turned and looked. "I don't see anyone. Who was it?"

"I'm pretty sure it was Loretta Tucci. I don't remember her mentioning at lunch that she was coming to Urbino today."

Betta inclined her head toward the banner hanging from the wall of the museum. "I'm sure she got an invitation to the opening tomorrow. She must have decided to come up a day early."

They went from the lights of the cathedral facade to the relative darkness of the street leading down the hill. A well-fed cat scurried from one doorway to another, looking for a mouse or some feline companionship, not noticing the two humans walking behind. At the bottom of the hill stragglers stood inside the bar next to the theater arguing the merits of the film they had seen.

"How about a coffee or mineral water?" Rick asked.

"I could use it."

Rick had his hand on the handle of the bar's door when they heard the faint sound of Betta's phone. She pulled it from her purse and looked at the number. "Why would he be calling now? He should be having a nightcap with Pilar."

"That's one way to describe it."

She pushed a button and put the phone to her ear. "Yes, Alfredo... Really?... Of course." She made a writing gesture to Rick, who pulled out a pad and pen from his pocket. "Go ahead— Rick will write it down." She repeated an address that Rick scribbled on the pad. "We'll find it. *Ciao.*" The phone went back in her purse but then quickly came back out. "They may have found the drawing. What was that address? I'll put it in my GPS."

"Go ahead, but I've still got the map they gave me at the hotel."

"Between the two we should find it. Somewhere near the botanical gardens, he said."

The address turned out to be directly behind them. Red and blue lights from two parked police vehicles bounced between the stone facades of the buildings and the tall wall that they faced. A shabbily dressed man with a five-day beard sat on the ground next to two trash cans, his back against the wall. A uniformed policeman stood above him writing on a note pad. Two other cops walked around shining flashlights on the ground. Near one of the police vehicles, a Fiat SUV, DiMaio nodded as he listened to a man dressed in a bath robe. Pilar, looking elegant, leaned against the second police car, her hands in the pockets of her coat. DiMaio noticed Rick and Betta approaching, said something to the man, and walked to them.

"What happened?" Betta asked.

DiMaio pointed with his chin at the robed man. "He lives in that building and heard the sound of someone going through the garbage. That is apparently something that annoys him, both for the noise and because people get into the trash and leave what they don't want all over the street in front of his house. He decided it was his civic duty to call the police. When my man arrived at the scene, he found that among the items that the guy had extracted from one of the cans was a leather case, which he heard was missing when I briefed everyone on the investigation."

"It has the drawing?"

"I haven't looked yet. It's in an evidence bag. Since you're the art cop, I was waiting for you to do the honors."

"Are we sure it's the right case?" Rick asked.

"Pilar said it is." He pointed a thumb at the SUV. "Let's take a look."

They walked to the back of the vehicle and DiMaio swung open the rear hatch. He reached in, took a pair of plastic gloves from a box, and handed them to Betta. While she slipped them on, he picked up a large plastic bag sealed at the top. The case looked like something used by an artist or an architect to carry his work, with a zipper around three sides and handles. A design had been tooled into the leather.

"That's the family seal." The words were spoken by Pilar, who had walked up behind them. "He hired a genealogy specialist to find it, but I always thought the whole thing was a scam. My ancestors were sheepherders and laborers, not the kind of people who spent their time or money creating a family crest. My father was trying to rewrite the family history, and the guy who found the seal was glad to help him."

DiMaio held open the plastic bag. Betta reached in, took out the leather case, and carefully unzipped it from one side to the other. She spread it open.

"It's empty. I must admit I was getting my hopes up."

"Are there any other compartments?" Rick asked.

"None." Betta closed the case and looked at the seal before turning it over. The back was without decoration. "Wait, here's a compartment." It was closed with a flap that had two snaps that popped open easily. She reached inside and pulled out a rectangular piece of paper and held it in her gloved fingers. "It's a ticket for the Galleria Nazionale delle Marche. It confirms what the museum director told us, that Somonte had come to his office."

"But Vitellozzi didn't mention that Somonte had brought the drawing with him," said Rick. "He said they talked about it, but he didn't say that he'd seen it."

Betta pulled her phone from her pocket and took a picture of both the ticket and the case before she slipped them back into the evidence bag.

"There's another possibility," said DiMaio as he sealed it up. "The ticket could be from an earlier trip Somonte made to Urbino."

"Or it wasn't his ticket," Rick said. "Someone put it there."

Betta sighed. "The bottom line is that we still don't have the drawing and that it's more likely he was killed to get it." She looked at Pilar. "I shouldn't be talking like this—it must upset you."

"No, I'm all right, really. Seeing the leather case brought back some memories, but they weren't especially pleasant ones. I'm fine."

DiMaio was about to put his arm around her but stopped when he noticed the other policemen watching them. Instead he turned to Betta. "Vitellozzi is the one key person in this case I haven't talked to yet. I'll go see him tomorrow and ask him if Somonte was carrying the drawing when they talked. If Somonte did have the drawing that day, I have to wonder why he didn't mention it to you two. It's not as if he didn't know the drawing was missing." He watched as the old man got to his feet and started down the street. The inspector walked to him and slipped something into his hand and got a puzzled look. Then he shuffled off under the glare of the man in the bathrobe. "We needed to give the *barbone* something for finding the case, even though it didn't contain the drawing."

"That was good of you, Alfredo," said Pilar.

DiMaio shrugged. "Perhaps you should go back to the hotel with Riccardo and Betta. I may be a while here."

"I'll wait."

"Alfredo, do you want me to go with you tomorrow to see Vitellozzi?"

"Thanks, Betta, but since you and Riccardo talked to him this morning, I should do the follow-up. I'm not sure which one I should see first, though, Vitellozzi or Professor Florio."

"Florio?" Rick asked. "Why Florio?"

DiMaio pointed at the building next to that of the concerned citizen, who was still standing in his bathrobe outside his front door. "That's Florio's office. And behind this wall are the botanical gardens. Either Florio is involved and is not very smart about hiding evidence, or he's being set up as a suspect. More likely it's neither and our murderer simply decided to dump the leather case here since it was convenient. Either way, I'll have to talk with Florio. I hope I don't have to listen to another harebrained theory about who killed Somonte."

—

Clad in a red UNM sweatshirt, shorts, and running shoes, Rick leaned over the counter and studied the city map with a groggy desk clerk who had just come on duty. Together they worked out a different route for the morning run. Rick had wondered if the steep streets could be avoided, but the only way to make it at all flat would be several turns around the parking lot below the castle, and Rick ruled that out as too boring. Instead, the clerk traced a *percorso* that would take Rick along the southern walls of the city, then on the appropriately named Via delle Mura before reaching a main street to return him to the hotel.

Rick raised the option of running along the road he and Betta used in and out of town, but the clerk ruled it out, saying the lack of path would make it too dangerous, even if there was little traffic at that hour of the day. Rick thanked him, stuffed the map into his pocket, and walked to the door.

Unlike the previous morning, the city saw no fog. The sun had not yet come over the spires of the palace, but enough light seeped through the sky that the streetlamps, though still lit, were not needed. After some stretching Rick ran to the corner and turned left and climbed the hill to the small square where they had received the call from DiMaio the night before. Except for a small sanitation truck emptying wastebaskets, it was deserted. He made a sharp turn and ran onto a street he hadn't been on before, Corso Garibaldi. Was there a law that required every city in Italy to name a street after the hero of the *Risorgimento*? The buildings on either side closed in on him, forming a stone canyon that echoed his footfalls. After a short distance, the western side of the duke's palace loomed above him, extending all the way past ornate balconies to the two rounded towers high above. Perhaps one of those balconies opened off Vitellozzi's office, a luxurious perk for the museum director. If his story that he'd received Somonte in his office was correct, they might have looked out over this street.

Rick lowered his gaze and jogged on as the surroundings changed from stony urban to natural green. Tall, leafy trees blocked any view of the buildings above him on the left, and on the right side ran a brick wall, beyond which opened up the splendid countryside of Le Marche. He could see for miles, which was exactly the reason the city's battlements had been built there. Some of the hills and valleys were thick with forest, while others showed patches of open fields. Here and there a tiny building broke up the green with a block of earthen brown. The street now changed names to Via Matteotti, honoring the anti-fascist politician murdered by Mussolini's thugs in 1922. Rick recalled reading about the case in an Italian history class. Unlike Somonte, Giacomo Matteotti had been stabbed to death.

Rick was beginning to get winded and recalled that Urbino's elevation was a mere fifteen hundred feet. After Albuquerque's mile-high trails, such elevation was nothing—was all this time in the lower altitude of Rome taking its toll on his endurance? He hoped not. Passing a grassy ravelin and rounding the rampart, he kept his eyes on the undulating terrain. It was made up of hills, not mountains, but farming must have always been difficult for the people of the region. Which may have been one reason why Federico da Montefeltro made his fortune as a soldier of fortune rather than a farmer.

Following the signs for the Porta Lavagine as the clerk had suggested, Rick began climbing the narrower Via delle Mura, which ran along the top of another layer of Urbino's wall system. He passed the Hotel Bonconte, which looked very pleasant, its windows facing the views below the walls. Too bad Alfredo didn't suggest they stay there; it looked like a winner. He stopped next to the wall and took out his map to pinpoint the hotel's location, noticing as he scanned it that the street running parallel below was the Via dei Morti. Why hadn't Somonte's body been dumped there? Shaking off the macabre thought, he put away the map and continued his run. The street was descending now, but he knew there would be another climb before he got back to the hotel, and it came at the Porta Lavagine, a narrow city gate where Via Battisti began the ascent to the city center.

Except for the window planters, the greenery was gone, and Rick was once again immersed in medieval stone and wood, or modern stucco and glass. But at least a few pedestrians now added a human feel to the street, making their way to a coffee bar, shopping for the pick of the best vegetables, or hurrying to an early appointment. A few glanced at him as he puffed past. Apparently early morning runners were not a rarity, perhaps thanks to the college students. At the top of the climb he found himself back at the intersection where he'd begun, a large loop complete. He considered but quickly rejected a final grind up Via Raffaello and back, instead loping down to the Botticelli.

Betta was coming out of their room when he was a few steps from the door.

"A good run, Rick?" She looked at the sweat stains and took a step back. "It appears so. I'll see you in the breakfast room. Enjoy the shower."

"And you look especially lovely," he called as she disappeared down the hall.

Twenty minutes later he sat downstairs with Betta enjoying a second cup of strong coffee with hot milk and peeling the rind off a Sicilian blood orange. Crumbs from the first part of his breakfast littered the plate. He glanced around the room, noting two tables of aging British tourists, or at least whom he thought to be British given the tea they were drinking and their shoes. Shoes, at least on older generations, were a giveaway for spotting Brits.

"Was Pilar here earlier?"

"I didn't see her. She may have had other sleeping arrangements last night."

Rick feigned shock. "I hope she simply got back late and slept in." He split his orange into pieces and popped one in his mouth. "Mmm; this orange is excellent. Have a slice."

Betta reached across the table but stopped when she heard her phone ringing. She took it from the table and checked the number. "Alfredo. Or Pilar using his phone. Hello?"

The smile disappeared as she listened. Rick could hear the voice of DiMaio but was unable to make out the words.

"We'll be right there." She hit a button to end the call. "It's Bruzzone, the art dealer. Someone tried to kill him."

# CHAPTER NINE

When Rick and Betta turned the corner, it was déjà vu from the previous evening. Two police cars, engines running and lights flashing, lined up in front of Bruzzone's art gallery. A uniformed policeman at the corner kept other vehicles from entering the street, while another standing next to the police cars ordered pedestrians to stay away from the gallery door and keep moving. As they approached, Rick remembered that he had considered extending his run up this street. Could he have missed the chance to be a witness to the attempt? Betta showed her identification to the policeman outside the door, and he waved her and Rick inside.

DiMaio stood next to the display case talking on his cell phone, but the action was inside the tiny office at the back of the shop. There Bruzzone, dressed in his same business suit, was bent over in the one visitor's chair squeezed into the space. He held a bloodstained cotton handkerchief to his forehead and stared at the floor. Behind him, between the still-cluttered desk and the wall, a policeman wearing rubber gloves worked a knife blade into a hole next to the bulletin board. DiMaio ended his conversation and slipped the phone in his pocket.

"This doesn't look good," Betta said.

The inspector glanced back at Bruzzone, whose chalky face contrasted with the red on the handkerchief. "No, it doesn't. He had just come in and was sitting at his desk checking emails when someone burst into the shop, raised a pistol, and aimed it at him. He hadn't turned on the lights in this room yet, so he didn't get a good look at the person. When he saw the gun, he ducked down behind the desk but hit the edge and took a gash out of his forehead. The man fired just as he was ducking under the table."

"He's sure it was a man?"

"He's not sure of anything, Riccardo. He thinks the guy was wearing a mask, or sunglasses, or something covering his face. What he remembers is the pistol, and how it was pointing at him, and how he instinctively ducked down. After the shot, he heard footsteps going back out and the door slamming. That's when he called us."

Betta looked around the room, which seemed unchanged from when she had been in the shop. Her hand lifted the hinged top of the glass case and then eased it back down. "Nothing was taken?"

"Nothing."

"Dottoressa Innocenti, is it not?" Bruzzone had gotten to his feet and was walking toward them.. He held the cloth with his right hand. "You will excuse me for not shaking hands." He looked at the bloodied handkerchief for a moment before pressing it back to his head.

"You may need some stitches, Signor Bruzzone. I'm sure the police will drive you to the hospital."

"Yes, yes, there will be time for that later. When the inspector is done with me. And this gentleman? Another agent of the art police?" He noticed Rick's cowboy boots but said nothing.

DiMaio introduced Rick as someone assisting him in the investigation. "Do you have any sense of why someone would do this, Signor Bruzzone?"

"It's obvious, isn't it?" He looked at DiMaio and then at Betta. "I was helping the police, of course, and whoever killed Somonte didn't appreciate it."

"What do you mean?"

"Well, Inspector, I mentioned some names to your colleague here, and someone must have found out."

"But—"

"You cannot be blamed, Dottoressa. This is a small city, and the arts community within it is even smaller. Word gets around quickly about something like a murder and stolen piece of art. So you must…"

He began swaying and Rick took hold of his arm.

"Thank you, Signor Montoya. I think I'm all right now. But perhaps I should have this head looked at. It's beginning to throb. Do you have any other questions, Inspector?"

"No. If I do I'll ask them later when you feel better. Let me get you into one of our cars to take you to the hospital." He took Bruzzone's arm and led him out the door.

"Rick, do you really think I'm responsible? I may have mentioned to some people that I talked to him, but…" She put her palm to her forehead. "*O Dio*, Bruzzone is right, isn't he? It's my fault."

"Betta, whoever took the drawing had to know that the authorities would interview anyone who had anything to do with it. Even if you hadn't mentioned your meeting with Bruzzone to anyone, it would be logical that he and all the others would be visited by the police."

She grasped his hand. "I hope you're right, Rick."

DiMaio came back through the door and stopped. "He'll

live, only because somebody was a bad shot. But if the gun-man—or woman—was standing here, it would not be easy to hit Bruzzone sitting at his desk." He put his outstretched hands together, pointed an index finger at the office, and squinted. "It would be a difficult target for a handgun, which is what I assume was used, and if the person had no firearms training, the tendency would be to shoot high." He lowered his arms.

"Betta is concerned about what Bruzzone said."

DiMaio shrugged. "You're no more to blame for this than I am, Betta. The real culprit is the guy who shot at him. My question is motive. Assuming the shooter is the same one who killed Somonte, why would he want to get Bruzzone? Does our killer think Bruzzone knows something and wanted to keep him quiet?"

"He was pretty quick to blame me," said Betta.

"Yes, you would be a convenient scapegoat, and that makes me suspicious," said DiMaio.

"If it was a warning to Bruzzone to keep quiet," said Rick, "I imagine he got the message."

DiMaio looked around the room and into the office where the policeman was still working away on the bullet hole. "Perhaps I should take advantage of his absence to look around his office. From the looks of it he won't notice that it's been searched."

"*Ecco*," said the voice from the office, and the policeman came out holding his hand palm up. The three of them peered into his hand where a small, squashed piece of metal lay on the gray rubber of the glove.

"Almost certainly a match for the bullet we took out of Somonte," said DiMaio. "Not a surprise, since we don't usually get two shootings here in a month, let alone a week. But we'll check to confirm it. Thank you, Sergeant."

The policeman slipped the slug into a plastic bag and made his exit. When he was out the door, DiMaio said, "I think I'll do a quick search of Bruzzone's office before getting back to the station. Can I ask you another favor, Riccardo?"

"Of course."

"The Spanish consul wants to talk with me. He may not speak Italian very well."

"Alfredo, unless the Spanish diplomatic service is very different from that of other countries, he has to speak Italian if he's assigned to Italy. But if you want me to be there just in case, of course I will."

"Thanks. I'll be back at the station in about a half hour. See you then." He started toward the office but stopped. "I'll be tied up with this crime scene for the rest of the morning after seeing the Spanish consul. Betta, why don't you go to the Galleria Nazionale and talk to Vitellozzi. What were we going to ask him?" He rubbed his eyes. "I didn't get much sleep."

"If Somonte had the drawing with him when he visited the Galleria. Of course, I'll go."

DiMaio rubbed the stubble on his cheek. "I appreciate both of you coming here, but I'm afraid it doesn't help you very much, Betta. The drawing is still missing."

"But Alfredo," said Betta, "the murder has to be connected to the drawing. It must be that whoever tried to shoot Bruzzone knows where it is. When we find the murderer, we will find the drawing."

DiMaio stared at her with tired eyes. "I know you want to find the drawing, Betta; we all do. But you have to face the possibility that Somonte's murder and the attempt on Bruzzone have nothing to do with the drawing."

They stood in silence until Rick spoke. "Something else occurs to me. To state the obvious, the person who killed

Somonte was the same one who came in here and shot at Bruzzone."

"That's correct," said DiMaio, "unless two people are involved in the crime and they took turns shooting at people. They would want us to think there was only one shooter. But I interrupted you, Riccardo. Go on."

"I was going to say that anybody who can prove they were somewhere else this morning when Bruzzone was attacked should be off the hook, even if their alibi for the night of the murder was weak. But if we have two accomplices, it won't matter."

DiMaio considered the observation. "Well, I didn't get much out of people when I asked them where they were the night of the murder, so I have my doubts that asking where everyone was this morning will help. But then I'm a confirmed pessimist and the lack of sleep is making it worse." He rubbed his eyes. "But, yes, let's find out where everyone was an hour ago. Betta, you can ask Vitellozzi, and I'll call Florio and Morelli. Rick, if you could call Garcia, that will cover him and Signora Somonte, though I doubt if they're involved."

Rick noticed that DiMaio left out one name. "We didn't see Pilar at breakfast this morning, Alfredo. Did you keep her out late?"

"No, I took her back to the hotel just after you left us last night at the wall. Well, not quite just after, but not very much later." He shrugged. "Perhaps she had breakfast with her stepmother."

Ten minutes later Rick and Betta walked into the Hotel Botticelli and asked for the room key. The desk clerk passed it to them along with a message asking Rick to call Signor Garcia, with his number. Rick took out his cell phone. "He may want to confess to the murder."

"Just so he gives me the drawing when he does." Betta held

the paper so Rick could use both hands to enter the number into his phone. A very short conversation in Spanish followed, and Rick put the phone back in his pocket.

"Well, this is curious. He said he needs to talk to me. We're going to meet in an hour, so I hope the Spanish consul doesn't take too long."

———

When Rick got to the police station the officer on duty told him to wait, that the inspector would be down shortly. It puzzled him as to why DiMaio wouldn't have him come to his office, but he shrugged and looked around the large waiting room, deserted except for three other people. A woman was with a young man in his early twenties, whom he guessed to be her son. She stared straight ahead; he kept his eyes on his phone, a wire running from it to his earbuds. Playing his uncle Piero's favorite game, Rick tried to guess why the two were waiting in the *commissariato*. The first possibility was a mundane one: the son needed some document that only the police issue, like proof of no criminal record, to be presented to another bureaucrat, in another government office, in order to get some public benefit. That was the most logical guess, but not very interesting. Better would be if they were there to report the disappearance of their husband and father, who had gone out the night before to bring home a pizza, and neither he nor the pizza had returned. He was straying from Piero's game, which was intended to sharpen powers of observation, and instead creating fiction.

Rick sized up the man in the corner, who was dressed in a dark suit with a starched white shirt and striped tie. In the few seconds that Rick was watching him, the man had looked at his watch twice. Who still wore a watch? Rick hadn't owned one in years, relying on his cell phone for the time, as well as for the news, GPS, sports scores, the weather, photographs, a dictionary, and notes to himself. He also made the occasional phone call on it. The man wasn't that old, but everything about him indicated he wanted to be seen as being older than he was. Rick the translator came up with a few appropriate words: Prim? Yes. Punctilious? Maybe. Pedantic? Perhaps. He was scrolling through his mental thesaurus when DiMaio appeared, looked around the room, and walked quickly to him.

"Thanks for coming, Riccardo. That's the consul sitting over there, and I'd rather not bring him up to my office or it could take forever. If you could start things off by making some excuse for me, that will help."

"*Ci penso io*," said Rick, using the Italian equivalent of "leave it to me."

The man watched them approach, his eyes lingering a moment on Rick's cowboy boots, and then got up when it appeared they were heading for him and not the woman with her son. Rick shook his hand firmly and spoke in Spanish, trying, but mostly not succeeding, to add a Castilian lisp.

"Señor Consul, I am Rick Montoya, the interpreter for Inspector DiMaio. He is mortified that he cannot receive you properly in his office, but he has been interrogating a prisoner there, and it is in—shall we say—some disorder. He hopes you will forgive him."

The consul's eyes widened and he looked at DiMaio, who, not understanding a word, smiled and bowed his head slightly before shaking the man's hand.

"But...but...I don't need a translator." The words were stammered in Spanish. "I mean..." He continued, but in Italian, "I don't need a translator."

"Excellent," said Rick, now in Italian as well. "Then I'll just sit here in case there is some word that either of you may need assistance with. It's my pleasure." The three sat on the bench, DiMaio in the middle inclined toward the Spaniard.

"How can I help you?" DiMaio asked.

The consul did his best to get back his composure. He took a deep breath and put a concerned look on his face. "I have come regarding the investigation of Manuel Somonte's murder."

"I assumed that," said DiMaio.

"He is, or rather he was, a most important man in Spain. He had many friends. In very high places, even in the Foreign Ministry."

"I see. It would be natural of them to be concerned that the investigation is being given the very highest priority by the Italian authorities. Anything less would be seen as unacceptable."

The consul nodded his head in a deliberate way. "I think we understand each other, Inspector. Now, if you would be so kind as to tell me exactly how the investigation is proceeding and what your conclusions have been to this hour." He leaned back and folded his arms over his chest.

DiMaio rubbed his chin and frowned. He was about to say something when Rick bent his head around the policeman's shoulder. "Signor Consul, I'm sure you can understand the implications of your question. Were the inspector to give you any details, it would mean that you would have to give implicit approval of..." Rick rolled his eyes toward the door from which DiMaio had just emerged. "Of the methods used by the authorities here. If that were to come to the attention of the press, it might put you in a rather delicate position. Of course, if that is not a concern..."

The Spaniard raised a hand. "No, no, I have complete confidence in the Italian police. I certainly didn't want to give the impression that I thought otherwise. My main concern was to convey the embassy's appreciation for the, uh, work that you're doing on behalf of a citizen of my country."

This guy will go far as a diplomat, Rick thought.

"*Buon giorno.*" The three men jumped to their feet as Pilar strolled toward them. On this morning she had gone casual: tight jeans and a turtleneck sweater. "If this is something important, I will not interrupt. I can wait over there." Rick detected something in her tone that was different from the previous evening. Didn't she sleep well? Had she and Alfredo had an argument?

"No," said DiMaio, "not at all. This is the consular representative of your embassy. Signor Consul, may I present Signora Pilar Somonte, the daughter of the deceased."

The consul's eyes widened in equal proportion to the squinting of Pilar. She took a moment to size up her compatriot before speaking in rapid-fire Spanish. DiMaio edged away, Rick right behind him.

"What's she saying?"

"I'll translate." Rick listened to Pilar and spoke in DiMaio's ear. "She is not happy with the support the consulate is providing... She just called him a pin-headed bureaucrat... Why had he contacted the widow and not her as well?... She plans to talk to the ambassador...she will also contact the Foreign Ministry when she gets back to Spain... She just called him another name I didn't understand that I'd guess is regional slang and not at all flattering."

The outburst had gained the attention of the woman at the other end of the bench, though her son was still deep into his cell phone. All during the tirade the consul nodded his head but said nothing except the occasional "*si*." Finally he mumbled a few words to her, excused himself to DiMaio, and made for the door.

Pilar stood there until he was outside. She turned to the policeman, then to Rick. "I'll have to see you later, Alfredo, when we're alone."

Rick watched her go, then looked at Alfredo, who was staring at the ground. Something was happening, but Rick decided this was not the time to ask DiMaio what it was. They sat down on the bench and said nothing for an uncomfortable minute before the policeman spoke. "Well, Riccardo, I'm so glad we all had the chance to meet the consul. It was certainly a pleasure chatting with him, wasn't it?"

"A lovely man."

More silence, broken by Rick.

"Pilar seems a bit agitated this morning, don't you think?"

"You could say that."

"It may be something in the culture. Iberian drama. Which reminds me that I ran into Signora Somonte yesterday outside in the parking lot. She was coming to see you."

"I'm sorry to have missed her."

"I'm sure you were, Alfredo. She asked me to tell you that you should not assume it was an Italian who murdered her husband."

DiMaio chuckled. "Her dislike of Pilar appears to know no bounds." He clapped Rick on the shoulder. "I can't thank you enough for what you did with the consul. I suspect I won't be bothered by him again."

Thanks to Pilar as well, Rick was going to say, but thought better of it. He looked at the woman and her son, and recalled his uncle's guessing game. "Alfredo, you don't happen to know why those two are in here, do you?"

DiMaio leaned forward, looked down the bench, and leaned back. "Signora Posilipo. She comes in every day at this hour to take orders for anyone who has to eat at their desk; then she brings the food back at lunchtime. She makes a dynamite *vincisgrassi*."

"The guy with her?"

"Her nephew. He teaches semiotics at the university."

They got up and started walking toward DiMaio's office. "Do you want a coffee, Riccardo? I need one; I've been up since six."

"Not for me. Garcia wanted to talk with me, and I'm meeting him in about fifteen minutes. You should come with me."

The inspector thought for a moment. "No, Riccardo, it would just take more time with the interpreting between Spanish and Italian. Plus, I have to go back to the crime scene at Bruzzone's shop. Garcia may well open up more without a policeman there. Did he ask to see me as well?"

"No."

"Then he wants to talk to you alone. Don't forget to ask him where he was this morning. You can tell me this afternoon what he said. I'm sure you'll remember everything."

"I'll try."

—

Betta had expected that the director of a famous museum located inside one of Italy's architectural treasures would have an impressive office, and that was certainly the case. She had been in many spectacular offices in Rome, starting with that of the Culture Minister, but they had nothing on the room where Vitellozzi toiled. To begin with, there was the view: the hills of Le Marche spreading like an undulating green carpet outside the windows. Her eyes then were drawn to the ceiling frescoes where a parade of allegorical figures marched among clouds and exotic birds. A wavy geometric pattern flowed through the tiles on the floor, and gilded *puti* looked down from decorations above doors and windows. With all of that in competition for a visitor's attention, no additional art was needed, but the museum director had hung two paintings in ornate frames on the wall opposite the windows. He didn't have the pick of the collection—the famous masterpieces had to be on public view—but Betta was sure there was enough art available that didn't fit in the main rooms to provide him with a good selection. She was surprised that he had chosen a rather obscure sixteenth-century artist whom she recognized only because she'd seen his work in the museum in her native Bassano. It was a style she favored, with deeper colors and thicker brush-strokes than were fashionable among the artists of that period.

Vitellozzi rose from his chair behind a desk made from one large plank resting on sawhorses of the same aged wood. A small stack of files made up the only paper on a working surface that also held a phone, computer, and cantilevered desk lamp. Unlike on the previous day, he wore a white shirt with a tie of conservative design. His dark suit jacket was draped over the desk chair, and he made no move to slip it on, a subtle indication of where he placed Betta in the pecking order of the Italian cultural world. That impression was confirmed when he motioned for her to take a seat at the meeting table at one side of the room rather than in one of the comfortable upholstered chairs arranged near his desk. This was to be all business, which suited her fine. The required coffee offer was made and politely declined, and he settled into the place at the head of the table.

"Thank you for seeing me again, Dottor Vitellozzi."

He waved a hand to indicate that thanks were not necessary. "You must forgive me for the chaos yesterday, but it ended well. By the evening, the exhibit was in place, and all that needs to be done today is to bring in the food and wine. We will see you this evening, I trust?"

"Yes, it will be a pleasure."

He pushed back the chair and crossed leg over knee. "It is on days like this that I am reminded how fortunate I am to be the director of a magnificent institution like this. Who would not want to work surrounded by some of mankind's most magnificent creations? And that includes this palace, of course." He leaned forward with a conspiratorial smile. "You know, this room may have been a hideaway for the duke when he wanted to get away from his court. There's no historical evidence to prove it, just conjecture, but I like to believe it's true. Can't you just picture him sitting here reading one of the many books in his famous library, occasionally looking out over the hills of his dukedom? Perhaps pondering the ideas of great philosophers or planning his next military campaign? Who knows what ideas were spawned in this very room?" He sighed. "But you have not come here to consider the life of Federico da Montefeltro."

It was a different Annibale Vitellozzi, and not just because he was more formally dressed. This was a contemplative, mellow museum director rather than a brusque, harassed exhibit-hanger. Betta had been ready for the same personality, and ready to dislike the man. Now she wasn't sure. Would he today be more likely to open up about Somonte?

"Yesterday I neglected to ask you if Somonte had the drawing with him when he visited you here."

Vitellozzi looked up at the mythological commotion on the ceiling as he tried to remember. "The drawing." His eyes returned to Betta and he nodded. "Yes, he certainly did. Had it in a leather case that he seemed quite proud of. I had not seen the sketch when Bruzzone put it on sale, since without any funds to purchase it, there was no reason for me to go look at it then. It would have only increased my frustration."

"As you must have felt when you finally did see it."

"I can't lie to you—I was angered as I held it in my hands. I'm sure that Somonte sensed my anger, but he seemed to enjoy it. He was that kind of person."

"So you think that was the purpose of his dropping in?"

"Ostensibly he came by to talk about the arrangements for tonight. As I told you yesterday, he was paying the bill for much of the event, and he wanted to know about the program. I was planning to recognize his contribution and thank him, of course, and I still will, though the tone will be more somber. His widow will come, I assume, and she will be the one thanked."

Betta changed the subject, but only slightly. "The leather case has turned up." She watched his reaction carefully.

"The...the case with the drawing? It was inside?"

"No, it was empty." She took her phone from her pocket and hit the screen while Vitellozzi watched with a puzzled look on his face. After a moment, she turned the screen toward him. "Is this the case he had?"

He went to his jacket, took out a pair of glasses, and put them on before returning to the chair and leaning toward the phone. "Yes, that looks like it."

"Which confirms what Somonte's daughter told us."

He flinched for a second time, but not as convincingly. "Daughter? Is she here?"

"Yes. I think she's planning to attend this evening."

"She will be most welcome, of course," he said, somewhat regaining his composure.

Betta could almost hear his mind working, likely thinking about the need to change his speech that evening. Pilar would have to be included when he recognized the Somonte family's support for the exhibit. He might also have been wondering if she and the widow would consider continuing that support in the future. Betta briefly considered telling him that the daughter and wife didn't exactly get along but decided it wasn't her role to do so. He would find out soon enough. Or perhaps he knew already. Was he really surprised to find out that Somonte's daughter was in Urbino? Betta was about to put the phone away when she thought of something else and pulled up another picture. Again she showed it to Vitellozzi.

"That's an entry ticket for the museum, of course. You can read it. Is that also some kind of clue in your investigation? Everyone who comes in here gets one, unless, like you, they have a pass from the Cultural Ministry."

His tone indicated that he had decided to go on the offensive. Betta turned off the phone and put it in her pocket. "It was inside the leather case. Perhaps put there when Somonte visited you the day he was murdered. Even major donors have to pay the entrance fee?"

"Only people who work at the Cultural Ministry can get in without paying. He might have been given the senior discount, but Somonte could afford to pay full price." He was growing impatient. "What is the next step for you, Dottoressa?"

It was a natural question, and Betta didn't know how to answer it, even had she known what her next step would be. "I am following up on some leads." She knew it was a weak answer and was quite sure he knew it as well.

He uncrossed his leg and leaned toward Betta. "Surely you have to believe that the person who killed Somonte has the drawing. Even if he was not murdered in order to get it, the killer must have it, or at least know where it is."

"I'm not sure which is worse: that this person has the drawing and understood its value, or did not and has thrown it away."

"If he knows the value, it may not turn up for a while. The killer could lay low and wait years to put it on the black market. But you are on the art theft squad; you know more about how such things work than I."

Was he baiting her? "For not knowing much about stealing art, your scenario is quite convincing."

"The scenario that I would prefer would be that it turns up a century from now in the archives of some museum. That happened recently in Milan at the Pinacoteca Ambrosiana. A page from a Leonardo folio was found in the wrong archive, having been misfiled a few hundred years before. The Piero drawing was lost for hundreds of years and miraculously turned up in someone's attic. It could happen again. And, who knows? This time it might find its way to this museum, where it belongs, among the other works by the master. I will hope for such an outcome, even though I will not be here to see it play out." He took off his glasses and placed them on the table before folding his arms across his chest.

"Perhaps you can afford to take the long view, Dottor Vitellozzi. In my office we are focused on the here and now." She stood. "Thank you for your time. And I very much enjoyed seeing this room. I can understand how you would enjoy working in it." The sound of a car horn blared from the street. "I suppose it's quieter in the morning. Do you arrive at the office early each day?" If he had been out shooting up Bruzzone's shop earlier, he might get why she was asking, but she couldn't figure out any other way.

"I've always been an early riser, and so I'm here early every day. It's the best time of day to get my work done, when no one is knocking on my office door. The rest of the museum staff doesn't arrive until after nine." He raised his arm toward the window. "This morning, I was here at about seven, and the view was spectacular."

Betta took note: he was here, but nobody saw him.

———

Rick tried to decide if San Giovanni Battista should be called a small church or a large chapel, but given its designation as an *oratorio*, it had to be the latter. The barreled wood ceiling was braced by heavy crossbeams that also held strings of spotlights that illuminated the art on the three walls. The left side was mostly bare plaster, covered in places with large fragments of the original frescoes. On the right wall it was a different story: the life of John the Baptist filled every square inch with movement and bright colors. In 1416, the Salimbeni brothers had joined forces to decorate the walls, including the *Crucifixion* behind the altar. There was so much activity that it was almost too much to take in, and Rick decided that if he came back with Betta, they would concentrate on one panel at a time. Which is what Lucho Garcia had apparently decided to do while waiting for Rick.

He sat on a plastic chair facing the depiction of John baptizing Jesus. In the panel, a crowd of robed and haloed saints knelt on one side of the river watching the two central figures. On the other side stood a group of men dressed incongruously in the elegant clothing of the fifteenth century. John tipped water from a shell over the head of a praying Jesus, and high above was the Almighty, flanked by angels, looking down on it all.

Rick sat down next to Garcia, and they studied the scene for several minutes before the Spaniard broke the silence.

"I would bet my salary that the men on the right were the ones paying the artist. Didn't they used to do that a lot, Ricardo?"

The use of the first name was surprising, but why not? The informality might help to open the guy up. "The patron of the work was often painted into the picture, Lucho, usually in a pious pose."

"Nothing has changed. Money still talks in the art world."

"I hope that wasn't all you had to tell me, because I knew that already."

He turned his head toward Rick and grunted. "No, that wasn't it. I wanted to talk about what is happening, from my point of view. I don't have anyone I can talk to about it, even if I spoke Italian. And if you share it with the inspector, that's fine with me…maybe it will help him in the investigation. I don't have anything to lose or gain at this point."

He pushed the fingers of his right hand through his long hair before rubbing the back of his neck. "As you can imagine, the death of Manuel Somonte has put me in a somewhat precarious position, if I might understate. When he took me on six years ago it was as a favor to my father, since our families were from the same village outside Oviedo. But he made it clear from the beginning, both to me and to my father, that I would have to earn the right to be kept on the payroll. I didn't want to let my father down, and I worked hard, so hard that Somonte brought me into the front office. This was not another favor to my father; I deserved it. In return, he taught me the ins and outs of the business but also schooled me in the things he loved outside the office, like his favorite artists and the plants. You could say that he treated me like the son he never had. Everything was going so well."

He took a slow breath and looked at the baptism on the wall. Rick thought it would be better to let him talk, so he stared with him in silence.

"Now it's all turned upside down. Pilar will be running the mill, and she doesn't want to keep me on, even though I have helped her in the past."

"How did you help her?"

Garcia's hand returned to the back of his neck, massaging away the stress that showed in his voice. "It was probably a mistake, but when I became her father's assistant she asked me to…well… keep her informed. She didn't get along well with him, hadn't for years, so she wanted someone in the front office to tell her what was going on, what decisions were about to be made, that kind of thing. She knew that he had come to trust me, telling me things that no one else knew. At the time I thought I was just being helpful, so that she didn't have to deal with her father. Mind you, it's not that they didn't ever talk. She was in the weekly meetings of the section heads, but he treated her like one of them. I also justified what I was doing by thinking it was helping the company, but really I was just being a spy. Somonte never knew, of course. When we got the news that he was dead, the only positive thought I had was relief that he would never find out I was spying on him. And that I would not have to do it anymore." He looked at Rick for the first time. "What a terrible thought, don't you think? After all the man had done for me, and I felt relief."

A gray-haired couple entered the chapel and walked to the right side, careful not to block the view of the frescoes for Rick and Garcia. They spoke a Scandinavian language, but Rick didn't know which. German, he could identify, but anything north of that sounded the same to him.

"I would have thought that helping Pilar would serve you well now, since she will be taking over from her father."

Garcia chuckled. "Yes, you certainly would think that, but it isn't turning out that way. Yesterday she tried to change the game, and I refused."

"I don't understand."

"Well, Ricardo, as you can imagine, her relationship with Isabella, Somonte's wife, was even more strained than it was with her father. The two women don't speak to each other, period. And what does Pilar want me to do, now that her father is gone, since she knows that I get along well with Isabella?" He didn't wait for Rick to answer. "She wants me to tell her what Isabella is doing."

"But if Pilar inherits the business, what does she care what the widow does?"

"That's the way Pilar is. I wouldn't be surprised if she contests the will to get more of the inheritance, just out of spite for Isabella."

Rick found it curious that Garcia kept using the widow's first name. Had he called her Isabella when talking to his boss? Very unlikely. What was more curious was the picture he was painting of a scheming Pilar Somonte.

"It also wouldn't surprise me if she tried to cozy up to the police inspector. It's the way she operates. She has certainly spent a lot of time in this country, so she knows how to be devious in both cultures."

The comment piqued Rick's curiosity. "She comes here often?"

"Two, three times a year. Supposedly on business to make contacts in the fashion world, but who knows what she does. The last time was just after the announcement of the donation to the museum."

"What are you going to do now, Lucho? I mean, when you return to Spain. From what you said it does not appear that Pilar is going to retain you in the business."

"Ah, but she may have to. Her father wrote down as little as possible about how the mill runs, but he confided in me. This may be the twenty-first century, but for commerce in northern Spain it's sometimes still the Middle Ages. I know the secrets about our employees, not to mention suppliers and buyers. Her father wove a web of relationships based on those secrets and I'm the only one who can navigate through it for her. Pilar isn't happy with the situation, but if she fires me she'll regret it, and she knows it."

"When you were spying—to use your term—you didn't describe this web?"

"I always found ways to avoid passing those details to her. At the time I was trying to be loyal to my employer, but now I think I was just planning for this day and didn't want to admit it to myself."

"What would you like me to do, Lucho?"

"You've already been a great help, just by listening to me rant, but I'm afraid it won't help find Somonte's murderer. If there were some way I could help, believe me, I would. He was not a perfect person, by any means, but he was like a second father to me. His killer must be found and punished."

The best Rick could do to reassure him was to say that Inspector DiMaio was an excellent police officer. Garcia stood and shook Rick's hand.

"I have to get back. Isabella is having her hair and nails done for the event this evening, and she doesn't know I'm here."

Rick suddenly remembered that he was supposed to check alibis for the time of the shooting. How could he do it tactfully? "There is a salon right at the hotel?"

"And a spa. She's been there since early this morning."

"Which gives you some time to relax. Have you been able to walk around the city at all?"

"I did, this morning." He checked his watch. "I really have to go. Thank you for letting me talk to you, Ricardo."

———

The gardens were twenty degrees warmer than on the street, turning a cool day into summer and adding weight to an atmosphere that was already heavy with the rich scent of plants. A trickle of sweat inched its way down DiMaio's neck and seeped into his collar, but more annoying was that Florio did not seem the least bothered by the humidity. On the contrary, the man thrived in it, happily pointing out every plant they passed by, noting its scientific name. It was like being back in high school

Latin class, taught by a priest who taunted the young DiMaio mercilessly when he couldn't recite his verb tenses correctly. He should have asked the professor to meet him out on the street. Finally, Florio realized that the policeman was not there for a botany lesson.

"But I suppose you are not here for a botany lesson, Inspector."

DiMaio took out his handkerchief and dried his palms. "No, Professor. What I wanted—"

"Before you get to it, I must tell you that I have another theory about the death of Signor Somonte. It came to me early this morning when I was watering the plants in my office. I always get to work early so I can do it unrushed, being sure that each one is sufficiently moist, except for the cacti, of course, which are on a separate schedule. I was also meeting one of my students, a brilliant young woman from Padova who is writing her thesis on phototropism in the aloe plant. But I am digressing."

"Yes, you are, Professor."

Florio gathered his thoughts, and DiMaio waited, none too patiently, hoping this wasn't another wacky idea from the pages of a murder mystery. He was disappointed.

"I recalled a quandary that Montalbano was in when Fazio insisted that the murdered doctor was the victim of a mafia vendetta. It seemed logical, since the man had recently stopped paying protection money to the leading crime family."

"Professor, we don't have any mafia presence here in Urbino."

"Exactly. Anyway, Montalbano knew something wasn't right; he could feel it in his bones. Being an experienced policeman, he knew that when something didn't smell right, there had to be a reason why."

DiMaio spotted an open sack of fertilizer and tried to breathe through his mouth. "I know how that is."

"Montalbano decided to go in the opposite direction from where the evidence was pushing him. Forget the mafia; someone was using it to throw him off the real track, which involved an insurance policy. I think that may be the situation in this investigation. Everything here says that Somonte was killed for the drawing, am I right?"

"For the sake of argument, let's say you are."

"Well, it could just be a ruse to keep you from focusing on the real motive."

"Which is?"

"The ransom."

"Ransom?"

"Absolutely. Somonte was kidnapped, and before they could send a ransom note, he tried to escape and was killed." Florio held out his hands, palms up, to show how obvious was his conclusion.

"Hmm. Very ingenious, Professor. A botched kidnapping. But before I follow that hypothesis, I must first tie up any loose ends on the one regarding the stolen drawing. Which is the reason I wanted to talk to you."

A large group of people were trying to squeeze past them on the narrow path between the plants. One of them looked at Florio and stopped. "Do you work here? We're looking for the place where the body was found."

"Just around that corner. The Spanish dagger. Very rare, but of course we have an excellent collection of rare plants." The group shuffled ahead and disappeared around the corner of the path. Florio returned his attention to DiMaio. "It's astounding how our attendance has shot up since the, uh, incident. I won't have to worry about my budget for this quarter. It should get the rector off my back. Now, what were you saying, Inspector?"

"We found the case in which Somonte was holding the

drawing. It was empty." He pointed toward the back wall of the gardens. "On the street behind here, in a garbage bin."

"That's almost in front of my office."

"I know. That's why I'm bringing it up."

"Do you think I threw it in there after killing Somonte?"

"You didn't really have an alibi for the time of the murder, Professor."

A grin spread across Florio's face. "This is delicious. I am really a suspect in a murder? But tell me, Inspector, would I have tried to hide the case at a place so close to my office? Isn't it obvious what happened here? Montalbano would have understood in an instant."

"I'm not Montalbano, Professor. I'm not even Sicilian."

"It's clear that someone wanted to keep suspicion far from himself, which was why the body was dumped in *my* botanical gardens, and the case thrown in a trash can in front of *my* office."

"So that you become a prime suspect, and the police are kept far off the trail of the kidnappers."

"Exactly. It makes perfect sense."

It made no sense at all to DiMaio, but something Florio had said would need checking. DiMaio tucked the thought into the back of his memory and turned to the priority at the moment: getting himself out of the humidity. A few minutes later he was out on the street in front of the gardens' entrance near several dozen people who were milling around on the steps waiting to get in. As he breathed in the cleansing fresh air, he spotted the pool under the decorative fountain and walked to it. Cupping his hands, he scooped up the water and splashed his face before drying himself with his handkerchief. He suddenly remembered that he hadn't asked Florio where he was earlier, at the time of the shooting. It was not important enough to brave the humidity, he decided. Florio was just not a serious suspect, and DiMaio had vowed never to enter the botanical gardens again.

At least there was one idea he got from interviewing the man. He pulled out his cell phone, took a breath, and hit a recently entered number. It was answered on the second ring.

"*Ciao*, Alfredo."

Her voice almost made the phone feel cold. "Pilar, I can't talk very long, but I have a question."

"Another question? What is it this time?"

"Do you know if your father had an insurance policy on the drawing?"

"Knowing my father, my guess is that he looked into what it would cost and decided he'd take the risk instead. But he always used Seguros Suarez, a company in Madrid. If he had insured the drawing, it would be with them. On the business side, the company was fully covered since he could write it off. Against fire, disaster, that sort of thing, we were, and still are, highly insured."

"What about life insurance?"

"When my mother was alive, he didn't have any. Macho Spaniard that he was, he thought he would live forever, I suppose. He also knew his family would inherit the business, so money would not be a problem for us. It all changed when he married that woman. She insisted on it. Is that all you needed to ask me?"

"Yes. That's very helpful. Thank you." He quickly hung up.

# CHAPTER TEN

The restaurant reminded Rick of a *churrascaria* where he had dined when he'd visited his parents in Rio. At the far side of the room, chicken, sausage, and various cuts of meat sizzled over the red embers of a grill, sending out waves of delicious scents. As he sniffed the air he realized that there had to be something primeval about the smell of meat on an open fire. When they were outside the restaurant and about to enter, DiMaio had mentioned that grilled meat was the place's specialty. Thanks to the aroma, their minds had been made up even before they sat down: it would be mixed grill and salads for all three, no menus needed. The decor of the restaurant complemented the open grill: dark wood beams, barrel vault brick ceilings, and cave-like arched doorways separating the rooms. They grabbed a passing waiter and put in their order, including a Rosso Piceno from a nearby vineyard that was the house wine.

"I'm sorry Pilar couldn't join us for lunch," said Betta.

Rick regretted that he'd neglected to tell Betta about the awkward encounter with Pilar in the police station. But did it matter? He would tell her later, and it would be interesting to see how their friend reacted.

DiMaio shrugged. "It's just as well. We can talk about the case openly."

It might have seemed like an odd comment to Betta, given how tight Pilar and Alfredo had been just the previous day. Rick was now sure that something was amiss between Alfredo and the comely Spaniard, and from the look on Betta's face, he suspected that she had an inkling of trouble. They watched the waiter return with the bottle, open it, and fill their glasses. Toasts were exchanged, and they took their first drinks of the dry, red wine.

"Why don't you tell us about your conversation with the botanical gardens director," said Rick. "I'm sure Florio figured out the murderer and motive, so we can spend the rest of lunch just enjoying the food."

DiMaio allowed himself a tiny smile. "I wouldn't say that, exactly, but he did have a theory involving a kidnapping gone bad. And he decided that the drawing case was found near his office in order to make him a prime suspect and divert attention from the kidnappers who were the real murderers."

"That must have upset him, being on the suspects list."

The inspector took another sip of wine. "Upset isn't the way I would have described him, Betta. It was more like I'd told him he'd be making a cameo appearance in a Montalbano mystery."

"Do you think—"

"No, Rick. My gut feeling is that there's no way Florio could have committed this murder. And as he pointed out himself, good detectives go by their gut feelings. What about your meeting with Garcia?"

Until DiMaio's earlier comment about them being able to talk openly, Rick had been dreading having to recount the conversation with Lucho, but now the pressure was off. He described the encounter, left nothing out, and when he finished the policeman was shaking his head slowly and rubbing his cheek.

"He doesn't paint a very nice picture of Pilar. What he said just reaffirms that it was a mistake bringing her in on the investigation."

Betta put her hand on DiMaio's arm. "It's not like she planned her father's murder, Alfredo. She's just been looking after her own interests. You can't blame her for that."

"Riccardo can tell you about the scene with the Spanish consul. It was a very different Pilar, even if the consul deserved what she gave him."

"She's under a lot of stress," Rick said. "And the reality of her father's death, even if they didn't get along, is starting to sink in."

"You may be right, Riccardo." He stared at his wineglass. "There was one bit of information Garcia gave you that I found curious."

"What was that?" Betta asked.

"That she comes to Italy often. Several times a year, wasn't it, Rick?"

"That's what he said, if we're to believe him. The last time was when the donation was announced."

"She didn't tell me about her frequent trips," said DiMaio. "Maybe she didn't want me to know about it, including what she was doing. Or who she was seeing."

The waiter appeared wheeling to their table a cart topped with a wooden cutting board, a platter, and three plates. The platter got their immediate attention. It was stacked with various grilled items that had just been taken off the flames and now oozed juices and scents. He opened a drawer, pulled out a menacing knife and long fork, and transferred the largest item from the platter to the cutting board: a slab of beef. With quick and sure cuts, he sliced it into pieces of equal size and divided them among the three plates. After sprinkling some salt and drizzling olive oil on the steak, he turned to the other meats. Each plate received a crisp sausage, a chicken thigh, and a cut of pork loin. The colors differed slightly: the sausage was a dark brown, the chicken a lighter tan, the pork almost white, and the beef went from crispy dark on the edge to rosy pink in the center. After setting plates in front of each diner, the waiter wished them a *buon appetito* and retired. Before picking up their cutlery, they leaned forward and breathed in the aroma of oil and rosemary mixed with the juices.

After a few bites, and more sips of wine, Rick continued the conversation.

"Is there a way you can find out when Pilar was in the country?"

DiMaio speared the sausage with his fork and cut it into three pieces. "The simplest way would be to check her passport, though they don't always stamp them at the port of entry, especially when it's a citizen of the European Union. Hotels send in the names of their guests to the local police, but it would take forever to track her down without knowing cities and dates." He smiled and took a bite of the sausage. "I could just ask her for her passport, but I don't think she'd be very cooperative."

More grilled meat and wine was consumed.

"The steak is definitely the top dog on my plate," said Rick. "Though the chicken is a close second."

After a discussion of the pros and cons of each, it was Betta's turn to report on her meeting at the Galleria Nazionale delle Marche.

"Vitellozzi was definitely in a more expansive mood. The exhibit was in place to his satisfaction, and he was taking a breather before the ceremonies this evening. Two things I found curious. First, he showed surprise when I mentioned

Pilar, saying he didn't know Somonte's daughter was here. I'm not sure I believe him, though I don't know why."

"A policewoman's hunch, like Florio told me this morning."

"Perhaps, Alfredo. It just didn't ring true, is all. I'm also not sure why it would be important, regardless of whether it's true or not."

"What was the other thing?"

She finished her last bit of chicken, leaving a clean bone. "Well, again, it was more the way he said it than anything specific. I asked him if Somonte had the drawing when he'd called on him, and he confirmed that he did. Since the museum hadn't bid on it when it was up for sale, Vitellozzi hadn't actually seen it before. But he didn't take it as a courtesy on the part of Somonte, letting him study it before it went to the museum in Sansepolcro. Instead, he was sure the man wanted to needle him about missing the chance to have it in the museum here."

"Somonte does not come across as a very simpatico person," Rick said. "Yesterday morning Morelli said that he did the same thing to him."

DiMaio had finished his food and picked up his wineglass. "Well, if he was trying to provoke someone, he definitely succeeded." He looked at the red liquid and put down the glass. "I have to confess that I neglected to ask Florio where he was this morning at the time of the shooting, but I'm having real trouble taking him seriously as a suspect. Did you two check alibis at your meetings?"

"Vitellozzi was at the office, but nobody was there besides him," said Betta.

"Garcia was wandering around the city by himself while the widow Somonte languished in the hotel spa, so he doesn't have a strong alibi either."

DiMaio nodded. "As expected. Morelli will likely be at the

galleria tonight, Betta, so you can try to pin down his morning whereabouts then. I'm not sure I'll be able to get there."

Another waiter came and took away their empty plates as the first waiter arrived, again pushing the cart. On it this time were three plates filled with salad leaves of different types, but all of them green. Again the drawer opened, and out came a soup spoon and a fork. He poured olive oil into the spoon followed by a dash of vinegar, salt, and pepper, then stirred the spoonful with the fork before adding it to one of the salad plates and gently tossing the greens to give it a slight coating. The process was repeated for the other two plates before he placed a salad first in front of Betta, then the two men. They all took bites.

"Just what we needed after that meat course," said Betta. "And exactly the right amount of dressing."

"Like with a good pasta," DiMaio said. "Just enough to coat it without losing the taste of the greens." The three pondered this bit of gastronomic wisdom before he changed the subject. "There was something else that came out of my conversation with Florio. It was when he ran his kidnapping theory by me, and I thought about what insurance Somonte might have had on himself. After I left the gardens, I called Pilar and she confirmed that her father had a policy, and his wife was the beneficiary. In fact, Isabella Somonte had insisted that her husband be insured. I would guess not a small sum, either."

"From the little contact we had with her," Rick said, "that would seem very much in character."

"Exactly. No great surprise there. But something else occurred to me, Betta. Could he have had any insurance on the Piero drawing?"

Her fork stopped in midair. "*O Dio*, why didn't I think of that?"

"I'm sure you would have, Betta. Your mind's been on other things."

"Rick, it should have been one of the first things I checked. Often the thieves contact the insurance company directly and a deal is cut to the advantage of both parties. The artwork is returned, the thieves get paid, and the company is relieved they don't have to pay the full amount on the policy. Naturally, we don't approve of such arrangements." She took a drink, but of water, not wine. "How can I find out what company insured the drawing?"

DiMaio held up his hands defensively. "You're getting ahead of things, Betta. Pilar didn't know if her father even had a policy on the drawing, but she said that if he did, it would likely be with the same company he used for the rest of his insurance." He pulled his small notebook from his pocket and flipped through the pages. He tore one out and passed it to Betta. "Here you are. Seguros Suarez in Madrid."

She glanced at the paper and stuffed it into her pocket. "We have a woman in the office who deals with insurance companies in these cases. I'll call her after lunch. Fortunately, she's a friend and won't ask me why it took so long to get the name."

"Come on, Betta, we've barely been here two days. And you've been busy working various angles to the investigation." She was sending off signals that Rick had come to recognize from similar situations, when she talked to him about the frustrations of her work. The perfectionist in her was not mollified by assurances from him those times, and it wouldn't be now. Better to change the subject and get her thinking about something else—preferably something else related to the case. "Have you changed your thoughts about Vitellozzi, after meeting with him a second time?"

It seemed to work. She pondered the question. "There

was something he said that, thinking about it now, was very curious. He talked about taking the long view, meaning that he's surrounded by works of art that have been in the collection for centuries and will still be in it centuries from now. He mentioned some priceless object that had been misfiled in a museum for decades and suddenly found. He implied that what is important is that the drawing turn up eventually, even if it is after we have all left the scene."

"So that makes you think he has it stashed somewhere," Rick said. "Why don't we steal down into the basement tonight when everyone is at the reception?"

"That's not a bad idea, Rick."

"I was joking, Betta."

Betta pushed at the leaves in her salad before spearing one on her fork.

"Did you hear that, Betta?" asked DiMaio. "Riccardo was joking."

Betta held up an empty fork. "Why don't you get a search warrant, Alfredo?"

"Based on Vitellozzi telling you that the collection will outlast him, and he hopes the drawing turns up someday? That would get a good laugh from the judge."

She concentrated her attention on the plate, carefully cutting a slice of lettuce.

———

"That explains it," said Betta after Rick filled her in on the encounter between Pilar and Alfredo at the police station. "Perhaps we were a bit too quick to assume that he would step away from his professional persona to become involved with someone connected to his investigation."

"He did become involved, Betta, but something soured the relationship. Clearly, he didn't want to talk about it, but he wasn't hiding the fact that it's over between them. We may never know if it was Alfredo or Pilar who caused things to go awry." A college student passed them, talking loudly on his cell phone. "Betta, you didn't tell Alfredo about your conversation with Pilar yesterday."

"Maybe it was just as well I didn't, given the way he's feeling about her. It's not relevant to the investigation." She stopped in her tracks. "But it may explain something that we couldn't figure out."

"What's that?" he said after returning to her side.

"You remember the slap in the cathedral?"

"It is etched in my memory."

"Well, Lucho told you this morning that he knew more about what the old man was doing than anyone in the company. Pilar understood that, and pressured him to spy on her father. But there was one secret Lucho may have known that he didn't pass on to Pilar."

"The purchase of the summer house."

"Precisely. She confronts him in the church, and he admits it. Wasn't 'inheritance' one of the words you managed to catch?"

"It was."

They walked along a narrow street before coming to a familiar corner. All streets in Urbino led to Via Raffaello, or so it seemed. They found themselves back on it and began the descent toward the hotel when Betta decided to call her office. Rick strolled over to the window of a shoe store while she talked on the other side. Like the shoe stores in Rome, or any other city in Italy he'd visited, the men's and women's footwear in this establishment were clearly separated. He knew this because he had taken on the habit of the locals while walking around Rome, that of perusing the windows of shoe stores. Somewhere he'd read that the Italian obsession with shoes started with the Etruscans, and, over the millennia, design changed while the love of fine footwear persisted. He found it curious that styles were the same in the capital as in the provincial cities—perhaps they all used the same distributors. This year, for men, the heavy-soled, industrial-looking shoe was in. It would take more than that to get him out of his cowboy boots. Next year, if the pendulum swung back to light loafers, he might be tempted. As he looked, trying to picture who might actually buy these shoes, his thoughts were interrupted by Betta's voice.

"She's going to check on it."

"Check on what?"

"The insurance Somonte might have had on the drawing. But it may take a while since protocol requires that they go through the Spanish police, and who knows what kind of bureaucracy that is."

"Unlike the streamlined Italian police."

"Do you make that kind of sarcastic remark around your uncle?"

"No, but he makes them around me all the time. Which reminds me—I should call him."

She squinted through the glass at the shoes, but Rick could tell that her mind was on other things. "I also talked with the guy I sent the pictures you took at Morelli's house last night. He promised to check them against the list of missing artifacts. That also might take some time, since Greek amphorae are reported missing all the time. It's not like checking fingerprints."

Rick glanced down the street. "Speaking of your friend Morelli, isn't that him?"

Betta followed his eyes. "It certainly is. And it looks like he just came out of Bruzzone's art gallery. Why would he be paying a call on Bruzzone?"

"He buys art, Bruzzone sells it. Isn't that the way it works?" He noticed her scowl. "You're right—it is a bit curious."

"Why don't we drop in at the gallery ourselves? Just to see how Bruzzone is doing after the attack this morning, of course." She tugged at Rick's arm but stopped for a moment and looked back at the rows of shoes. "Who buys those things?"

They walked past the house of Raphael to Bruzzone's shop, where a bored policeman stood outside smoking. He must have seen Betta and Rick with DiMaio at the *commissariato*, since he quickly stamped out his cigarette and opened the door for them. They thanked him and entered the shop, which looked as it had earlier that day except the door to the office in back was ajar rather than wide open.

"I'll be right with you."

A moment later the door opened and Bruzzone peeked out. For an instant he didn't recognize them, causing Rick to wonder if the gash on his forehead had affected his faculties. A square white bandage, perhaps larger than it needed to be, covered the wound. Color had returned to his face since the morning, but his body language indicated he was still somewhat in shock.

"Dottoressa Innocenti and Signor Montoya. It is good to see you again, and it gives me the opportunity to thank you. I was in no condition to remember such niceties this morning."

Betta took his hand in both of hers. "No need for that, Signor Bruzzone. We wanted to see how you were doing."

"Much better, thank you. Much better. I wish I could offer you some coffee, but I haven't had time to load my machine." He smiled. "It isn't very good coffee, so you are fortunate. Have you heard anything from the inspector regarding…" He raised his hand to his forehead without touching the bandage.

"We know he's been working hard on various leads," said Rick, knowing he didn't sound convincing. "You're able to get back to your regular routine of work?"

"Oh, yes. The clinic took good care of me and told me to go home, but I had work to do here. Word must have spread around the city about the incident, since several people have called or stopped in to check on me. Cosimo Morelli was just here."

"Morelli?" said Betta. "The art collector?"

"Yes, he even showed some interest in those miniatures, something I found very strange. It's not the kind of art he's ever collected, as far as I know. Maybe he was just trying to make me comfortable after the attempt on my life, although making someone feel comfortable is not in Cosimo's nature, in my experience. Just the opposite. I think he just wanted to snoop."

"Perhaps he's concerned about his own safety," Rick said.

Bruzzone thought about it. "I hadn't considered that, but it could be. Anyone who had contact with Somonte could be in danger, and there aren't that many of us. That may have been why he asked about the police investigation."

"What did he want to know?"

"He asked if you police had any suspicions about who took the shot at me. That would be a natural question if he's worried about his own safety and he didn't want to ask Inspector DiMaio directly."

Rick considered what Bruzzone was saying and found it curious that the man hadn't put two and two together to realize that Morelli himself was a suspect. And as a suspect in the murder, he had to be a suspect in the botched shooting that morning. The gash on the head was clouding his thinking, after all. "What did you tell him?"

Bruzzone held up his hand in a helpless gesture. "What

could I tell him? I said the police were checking to see if the bullet was from the same gun that killed Somonte. Have you confirmed that yet, by the way?"

"We haven't talked to the inspector since we left here this morning," Betta answered.

Rick marveled at her deflection. "What else did he say?"

"When I mentioned that you were here this morning with Inspector DiMaio, he said he'd met you both. He asked if I'd ever had any contact with the art theft squad before. Can you imagine such a question? Certainly not, I told him." His eyes jumped to Betta. "I don't want to give the impression that I'm against what your office does, Dottoressa. Obviously, if I can ever be of assistance, I—"

"We understand perfectly, Signor Bruzzone."

The door opened behind them and a balding man dressed in a suit entered. He gestured to signal that he didn't wish to interrupt the conversation.

"An old friend and loyal client," said Bruzzone. "Word travels fast around Urbino, especially when the news is something as exciting as this." Again he raised his hand to the bandage, but stopped short of touching it.

"We will leave you to your friend," said Rick. "We're glad you're recovering quickly."

Bruzzone thanked them, and they walked out to the street. The policeman had changed his position from one side of the door to the other and gave them a conspiratorial nod as they passed.

"Somebody could still walk in and shoot him," said Betta.

"But he wouldn't get very far after he did."

They started down the street, which had been taken over by afternoon tourists. Just above them a woman carrying the standard tour guide umbrella was lecturing in Italian to a large group about to enter the house of Raphael. Another gaggle stood several doors down, in front of the San Francesco church, but for them the language was German. Rick noticed that every German listened intently to their leader while half the Italians talked among themselves while occasionally glancing up at the tour guide.

"We have some time now, Betta—why don't we visit the Casa di Raffaello?" At that moment, the group of Italians surged toward the door where at the most two people could enter at one time. It reminded him of lift lines in the Dolomites, but fortunately here nobody was wearing skis. Down the street the Germans were moving in orderly pairs into the portico of the church.

"Too crowded," answered Betta. "Maybe tomorrow morning. But I have an idea. You and I have been to the street behind the botanical gardens, but not the scene of the crime itself. Aren't you curious to see it?"

"I am, now that you mention it. Maybe we'll run into DiMaio's friend Florio."

They turned and started climbing. The street seemed to get steeper every time they walked it.

"That was interesting what Bruzzone said about Morelli," said Rick. "After listening to you interview him at the station, and meeting the man last night, I have a hard time picturing him as the concerned friend dropping in to give comfort. He was definitely probing."

"No question about it."

A sign appeared for the Orto Botanico, and they followed it.

———

"Wait here," said DiMaio. "I just need to check messages."

The driver, a young policeman, nodded and turned off the

engine of the squad car. His boss bounded up to the entrance to the *commissariato* and pushed open the door. Immediately, he realized his mistake. Why hadn't he parked behind the building and come in the back door? Waiting in the main lobby was the journalist who had ambushed him two days ago, wearing the same earnest look on her face. At least she had changed sweaters, though the jeans looked to be the same.

"Signora Intini, I don't have anything new for you, and I'm in a great hurry."

"Our readers have a right to know what is happening, Inspector. It is not every day that we have a murder in our city."

DiMaio kept to himself his opinions about the public's right to know. What he wanted to ask was her source for the details about how Somonte's body was found, but he knew she wouldn't tell him. As he thought about what tidbit, if any, to feed her, she spoke up herself.

"I understand that you met with the Spanish consul. Can you at least tell me about that?"

"How did you know that?"

"Just a journalist's hunch. I called the Spanish embassy in Rome and they told me. So you did meet with the consul?" She pulled out her notepad and waited.

She was obviously proud to tell him how she dug up a source, making him think that perhaps he could play on her ego and ask her who told her about the body. He rejected the thought as soon as it appeared in his head. "I did meet with the consul this morning in this very spot. We had an open and productive exchange. He assured me that the embassy will do everything possible to assist the Italian authorities to find the perpetrators of this terrible crime, and I expressed my appreciation and assured him in return that we will not rest until it was solved." He waited while she scribbled in her pad.

"That's it?"

"That's as much as I am allowed to tell you. Diplomatic entities do not have the same regard for the need of your readers to be informed as do you. As I'm sure you will understand, my hands are tied."

She looked down at her notes and back at DiMaio. "But—"

"I really must go. Don't worry, I still have your card." He turned and walked quickly away.

She called after him. "Is it true there's someone from the art police here?"

DiMaio had disappeared into the rear of the building.

—

When Rick and Betta arrived at the entrance to the gardens, they found a crowd of people sitting on the steps and others standing in front of the fountain. Without knowing the profile of a botany aficionado, it wasn't clear to them if everyone was waiting to see the murder scene, the other plants, or both. Betta surveyed the group, nodded her head to Rick, and made her way through the people seated below the doorway. He followed, noticing the scowls on those waiting to get in. At the ticket counter they encountered another scowl, that of the woman sitting behind it.

"We're only letting in small groups at a time," she said, and held up two pieces of paper with numbers written on them. "Wait for me to call; it will be about a half hour."

Betta looked at the numbers but didn't take them. Instead, she pulled out her identification. "We're from the police. Inspector DiMaio sent us to take a look at the crime scene."

The woman's eyes widened, and for a moment she didn't speak. Then she turned her head toward the garden depths.

"Nino! Police!" A nervous smile tightened her face when she looked back at Betta. "He'll be right with you."

They heard the crunch of shoes on gravel and a man appeared from among the fronds. He wore green overalls embroidered with the logo of the Orto Botanico over a darker green shirt. Perspiration covered his face and neck, but he made no attempt to wipe it with the handkerchief protruding from his pocket. When he noticed that one of the policemen was in fact a policewoman, the handkerchief came out, but only to dry his hand that he extended to her.

"Fantozzi, *piacere*. Inspector DiMaio was here this morning speaking with Professor Florio. I didn't know that more police would be coming. Of course the inspector didn't want to speak again with me, only with the professor."

Betta noticed the annoyance. "Which is why we are here, Signor Fantozzi. If you don't mind going over again what happened that morning."

The man grinned. "Certainly not. If you could wait just a moment, I will get rid of the people looking at the plant now. Excuse me." He hurried off into the greenery and a few moments later reappeared, herding a dozen people who glowered at Rick and Betta as they left the building. "Now, if you'll come this way, please."

They followed behind him, Rick's cowboy boots crunching as they dug into the gravel. Rick noticed the rise in humidity and temperature as soon as they stepped from the entrance area into the verdant garden proper. Both increased even more when they entered the greenhouse. The path took a sharp right turn, and Fantozzi stopped next to the Spanish Dagger.

"Here it is. This is the exact place where I found him. I was a bit shaken up, I don't mind telling you. I'm not used to finding bodies when I make my first rounds in the morning. My heart pounded, and I broke out in a sweat."

Even worse than normal? Rick was tempted to ask as he wiped his own brow with his handkerchief. Betta appeared not to notice the heat, reminding him that women don't sweat, they glisten. "Tell us what you saw. We heard it from the inspector but would like to get it from your point of view, you being an eyewitness."

Fantozzi clearly relished the opportunity. "I came around the corner, past the cacti, and almost immediately knew that something was amiss. This was even before I saw the body. Since I spend so much time working here, I must have some kind of antenna system that alerts me to changes. The way leaves move, odors, whatever it is, I knew then that something was wrong. Then I saw the figure sitting there, and my immediate reaction was that some drunken tramp had somehow found his way in here and fallen asleep. When I took one step closer, of course, I knew who it was." He paused for dramatic effect. "Signor Somonte, the very person who was to visit the gardens the next day. It was then that I realized that he was leaning against one of the very plants that he had donated. How... what's the word?"

"Ironic?"

"Exactly. Thank you."

"Please tell us how the body looked," said Betta. "You knew immediately that he was dead?"

"Oh, yes. And not just from the bloodstain on his shirt. Even though he looked like he was sleeping, there was something clumsy about the way the body was arranged. I say arranged because he would not have ended up in that position on his own. Not on your life."

"How was he arranged?" Rick asked.

Fantozzi looked around to be sure that nobody else was watching, then got down and sat himself in front of the tall plant. Leaning back, he tilted his head slightly to one side. "He was like this," he said with eyes closed to give more authenticity. Careful not to put too much weight on the plant, he got back to his feet and brushed himself off.

"That was when you called the police."

"Uh, it was Professor Florio I called first. He told me he would contact the authorities and to get out to the street and wait for them. He was adamant about not touching anything. He knows all about those things from the books he reads."

"So we've heard," said Betta. "And you did what you were told."

"Certainly. But the professor arrived before the police. He must have been in his office." He pointed behind him with his thumb. "It's on the next street over."

"Yes, we know. How do you think the body got in here? You must have some ideas."

Fantozzi beamed. It appeared that nobody had asked him his opinion. "Well, as you know already, Signor Somonte had his own key to the gardens. Ceremonial, but it worked. I think that whoever killed him forced him at gunpoint to come here, made him open the gate, and shot him in front of his plant."

"Then propped up the body."

"Exactly, Signora."

"So it didn't have to be someone he knew."

Fantozzi used a finger to wipe a drop of sweat from his nose. "I hadn't thought of it, but that's true. Just someone who knew that he had the key to get in here."

"Thank you for your insights, Signor Fantozzi. We should leave you to your work and let all those people come in to see the gardens."

"Most of them aren't interested in the other plants, just Somonte's. Yesterday a woman came in with her little daughter to show her. Disgusting. But it certainly is making Professor Florio happy."

Outside, Rick and Betta breathed in the cool afternoon air and splashed their faces with water from the fountain pool. "I wonder if they put this here just for the people coming out of the heat inside," Rick said. "If I knew my Latin, I could read the inscription."

As usual, Betta had her mind on the missing drawing. "We didn't get anything out of that except perspiration."

"Except that we're pretty sure the murder was connected to the missing drawing."

She shook her hands of excess water and looked at Rick. "How can we be sure?"

"How many people had seen the drawing?"

Betta put some thought into the question. "Obviously all the people we've interviewed. But remember that there was an article in the paper a few days ago about the donation. Vitellozzi mentioned that when we talked to him. My guess is that there was a picture of it accompanying the story."

"It must also have mentioned that Somonte was stopping in town on his way to Sansepolcro and that the drawing was of great value."

Betta rubbed her eyes. "Too much of a temptation for your normal thief. All he had to do was track down where Somonte was staying and shadow him. And by carrying the drawing around, our victim made it easy." She sighed. "We're back to suspecting half the population of Urbino in a robbery that turned violent."

"Not exactly. I believe what we just heard back there in the humidity brings the suspects list back to the serious art experts."

"Nothing he said could have been different from what he told Alfredo that morning."

"Perhaps, but Alfredo might not have spotted it. I refer to Fantozzi playing the role of a cadaver, and playing it well.

Didn't it remind you of something? He closed his eyes and tilted his head."

"*O Dio*, of course. The sleeping soldier in Piero's painting in Sansepolcro."

"Whose face just happens to be the subject of the missing drawing. Which means that our murderer not only knew about the drawing but also knew that it was a study for the painting. And he was familiar enough with it to set up Somonte's body to mimic the sleeping soldier. Pretty macabre."

"Also pretty sophisticated. Our suspects list remains small."

"And, Betta, it increases the chances that the drawing is in the hands of someone who understands both its artistic and monetary value."

# CHAPTER ELEVEN

The Palazzo Ducale was made for nights like this. During his reign, Federico da Montefeltro staged scores of events here that were the height of elegance and ceremony, but those were different times. Tonight's opening would not approach the duke's flair for decadent opulence, but the massive structure was doing its best to re-create something from its past glory. The *piazza* in front was lit by a line of torches inserted into wrought-iron sconces flanking the shuttered windows of the second floor, casting pale, flickering light onto the stone pavement. Raphael would have felt right at home in this atmosphere, though perhaps puzzled by the single spotlight illuminating his young face on the exhibit banner.

Rick and Betta walked through the square toward the entrance. Fortunately, they had both packed something a bit more formal for the trip, just in case something came up that required more than business casual. Rick had a blue blazer, his only white shirt, and a favorite burgundy tie, along with his dressier pair of cowboy boots. Betta, whom Rick decided could look good in a flour sack, wore the classic black cocktail dress and low heels. In place of business-hour gold studs in her ears, small hoops, which he'd never seen before, hung below her close-cropped black hair. At the hotel she had thrown him a curveball by not using her usual Dahlia Noir and challenging him to name what she'd sprayed on. He'd nailed it—Habanita—and now as he caught another whiff of it he was tempted to warn her never to question his perfume acumen. He resisted, not wanting to spoil what he hoped would be a very pleasant evening.

Another pleasant evening.

Since she'd moved to Rome to join the art theft squad, there had been ups and downs in their relationship, but lately it had moved into a very relaxed phase. Not that they took each other for granted. Each had other friends, both from their work and going back to before they'd met, but there was an unspoken understanding that they would be together whenever they could. Was it time to have a chat about where it was all going? Betta was not one to keep things inside, he told himself; when it becomes an issue for her, she'll say something.

Garlands of flowers festooned the grand staircase leading to the second floor where museum guards directed them toward the room of the special exhibit. It was the route they had taken on their previous visit, and it was impossible not to stop and admire some of the paintings they passed. One was *La Città Ideale*, the ideal city, attributed to Piero della Francesca but not definitively identified as his, despite the rigid perspective for which the painter was known. Unique for its long, rectangular shape, it showed pristine lines of buildings on either side, drawing the eye to the round structure in the very center. An already haunting canvas was made more so by the total absence of human beings. Rick wondered out loud: "Could that have been the artist's message, that the ideal city would lack people?"

"I don't think so," said Betta. "There is a hint of humanity there with the slightly open door to the building in the center. It's as if he wants us to enter. And there are some plants hanging down from a few of the windows, put there by people. Perhaps everyone is inside the center building, having a meeting."

"Or watching a movie."

Double doors offered wide access to the exhibit room. As they approached, the voices of the guests became more pronounced, a strange contrast to the silent halls they'd just traversed. Betta paused and took his arm as they got closer.

"Most of the people here tonight will be one of three types, Rick. First will be the city's upper crust, not all that interested in the artwork, more in seeing who else is here and being seen by the others. Then the local politicians, whom I assume Vitellozzi has invited. They will also pay more attention to the other guests than to what's on the walls."

Rick tried to think how he would translate the word *schmooze* into Italian. "I know their kind from the diplomatic receptions I've been to. While talking to you they're looking over your shoulder to see if there's someone more important they should be cultivating."

"Exactly. But you could say that of just about anyone. The third category is the art professionals. They will wander around and look at the paintings, even though they've seen them a hundred times before, some of them on the walls of their own museums. What they will enjoy most will be gossiping with each other about who is up and who is down in the art community. There's always someone ready to retire or rumored to be moving to another job, and they'll talk about the leading candidates to take their place. Or insinuate that they themselves are under consideration for the position."

"I trust that you fall into the third category, Betta?"

"*Magari*," she said, using a word that could be translated in various ways, including "fat chance." She pulled his arm and they walked into the room. "Tonight there's a fourth group, those trying to figure out who possesses the missing drawing. There are only three people who are in that elite company, two if Alfredo doesn't show up."

Rick raised his hand to salute. "I understand my mission."

They stepped through the door and immediately encountered Vitellozzi, who had positioned himself to receive his guests. Despite the bustle of activity behind him, he was as relaxed as when Betta had seen him that morning.

"Dottoressa Innocenti, Signor Montoya, thank you for coming. The hour has finally arrived, after years of planning, and I'm pleased you will share it with us. Please get something to drink and enjoy the exhibit."

"Thank you, Dottor Vitellozzi," said Betta as she shook his hand. "And congratulations—it looks wonderful."

They moved ahead while the director turned his attention to the next group of arrivals. Rick deftly took two flutes of wine from a passing tray and gave one to Betta. "To our search," he said as they tapped glasses and surveyed the room. When they had been there during the setup, Rick had not noticed that, except for some wood decoration around the doors, the room was completely bare. No doubt the room selection was deliberate, since the stark walls would in no way detract from the magnificent art hanging from them. The star this evening was Raphael, not the architect of the palazzo.

Immediately, they noticed people they knew.

Cosimo Morelli stood in front of a framed female portrait, but his attention was on the woman standing next to him, who displayed more than a minimum amount of cleavage and acted bored. "That's *La Muta*, the Raffaello from the collection here,"

Betta said. "It appears that the woman talking with Morelli is equally mute. No doubt in awe of his repartee."

"Or paralyzed by the strength of his cologne. Let's forget Morelli for the moment and say hello to Bruzzone. That must be his wife with him."

The art dealer had traded the white dressing on his forehead for a more subtle, skin-colored bandage. The woman standing next to him appeared to be somewhat older, though the strain on her features could have been as much the result of the morning's excitement as the aging process. The two did not speak as they studied two portraits hanging side by side. The man and woman in the paintings were inclined toward each other but stared directly into the eyes of the viewer with a smug self-confidence.

"*Buona sera,* Signor Bruzzone."

His body tensed and he turned quickly. "Ah, Dottoressa Innocenti, *buona sera*. And Signor Montoya. Let me introduce my wife." Handshakes were exchanged. "These people came to my aid this morning, *cara*. You'll remember I told you about them."

"Thank you for helping Ettore." Her face showed exhaustion, but she forced a smile.

"We were just admiring the Doni," said Bruzzone. He pointed at the portraits and Rick detected a slight shake in his hand. "Agnolo and his wife, Maddalena, he a prominent Florentine merchant of the time. They are the model of Renaissance wealth, don't you think? 'Look at us,' they are saying, 'we are so rich we can afford to buy not only these fine clothes but to hire Raffaello to paint us.' The master did a fine job conveying the snobbishness of these two, do you agree?"

"Absolutely," Rick answered as he gazed at the two faces on

the wall. "The scenery in the background, Signor Bruzzone. Am I mistaken, or is it reminiscent of—"

"Leonardo. Yes, very good. It was painted when Raffaello was studying his work. The way the two bodies are posed is also very much like a Leonardo da Vinci portrait." He moved his eyes from the painting to Betta. "Is the inspector coming this evening?"

"He didn't say," she replied. "He's quite busy on the case, as you can appreciate."

"I hope it gets resolved soon. Don't you agree, *cara*?"

His wife nodded but said nothing.

Betta saw her lack of response as a sign that they should move on. "Signor Bruzzone, Signora, a pleasure to see you. If you'll excuse us, we'll look around at the other pieces."

They started walking to the other side of the room, but after a few steps Betta pulled on Rick's arm. "Bruzzone seemed a bit on edge."

"As would be expected after what he went through this morning. He'll probably be looking over his shoulder until DiMaio finds the person who shot at him."

The guests moved around the room in slow motion, stopping at one masterpiece before sliding off to the next. Most of the women wore black dresses, as if they had decided they should not compete with the colors of the paintings on the walls. The men had done the same in their choice of suits, and even their ties were subdued in hue and design.

"Look who just arrived." Betta's eyes were back at the doorway, where Pilar was engaged in conversation with Vitellozzi. "I'm not that good at interpreting body language, but my guess is that they are not meeting for the first time."

"Interpreting is my business, *cara*, and I would agree with you. Look at that—she just laughed and touched his arm.

Those two are definitely not strangers, and they don't seem concerned about anyone knowing it. The question is, did they meet for the first time this week, or on one of her previous trips to Italy."

"And would it have any bearing at all on the case?" She studied the two, who were still chatting at the doorway. "This morning when I talked to him he claimed not to know that Somonte's daughter was in town. He could have gotten her phone number and called to be sure she knew she was welcome tonight. Or, he was lying to me and they'd already talked, but he didn't want me to know."

Pilar noticed that other arrivals were waiting to greet Vitellozzi. She said something to him and entered the hall, which was starting to fill with people.

Rick nudged Betta. "Now look who's here." In contrast with the jeans she'd worn when ambushing DiMaio at the police station, the newspaper reporter wore a skirt and blouse, but she still held tightly to her pen and pad. This evening she was accompanied by a photographer, who snapped pictures of Vitellozzi as he answered her questions. "She covers all the beats, it appears, from murders to culture. Let's avoid her—she'll remember we were with Alfredo the other day."

It was too late. She was already walking quickly toward them.

"I'm Laura Intini," she said as she flashed her press card. "Didn't I see you with Inspector DiMaio? Were you at the *commissariato* in connection with the homicide investigation?"

Rick stepped in before Betta could reply. "Is there a homicide investigation? We are old friends of the inspector and dropped by to say hello. Who got murdered?" He looked expectantly at her while Betta remained silent.

Intini wouldn't take the bait. "Is Inspector DiMaio coming this evening?"

Rick and Betta exchanged shrugs. The reporter mumbled something and walked away with her photographer in tow. Immediately, she found a couple who looked ready to have their picture in the newspaper to show they were at the cultural event of the year. While they talked, the photographer clicked away.

"Everyone so far wants to know if Alfredo is coming," said Betta. "Do you think he'll be here?"

"I think he said something about avoiding the place since the mayor will be in attendance. That may be who our journalist is talking to now."

Most of the throng talked in the center of the room as if there was nothing to be seen on the walls, and the decibel level rose accordingly. The bar set up in front of the tall fireplace was doing a brisk business, which added to the noise. Rick noticed a man in a dark suit standing against one wall, one of the few with no glass in his hand. His eyes moved around the room.

"That guy's got to be security," he said to Betta in a lowered voice.

"Maybe a plainclothes cop keeping an eye on Bruzzone."

"I forgot about that. You could be right." He took a drink from his glass. "This stuff is pretty good. Vitellozzi hasn't spared the expense, it appears."

"He's using Somonte's money for it. Look, Loretta Tucci has made the trip here from Monterchi. And she's chatting with her fellow museum director from Sansepolcro."

"Engaging in shop talk about running their museums. But, no, you said that the art professionals would be gossiping about the next opening in the world of Italian cultural professionals. The two of them must aspire to higher positions, wouldn't they?"

"Absolutely, Rick."

They walked to where the two women were engaged in conversation. Tucci looked up. "Betta and Riccardo, I thought I might see you here. Let me introduce Tiziana Rossi."

"We've met," Betta said as they all shook hands. "Dottoressa Rossi received us two days ago at her museum in Sansepolcro, but unfortunately things didn't go as planned."

"I hope you are getting closer to finding the drawing," Rossi said. "The museum was devastated with the news that it had gone missing. The whole town of Sansepolcro was so excited that it was coming home."

"No news yet, I'm afraid, but you'll be the first to know."

It was as if both women sensed Betta's discomfort. Tucci changed the subject. "Isn't this a magnificent exhibit? It must be the first time so many Raffaellos have been in the same room—a definite triumph for Vitellozzi. He must have been working on it for years."

"That's what he told us," said Rick. "Getting works on loan from other museums is a delicate process, apparently. But you two certainly know more about that than I."

"The *Madonna del Parto* never leaves Monterchi," said Tucci. "It's all we have, so without it nobody would come to our museum. Your situation is a bit different, isn't it, Isabella?"

"I get requests for loans frequently, mostly for the Pieros, of course. With us it's usually a financial transaction since we don't often mount exhibits and need some piece from the other museum. But we don't lend out more than one major work at a time. Visitors become annoyed when there is a sticker on the wall in the place of a painting they've come to see. People often travel a long way to visit Sansepolcro, and we don't want to disappoint them."

While her colleague was speaking, Rick noticed Tucci's eyes wandering around the room. It confirmed Betta's observation that these events were as much for networking as anything. Everyone feigned interest in the art, but for many present this evening, it was secondary. At that moment, one of the museum staff interrupted their conversation.

"Signor Montoya? Dottor Vitellozzi asks if you could please give him some assistance." They all looked back toward the door and saw the museum director standing with Signora Somonte and Lucho Garcia. The three were smiling woodenly at each other but not speaking. Rick concluded that she must have shopped in town for something more appropriate for widowhood than the wardrobe she'd brought with her. It was a subdued dark-gray dress that came down well below her knee, though it still showed off her curves. Garcia's suit was dark with a dark-blue tie.

"I think he needs an interpreter. If you ladies will excuse me." He walked quickly to the museum director. "Can I help, Dottor Vitellozzi?"

"If you wouldn't mind, Signor Montoya. We were not communicating well, to say the least, and Signor Garcia suggested that you might interpret, as you did for the inspector at the hotel."

"Certainly."

"Please tell the signora that she has my deepest condolences for the loss of her husband."

Rick went into his well-practiced consecutive interpretation routine. Signora Somonte and Vitellozzi exchanged appropriate pleasantries, and he told her that he would be noting her husband's contribution to the event when he addressed the guests later in the program. She thanked him and said she would be pleased to say a few words herself, something that clearly took the museum director by surprise. He asked Rick to interpret for her, and Rick said he would be honored. Vitellozzi offered to take her around and tell her about each of the works displayed, but Garcia stepped in, saying he was familiar with them and could do it. Besides, he added, the director was busy with the other guests. Vitellozzi thanked him. Everyone shook hands and Rick returned to Betta, who was still standing with the two museum directors.

"You've already earned the price of tonight's ticket, Rick."

"And I'll get overtime later when interpreting the signora's remarks."

Tucci's eyes widened. "She's going to address the crowd? The way she just tossed down that glass of prosecco, it could prove interesting." They watched as Signora Somonte put her empty glass on a waiter's tray and took a full one. "Extremely interesting."

"Ladies," said Betta, "Riccardo and I had better see the art before he's put to work again, if you'll excuse us."

They did, and the two of them drifted to the other side of the room where *The Marriage of the Virgin* hung. Three people, who did not appear to be together, studied it while sipping from their glasses. The scene was an open square below a round, domed temple in the distance. The priest, ornately robed, held the hands of Mary and Joseph at the point when the groom was putting the ring on her finger. A group of women stood behind Mary, an equal number of men in back of Joseph.

After looking at the painting for a few moments, Rick turned to Betta. "You're the art expert—tell me about this one."

She took a deep breath. "You can read next to it that it's on loan from the Brera in Milan, but it was originally commissioned by a patron for a church in Città di Castello. We drove near there yesterday. Given the rounded top, it was probably intended to be put above an altar. The perspective is done perfectly, taking the eye to the vanishing point at the temple door, which led to speculation that Raffaello had studied Piero's treatise on perspective. The temple is painted so perfectly that some art historians think he worked from a wood model, but that's never been proven." She pointed with her hand. "The figures in the foreground are of course the stars of the work. You can see that Joseph is the only male wearing a beard, and the only person barefoot, which likely foreshadows the arrival of his son. Every aspect of the painting has a meaning, of course."

"I could not help overhearing," said a voice behind them. They turned to see a thin man peering at the painting through round glasses. "You must be an expert on Raffaello."

"Not really," said Betta. "Is this the first time you've seen this work?"

"Yes, indeed it is. We who live here in Urbino are delighted that it's all been brought here, even if it's just for six months. He was born in Urbino, you know."

"We'd heard that," said Rick.

"Yes, indeed. One of our main streets is named for him. The house where he was born is located on it."

"We've been meaning to go during our stay here. You are a local—what else should we not miss while we're here?"

The man pursed his lips and thought. "Well, this palace is the reason why most tourists come to Urbino, and you're here tonight. But there is much to see in the regular collection, so you must come back. The other attraction that shouldn't be missed is the Orto Botanico."

It dawned on Rick who the man was. His eyes shot over to Betta and back to Florio. "Urbino has a botanical garden?"

"Oh, yes, a fine one." He looked left and right and leaned forward with a conspiratorial smile. "I'm the director."

"Really? Well, we will have to make a visit, won't we, *cara*?"

"Absolutely," Betta answered. "But didn't we read something

about the gardens in the newspaper? We always make a point to read the local paper whenever we travel."

Florio kept his voice subdued. "A very nasty business, indeed. A man was found dead there. Surprisingly, people have been coming to the garden the last few days just because of that. And what brings you two to Urbino? The art, I would imagine."

Rick answered. "Certainly that, but I'm an interpreter. In fact, it looks like I'm about to go to work, if you'll excuse us." He took Betta's hand and they walked toward the small stage where Vitellozzi had just stepped to the microphone. Behind him a man surveyed the crowd like he owned them, and Rick guessed him to be a politician. It was the Galleria Nazionale delle Marche, after all, so it would make sense that a representative of the region be present. Next to him stood the Widow Somonte, fortunately without a glass in her hand. Lucho was a few steps away watching her carefully. A man with a deep tan stood next to the director. He wore a meticulously tailored suit and looked vaguely familiar. "Betta, do you know either of those two men with Vitellozzi?"

"The one on his right is the undersecretary of culture. I heard he was going to be here."

"So you know each other."

"Be serious. He's probably never even met my boss, let alone people like me. We're not even in the same building." She glanced back. "What did you think of Professor Florio?"

"Not exactly the cold-blooded murdering type. Alfredo should cross him off his suspects list."

"I think he already has. You really should have told Florio we went to his gardens today. It would have been fun to see his reaction. Look, he's over talking with someone else. I'm guessing he's searching out the visitors to tell them the real action in Urbino is among the plants."

The guests were starting to notice the people who had taken their places on the podium and began to quiet down. The waiters also sensed that the formalities were about to begin and retreated behind the bar. While the dignitaries spoke, the waiters would fill glasses for their next turn around the room. Rick squeezed Betta's hand and walked to the rear of the podium, ready to step up when needed. He hoped that the Widow Somonte had changed her mind about speaking, but she was still next to Vitellozzi. Lucho continued to hover nearby. The director stepped to the microphone, tapped it a few times to be sure it was working, and identified himself before welcoming everyone to the event. Then he began to describe the planning that had gone into bringing all the works of art together, making Rick wonder how long he would drone on before introducing others who would no doubt drone on as well. He thought Betta had to be wondering the same thing and looked out into the crowd to catch her eye. She was nowhere to be seen.

—

A series of similar corridors led to Vitellozzi's office, making Betta glad she had paid close attention to the route that morning. In case she ran into a museum employee, she was ready with the excuse that she had gotten lost on the way to the ladies' room. The palace had hundreds of rooms, after all, so it would be understandable that a visitor could get confused, as long as there was a bathroom somewhere in the vicinity. Fortunately, she met no one, and the halls were almost silent except for the sound of Vitellozzi's voice just barely audible far behind her. After a turn down another hallway even that sound faded to nothing—when the duke built the *palazzo* he had made sure the walls were thick. She came around what she remembered to be the last corner and spotted the office, marked by a simple *direttore* nameplate in brass next to the closed door. Would it be locked? She turned the handle, pushed it open, and stepped inside. Better to close it, since her excuse would look weak if someone walked by and saw her inside. This was not a room anyone could have mistaken for the *toilette*.

Fortunately, Vitellozzi had left the lights on, and she could see that everything looked the same as it had that morning. Her eyes again darted to the ceiling, but she forced herself to keep her attention on the desk and surrounding furniture. If she was to find anything of interest, it would be there. The outside view was less of a distraction at this time of day. Dusk had turned the hills from shades of green to grays and blacks, and the sky had darkened so much that a single star shimmered high above the horizon. She walked quickly to the desk. The files that had been stacked on one side were still there, perhaps lined up even more neatly. She took the top one in hand and found it stuffed with spreadsheets that she realized were income and expenses for the museum, arranged by months. Such was the drab reality of running a public institution, even a glamorous museum like this one.

The next file was thicker and more interesting. It held correspondence to and from the museums that had lent works for the exhibit Vitellozzi was speaking about at that very moment. As fascinating as the letters were, they would not get her any closer to finding Piero's drawing, and time was passing quickly. She put the file back under the first file and noticed that something at the bottom of the pile was different in size, small enough that the files hid it from view. Logic—and neatness— would dictate that the smaller item be placed on top. She lifted the stack and found not another file but a paperback book with a white cover. Immediately, she recognized it as one in a series on famous artists, several titles of which she had read as a student at the university.

This one analyzed the works of Piero della Francesca.

Why had it been tucked in at the bottom of the stack? It had to be so that she wouldn't notice during her morning visit. However, the museum was famous for its works by Piero, so it would be logical that Vitellozzi should keep a reference work about him on his desk. Did he simply want to avoid the discomfort that would come with a question from his police visitor? Somehow, he didn't seem the kind of person to be bothered by such things. If anything, he would put it out in the open to provoke her.

She was about to slip it back under the files when she noticed a card peeking out of the middle of the book. Her finger opened to the marked page, revealing a color print of one of Piero's more famous works, the very one she and Rick had seen two days earlier in Sansepolcro.

Below the standing figure of Christ lay the sleeping soldier with the face from the missing drawing.

Why was the page with this particular illustration marked? Once again it was at the very least curious, and possibly suspicious, but still merely coincidental. Before replacing the card between the pages, she turned it over and found that it was the business card of Manuel Somonte, with his contact information printed in Spanish. Had Somonte left it when he'd called on Vitellozzi just before his murder? Betta ruled that out since the card was bent and smudged. Even if the card had just been inserted to mark the page, the museum director had received it from Somonte longer than three days ago. She noticed faded letters under the printed words that she strained to read.

Her concentration was broken by the faint sound of applause. Were the ceremonies over? She couldn't have been away from the exhibit hall that long, but maybe she'd lost track of time. She quickly replaced the card and put the book back under the stack of files. More applause.

Betta hurried from the room and closed the door behind her.

Rick stood ready behind the riser and kept an eye on the door at the far end of the room. After Vitellozzi's opening remarks, the culture undersecretary had conveyed the minister's anguish in not being able to attend and then offered his own two cents—or was it two euros?—about the importance of the event to the cultural life of Italy. His talk was mercifully short, but the next speaker's was not. The president of the region expounded on the artistic patrimony of Le Marche, starting with Raffaello and going through a long list of worthies whose names meant nothing to Rick. He was reminded of the cynical Italian phrase *illustri sconosciuti*—illustrious unknowns. As the man appeared to be winding down, Betta came through the far door and flashed Rick a thumbs-up sign. He gave her a theatrical frown and head shake in return. His attention snapped back to the formalities when he heard Vitellozzi talking about Manuel Somonte, the late benefactor of the museum and contributor to this fine exhibit, recently and tragically struck down. Rick stepped quickly to Isabella Somonte's side and began giving her the Spanish translation in a low voice. She gave him a blank stare and then realized why someone was whispering in her ear before she looked back at Vitellozzi, who was asking everyone to welcome Signora Somonte. There was polite applause.

"It is time for you to say a few words," Rick said gently.

Lucho appeared at her side, took her arm, and guided her to the microphone. The crowd waited patiently, unsure what to expect, while Isabella stared back at them. Seconds passed.

Rick leaned toward her. "If you'd rather not—"

"I will speak." She began to sway, clutching at the microphone, and might have fallen if Lucho and Rick had not steadied her. "Translate every word," she ordered.

Rick nodded and looked at Lucho, whose face was grim.

"My husband is not here tonight," she began. "Had he not come to your *beautiful* city, he would still be alive."

Rick put her words into Italian, but without the derisive tone she'd given to the word "beautiful." This was not going to be easy.

"I could never understand Manuel's fixation on Italian art. After all, we have great Spanish artists. Why did he have to come here? His mother was Italian, but was that reason enough? It would not be for me, but I am one hundred percent Spaniard." She pounded her fist on her chest and again nearly lost her balance. Lucho was there to steady her.

As Rick translated, he noticed Pilar standing in the back of the crowd, enjoying the spectacle while everyone around her watched in transfixed disbelief. Vitellozzi stared at the ground, his arms folded over his chest. The regional president, perhaps used to dealing with awkward situations in public, maintained a stiff smile, while the culture undersecretary stared at the ceiling. Rick finished translating the sentence and turned back to her. For a moment he wondered if she was finished, but she snapped out of her daze and continued.

"I know…" she began and started to sway, causing Lucho to step forward and take her arm. She stared at him almost without recognition, before looking back at the people standing in front of her. Her eyes seemed to be searching. "I think…no, I am certain…that someone in this room—"

Rick was wondering how to interpret when Lucho leaned toward her and spoke into her ear. His voice was soft but firm. "Isabella, it is time to go. You have had a long day." He shook his head at Rick and led her to the rear of the riser. She didn't resist. A museum guard helped her down the step and the two Spaniards walked slowly to the door. The eyes of everyone in the room followed them until they were out of sight.

Vitellozzi stepped to the microphone. "As you all can understand, Signora Somonte has been under a great strain since her husband passed away. It was courageous of her to come this evening, and we are very appreciative that she did. This ends the formalities; please enjoy the art."

The waitstaff took the words as a green light to begin circulating among the invitees, but everyone else stood planted in their places. It took several moments before anyone spoke, and when they did it was in low voices. Vitellozzi stepped off the platform and waded into his guests, smiling and shaking hands, even of those he had greeted previously. He broke the ice to some extent, as did the waiters, whose flutes of prosecco were quickly snatched from their trays. Before the ceremonies, everyone had appeared more interested in each other than the art. Now, almost reluctantly, they honored Vitellozzi's request and turned their attention to the paintings. Rafael's self-portrait, which had graced the poster seen around Urbino, drew the largest numbers.

Rick stayed a few moments on the riser surveying the scene. Betta was back to chatting with the two out-of-town museum directors. Morelli was sipping prosecco and looking deep into the eyes of a woman, but a different one. Florio had cornered two couples and was likely expounding on the wonders of his gardens. Bruzzone was nowhere to be seen, nor was the man whom Rick had suspected to be his police guard. The man had been showing signs of nervousness earlier, and Signora Somonte's rant might have persuaded him and his wife to head for home. Intini, the journalist, had somehow found Pilar and was scribbling into her notebook as they talked. Or had Pilar found the journalist? Rick stepped down and walked toward Betta, picking off two glasses from a tray on the way. She noticed him, excused herself, and met him in the center of the room, taking the glass.

"Thank you, Rick." She smiled and took a sip.

"Please tell me that you weren't snooping around the palace during the speeches."

"I may have gotten a bit disoriented while searching for the ladies' room."

"Well?"

She told him what she had found, doing her best to make it sound like the book and bookmark were the equivalent of a smoking gun. He wasn't convinced.

"The director of a museum that specializes in the works of Piero della Francesca has a book on his desk about Piero, and a card in the book is from one of the museum's benefactors? Not exactly overwhelming evidence. Alfredo won't need to take out his handcuffs quite yet."

"But the painting on the page that was marked? *The Resurrection*, from the museum in Sansepolcro? It's a lot of coincidences."

Rick shrugged. "Maybe it's his favorite Piero painting."

She was about to argue but nodded instead. "You're right. It proves nothing." She sipped her wine and looked over Rick's shoulder. "Here comes Morelli."

"I can almost smell his cologne."

Morelli walked to them and bowed slightly. "Good evening to the Rome contingent. Are we here to enjoy the Raffaello exhibit or to arrest someone for stealing some masterpiece?"

"We would love to do both, Cosimo," Betta answered. "Are

you here to enjoy the art on the walls or to find a buyer for your newly acquired drawing?"

Morelli forced a smile. "As you well know, Betta, my collection does not extend to pencil sketches, even those of great artists. I prefer other kinds of art, especially art that will last centuries."

"You tried to buy it, if I'm not mistaken."

"Yes, and when I didn't get it, I recognized my error and returned to the collecting I know best: paintings and Greek artifacts." He turned his attention to Rick. "It was a shame you did not translate the final words of Isabella Somonte. From the little Spanish I know, it might have been of interest to those gathered."

"Have you spent much time in Spain, Cosimo?" Rick asked.

"A few business trips, though I mostly deal in Italian and Greek olive oil."

"You must have visited your friend Manuel Somonte."

Morelli's smile faded. "Olives are grown on the Mediterranean shore of Spain, Riccardo. Somonte lived in the north, which is mostly known for mountains and sheep."

"Yes, of course," said Rick. "But you didn't answer my question."

"Questions posed in jest do not need an answer. Have you found your drawing, Betta?"

"Is that question asked in jest as well, Cosimo? If we had the drawing, you and everyone else in town would have heard about it."

He nodded. "Very true. I hope it turns up before tomorrow afternoon. I'm leaving on a trip to Greece and will be there for ten days. It is very difficult to get news from Urbino when one is on an isolated island."

"You may want to check with Inspector DiMaio before you leave town," said Betta with a sweet smile.

"He called me earlier to ask where I was early this morning, but he didn't tell me why. Police harassment, I'd call it. Why would I want to check with him about my trip? It's none of his business."

"Not that you are a suspect in his homicide case, of course, but you know how police are. They don't like people connected to an investigation flying off to other countries, especially isolated islands."

"Our mayor is here tonight. I will talk to him about whether I can be allowed to leave or not. And since I may not see you before my departure, have a pleasant trip back to Rome." After another slight bow, he melted back into the crowd.

"A delightful fellow," commented Rick.

"I'd love to catch him at something. I haven't heard back from my office on the amphorae you photographed. Of course they've only had the picture for a day."

The noise level in the room had increased, thanks to the wine which continued to flow. Canapés also circulated on trays, but the waiters carrying glasses were more popular with the guests who now gathered in front of the artwork. One of the paintings, a portrait of a woman, only had a few people studying it, and Rick suggested that he and Betta go over so that the subject wouldn't get an inferiority complex. It was the picture Morelli had been standing in front of when they arrived.

"*La Muta*," said Betta. "It is the more important of the two Raffaellos in the museum's permanent collection, so most of the people here have already seen it."

The woman was seated with her hands folded on her lap, looking directly at the artist with Mona Lisa–like indifference. The plain background accentuated the elegance of her dress, its folds picking up the light coming from her right. A long neck mirrored other works in the room, including the artist's self-portrait, but her most striking feature was her hands, adorned by rings and holding what appeared to be a piece of parchment.

"Why is she called the silent one?" Rick asked.

"It's unclear, if I recall my Raffaello course at the university. It could be the way her lips are tight, like someone who is averse to speaking, but it may refer to us not knowing the identity of the sitter, though there are various theories on that. The positioning of the hands was almost certainly influenced by those of the *Mona Lisa*, which Raffaello saw before painting this portrait."

"The hands are beautifully painted. I doubt if she's washed many dishes."

"Probably not."

They studied the painting for a few more minutes before Rick noticed two people carrying on an animated conversation near the door. "Alfredo has arrived."

Betta looked to see DiMaio standing silently with arms folded while Vitellozzi moved his hands and talked. At the end of what had to be his explanation of something, the director gave the policeman a "What's the big deal?" shrug. Whatever he'd said, Alfredo did not appear to be convinced. His face indicated that the discussion was ended, and he looked around the room. He spotted Rick and Betta, said something to Vitellozzi, and strode toward them between the invitees.

"It didn't appear that you were congratulating our museum director on the event," Rick said when he reached them.

"*Ciao*, Betta; *ciao*, Rick. No, I was asking him where he was at the time Bruzzone was shot at, and he didn't have much of an answer. I also inquired about something I found out when we did a check of travel records." He looked even more fatigued than when they'd seen him at lunch. The circles around his eyes appeared darker, as did his unshaven face.

"And that would be?" asked Betta.

"Vitellozzi flew to Madrid twice in the last couple years." DiMaio flagged down a waiter and took a glass from the tray. "The first trip was around the time Somonte purchased the drawing, the second a few months ago, just before it was announced that the donation would go to the Sansepolcro museum." He took a long drink of the wine. "This is just what I needed."

"I suppose he told you he was consulting with his major donor about support for the museum, including this exhibit."

"That's precisely what I expected him to say, Betta, and he didn't disappoint me. He also said that losing Somonte, such a great benefactor, will be a major blow to this museum."

"Meaning," said Rick, "'I didn't kill him so take me off the suspects list.'"

"Exactly. And he has a point. But guess who else has been traveling to Spain." He started to raise the half-empty glass to his lips.

"Morelli?"

DiMaio lowered the glass and looked at Betta. "How did you know?"

"Do you think we're just here to enjoy the art? He told us a few minutes ago."

"And, Alfredo, Betta got it out of him without any heavy-handed interrogation methods, I might add. He said he was buying olive oil in the south, the other end of the country from Somonte's wool mill. Which rings true. It's not as if he and Somonte were close friends, Alfredo."

DiMaio let out a deep sigh that immediately turned into a yawn. "Sorry." He looked around the room. "What other information have you two dug up?"

Rick and Betta exchanged looks.

"Tell him," Rick said.

She recounted her visit to Vitellozzi's office, which didn't appear to concern DiMaio greatly, perhaps because he was too exhausted to become upset. "You get points for the initiative, Betta, but there isn't much there for me to work with."

Rick was about to say that his reaction was the same, but he held his tongue. Instead he said, "You missed the excitement when an inebriated Signora Somonte addressed the group."

That got the policeman's interest. "Really? What did she say?"

"Not much, except that she blamed Italy for her husband's death and almost said that she thinks someone present this evening is responsible. Then Garcia hustled her off the podium."

"The rant of a grieving widow. I wish I could have seen it. She could have at least done me the favor of narrowing it down to a half dozen names." He deposited his glass on a passing tray. "You two enjoy the art. I'm going to do my best to avoid our mayor and that journalist, both of whom I spotted when I came in. I'm going to slip out and return to the office." He left their side and took a circuitous route to avoid encountering Pilar Somonte, who was talking with a woman twice her age.

"Betta, has something crossed your mind about Vitellozzi's trips to Spain?"

"That he went there to convince Somonte to donate the sketch to his museum, and when the man refused, he found other means to get it? Which is why he had the book in his office marked with Somonte's card, one that he must have been given on one of those trips."

Rick kept his eyes on Pilar. "That's possible, of course, but it's not what I was thinking."

She took his hand. "And what were you thinking?"

"That Vitellozzi may have gone to Spain to see someone else."

——

Betta and Rick had eaten enough canapés so that regular dinner didn't sound appealing. Nor did the idea of going back to the hotel, thanks to all the theories about the investigation running through their heads, none of them making much sense. A wine bar they'd passed earlier seemed like a good alternative to a full restaurant meal and would give them the opportunity to unwind and talk about what they'd heard during the exhibit opening. Located near their hotel, the place was not much wider than the window and door that faced the street, but went back deeply into the building. Behind the bar that ran along the right wall, two women in long white aprons served up wine and small plates of food to go with it. The clientele was young and casually dressed, likely university students, making Rick feel aged in his jacket and tie. The air was filled with animated conversation and the smell of what in Spain would be called *tapas*. The largest tables could accommodate four people, but most of them held only two. One had just emptied, and Betta took possession of it while Rick turned to the bar.

"After that prosecco, I'm ready for something red," she called to him as she sat down. The height of the table was matched by stools with sturdy backs. Rick asked the barmaid for two glasses of a local red of her choice, and returned to the table holding a scribbled card with the evening's fare. He passed it to Betta.

"It may be the aromas in this place," said Rick, "but all of a sudden I'm hungry." He looked at the plates at other tables.

"After that big lunch we had, you're hungry again?"

"We didn't have pasta at lunch."

"Did you always have pasta at lunch when you lived in America?"

"This isn't America."

She shook her head and moved her eyes over the menu card. "Some bruschetta, for sure. Oh, and look at this: *formaggio di fossa.* That's a local specialty. I remember having it years ago when I came here with my parents. I thought it was a funny name. If those two aren't enough we can order something else."

She passed the menu back to Rick, who perused it quickly. "Cave cheese?"

"It's semisoft, made with sheep or cows' milk, and has a sharp flavor. According to tradition, the cheese was stored in pits inside caves to keep marauding armies from discovering it. But they still let it mature in them today to give it the unique taste."

"Sounds like a gimmick." He walked to the bar and put in their order. The wine had been poured so he brought the two glasses back to the table. "She said this is a Rosso Piceno from a vineyard owned by her brother-in-law. We'd better tell her it's wonderful even if it isn't." They tapped glasses and sipped. "Fortunately, it's good."

They didn't talk for a few minutes until Betta broke the silence.

"We have to admit it; this investigation is going nowhere. The Piero drawing could be in someone's suitcase halfway to China, for all we know. If it never goes on the market, it's gone forever, or at least for our lifetimes. The only result of this investigation is that it will show up as a negative report in my personnel file."

"Not every case ends successfully, Betta. They can't hold this against you."

Her lips formed a bitter smile. "I work in a bureaucracy. Anyone who wants to get past me on the promotions list will be sure the system remembers that Betta Innocenti was the one who lost the Piero drawing. I can easily name a few who are watching this case very closely, ready to pounce."

This line of conversation would not go anywhere, he knew. Better to get her mind on something other than the backstabbers in her office. "Why don't we go over the various players in this affair, Betta? Maybe something will jump out. That's what they do in the crime novels."

She laughed, but it was not a happy laugh. "We should be consulting with Florio…he's the expert on crime novels." She took another drink of the *rosso*, which seemed to help her attitude. "You're right. Then let's start with our museum director. We just found out that he has also made some trips to Spain, and you have insinuated that he may have been interested as much in Pilar as her father."

"Just a thought."

"They did seem pretty cozy tonight when she came in. If we take your line of thinking to its logical conclusion, Pilar didn't get along with her father and wanted to take over the business, and Vitellozzi wanted the drawing for the museum, thinking he could talk the widow into changing the donation."

Rick nodded. "The drawing conveniently turns up, he gets the widow's ear, and it ends up in Urbino's Palazzo Ducale, after all. Of course she could sell it again. That would be what I'd expect of the woman. Probably sell it to another Spaniard."

A young man wearing a white apron appeared at their table carrying two dishes that he put between them. He looked so much like one of the women behind the bar that he had to be her brother. From the apron pocket he extracted silverware wrapped in napkins, placed them next to the plates, and wished them a *buon appetito*. The bruschetta was what Rick expected: a meaty paté spread over toasted slices of crusty bread. The other plate was different, and they both leaned closer to take in the arrangement of items. Pieces of the same crusty toast over-lapped each other on one side, a white slab of the cheese was in the middle, and a small cup of what looked to be fruit preserves sat on the other side. Betta explained that a slice of the cheese went on the toast, and then a bit of the preserves—which they realized were cherry—would be spread lightly over the cheese. The sweetness of the fruit, she assured him, would be a needed contrast to the tartness of the cheese.

Rick followed the directions and found that she was exactly right. "What about Florio?" he asked after his second bite. "I know he's difficult to take seriously, but the murder did take place in his gardens, and he is definitely milking it to the maximum."

"Not to mention that he knows all about planning a murder from reading mysteries."

"You don't sound convinced."

"No, Rick, I'm not. Let's move on to Morelli."

He tried the bruschetta. It was unlike and perhaps bet-ter than the bruschetta at lunch yesterday. "It's a good thing there's an even number here so we won't have to fight over the extra piece."

"Take one of mine. You said you were hungry."

"You are too kind, Betta. All right, back to Morelli, the man you love to hate. He does make a good villain, I have to admit, and he doesn't have a real alibi for either the night of the murder or this morning's attempt on Bruzzone. His motive, of course, is the drawing. He wanted it, didn't get it, and held a grudge for missing out. By killing Somonte, he both gets revenge for being humiliated by being out-bid, and he gets the drawing that he can enjoy in the privacy of his own home."

Betta sipped her wine. "I may be wrong, but I don't think his ego would allow him to possess a work of art that he couldn't show to his guests."

Two people left the table behind them and were quickly replaced by a pair of students who squeezed past Rick and Betta to lay claim to the empty places. Groups stood by the door keeping an eye on the room, ready to pounce. The place was getting more popular as the evening progressed.

"Thank goodness we got here when we did," said Rick. "Do you want another wine? We can try a glass of something different."

"Why not? At least I can tell the people at my office that I discovered some new wines, even if I didn't discover who took the drawing."

Rick was not happy with her self-pity. It wasn't his favorite side of Betta, but he just shook his head and took the two steps to the bar. After consulting with the barmaid, he returned to his seat. "I told her the Rosso Piceno was excellent and asked for something else local. She's pouring something from the hills between here and Pesaro, called Focara Rosso. You did want to stay with red, didn't you?"

"Yes, for sure." She took another bite of the cheese on toast. "Who's next? How about the Spanish contingent? Signora Somonte may have a strong motive, especially if Garcia was more than just her husband's special assistant. With Somonte out of the picture, she gets a hefty inheritance and her boyfriend full-time as a bonus."

"It would have been easy for Garcia to follow him as he left the hotel and then pulled the gun." Rick raised a hand to hold a thought. "Wait, how about this: knowing his boss had a key, he might have talked Somonte into showing him the gardens and then done him in when they got there. We've always assumed that the murderer forced Somonte there at gunpoint, but perhaps that wasn't necessary."

"And the grieving widow is waiting for him back at the hotel. That's possible."

Rick noticed that the woman behind the bar was pouring two glasses of red wine. He got off the stool and asked if it was theirs, and when she nodded, he brought them back to the table. When he put one in front of Betta, he noticed that the two serving plates were almost empty. "Do you want me to order something else?"

"Not for me," Betta said, "but go ahead if you're still hungry."

"No, this glass of wine will do it. Where were we?"

"Discussing the Spaniards. But because of the attempt on Bruzzone, it makes more sense that our murderer is someone from here in Urbino, which brings us back to our favorite private collector and museum director. And that takes us to Bruzzone's own theory that the person who shot him found out that he'd suggested to me that the police talk to Vitellozzi and Morelli. One of them got word of what he'd said to me, was not happy about it, and stormed into his shop with the gun."

Rick put down his glass after a drink. "You're forgetting the other possible motive, Betta. Alfredo came up with it after they took Bruzzone off to have his head bandaged up."

She was about to take a drink but lowered her glass. "And that was?"

"The person who shot at him was not upset about what he'd said to the police but rather by what he might say. Bruzzone may well have more information to tell the cops, and the murderer wanted to be sure he kept quiet."

"He would have kept very quiet if the bullet had hit him rather than the wall."

"If that theory is correct, it's no wonder he was so nervous tonight when we talked to him."

"Let's see how nervous he is tomorrow when we speak to him again." She stared at the glass but didn't drink. "Do you know what worries me the most, Rick?"

He reached across the table and took her hand. "It's the drawing, isn't it?"

A half smile formed at the corner of her mouth. "You know me too well." She squeezed his hand, then withdrew it to pick up her glass. "I think this is better than the first one."

# CHAPTER TWELVE

The ring came at the perfect time. Rick stopped, leaned forward with his hands on his knees to catch his breath, and pulled the phone from his pocket. As he expected, the call was from his uncle, the only other early riser he knew. He guessed that Piero had reviewed the case on his computer screen and thought, correctly, that now was a time his nephew would be free to talk.

"Commissario Fontana, it is an honor to speak with you."

"The pleasure is mine, Riccardo. From your voice I suspect I have found you, as I expected I would, in the midst of your morning run. I hope this is not inconvenient."

"Not at all. I have just climbed one of the steeper streets of Urbino and can use the respite, if you'll excuse my panting. I imagine you are calling to see how the case is progressing."

"You imagine correctly. I have been following DiMaio's reports, and reading between the lines I get the sense that he has reached a dead end."

"That's it in a nutshell. Last night at the big art opening at the Palazzo Ducale we spoke with several of the people involved, but we didn't get much from them."

Piero took a moment to respond. "The reports I read don't

say much about the missing drawing, but I suspect that there is nothing new there as well. How is Betta taking it?"

It was just like his uncle to worry about Betta. Piero didn't disguise his fondness for her, and would be more than happy if she were to become part of the family, but he would never say that to Rick. Such meddling was something an Italian mother would do, not an Italian uncle. At least not this Italian uncle.

"She's frustrated, as you can imagine. She thought Sansepolcro was just going to be a ceremonial event, representing the ministry at the donation of an important work of art, and then it turned into an investigation. You could see her excitement. But that's starting to wane, even though it's been only three days."

"Homicide cases start to go cold immediately, and I would assume it's the same with stolen art." Again there was a short pause. "Do you think DiMaio is handling this case well?"

Rick recalled that after the Bassano investigation he had asked his uncle to put in a good word about Alfredo. He hoped Piero was not having second thoughts about doing so. "As far as I can tell, I would say he is, but you probably see more than I do from reading his reports."

"Reports never tell the whole story."

The whole story would include DiMaio's initial relationship with the daughter of the victim. Rick would wait until getting back to Rome to mention that detail to his uncle. If then.

"Riccardo, I have to go. Let me know when you're coming home. *Baci per* Betta."

"*Ciao*, Zio." He stuffed the phone into the small pocket, took a few jumps in place, and started back toward the center of town. Running downhill, especially down a steep hill, required considerably more care than staggering uphill, as Rick had done at the start of his run. He was at the end of the loop, which had taken him to the tops of both of Urbino's principal hills and now descended Via Raffaello. The street was starting to come to life, making the avoidance of groggy pedestrians another concern. He slowed as he passed the house of Raphael, vowing that this would be the day to make a visit. It was almost across the street from Bruzzone's art gallery, where they would be making a call after breakfast, so why not visit the birthplace of the city's most famous native as well? He passed the gallery and didn't see any movement inside, but that was to be expected given the early hour. A few steps later he made the turn to start down Via Mazzini, and a minute after that he turned onto the Hotel Botticelli's street. When he got to the room, Betta had already gone to breakfast. He showered, dressed, and went down to join her. As always after his morning run, he was in need of calories.

He looked around the breakfast room and quickly spotted her sitting alone at a table in the corner, her cell phone and a folded newspaper next to her plate. As he worked his way among the other tables, he noticed her face and became concerned. She stared down at the cup directly in front of her with an expression indicating she had just lost her best friend. When he sat down, she barely glanced up.

"What's happened, Betta?"

"I just talked to my boss in Rome. He's pulling me off the case."

"That's all?" He poured hot coffee and hot milk into his cup.

Now she looked at him. "Isn't that enough? Just what I feared would happen has happened. He said to turn the investigation of the missing drawing over to the local police and come back to Rome."

"He must have some other case for you to work on." He added sugar to his cup and stirred while checking out the buffet.

"I hate to think what that might be. Rick, we were almost there. I could feel it."

He hadn't felt it; he had the impression they were spinning wheels, but he kept the thought to himself. What he now felt was hunger. "Let me bring back some breakfast and you can tell me what's in the paper." He got to his feet. "What can I get you?" Her answer was a head shake, and he walked to the buffet, still well stocked despite several tables of tourists. He took a plate and filled it with an almond croissant, a yogurt, a crusty roll, two small plastic containers of Nutella, and an orange. When he got back to the table, he was relieved that Betta's face had the suggestion of a smile. "Something good in the paper?" He poured more coffee into his cup.

"Some comic relief. The story on the front page is written by that journalist we saw at the event last night. She cites unnamed sources who told her, under the condition of anonymity, that the leading suspect in the murder of Somonte is none other than…?" She looked at him over her half glasses.

"Since you're laughing, it must be Florio."

"None other. And he has to be the anonymous source."

Rick took a bite of the croissant. Almond was his favorite, along with chocolate. "How can you be sure? Alfredo could have told her that to have some fun."

"The article also notes the jump in attendance at the Orto Botanico, with numbers."

He nodded. "You're right—it was Florio."

Slowly the plate in front of him was emptied, and Betta decided to help him with half the orange, after which she went to the buffet and brought back a yogurt for herself. She pulled back its cover and picked up a spoon. "Let's take a different route back to Rome. Along the Adriatic?"

Rick was happy to get her mind off her work—or lack of it. "We could also go back to Sansepolcro and then straight south around Perugia. We could have lunch at the place outside Todi where we ate on our Orvieto trip. Or if we're hungry before that, there's the Tre Vaselle in Torgiano, just south of Perugia."

"You're filling yourself up on breakfast and already planning lunch?"

"We're in Italy, Betta. It's the law." That managed to get a good smile from her. "But before we depart, let's go to Raphael's house. I ran past it this morning and realized it's the one important sight in Urbino we haven't visited."

"Certainly, Rick." She pushed her empty yogurt cup to the side and picked up her cell phone. "Let me call Alfredo to tell him that the investigation is now completely in his hands. And I'll pass on our agreement with him that the attack on Bruzzone yesterday morning may have been a warning to keep him quiet." She started hitting buttons and then paused. "At least last night it sounded to us like a good theory. Now in the light of day I wonder if it was just the wine talking."

"That will be for Alfredo to decide." He picked up his cup and found that the coffee was cold.

———

Rick and Betta came to the Piazza della Repubblica and turned left to start the climb up Urbino's main street. Via Raffaello was busier than when Rick had jogged down it earlier. A good number of the people they saw were tourists, but most were pensioners and other locals gossiping and enjoying the pleasant weather. The San Francesco church was not yet open, though it must have been about to since a group stood waiting outside the closed doors. Just past it in the small courtyard people sat at tables under large umbrellas enjoying their last taste of coffee and watching the passing pedestrians. Humans were not the only ones enjoying the fine morning. While their masters chatted, two dogs—who by their shapes and coloring could have been related—eyed each other with tongues flapping. Just ahead was Bruzzone's gallery.

"He must not be in yet," said Rick. "No police in front."

"I think you're right. I doubt Alfredo would have pulled the guard off only twenty-four hours after the attempt."

Casa Raffaello had the same fifteenth-century look as the other stone buildings on the block but was set apart by a banner hanging from the facade. They walked up a short step into the hallway where they bought tickets, were given a brochure, and pointed toward the stairs. After taking the stone steps up to the next floor, they found themselves in the spacious room appropriately called the Sala Grande. Rectangular paving stones, which Rick guessed not to be the originals, covered the floor. This was the heart of the home, where the family had gathered in front of a large, deep fireplace, where they ate at a long table, and where guests were entertained. Carved decorations filled in the space between ceiling beams that had their own carvings to match. While the house was not a palace in the English sense of the word, this room said that young Raphael had enjoyed a comfortable childhood. Large, dark paintings, mostly of religious themes, hung from the walls. None of them were originals by the master himself.

The only decoration in the next room, except for a fresco painted on the wall, was two chairs and two small framed paintings. The room was identified in their brochure as the Camera di Raffaello, which would indicate that this was where the artist had slept, or perhaps where he was born. The small fresco was clearly the most important feature of the room, and perhaps the entire house, since cords and stanchions prevented visitors from getting too close. It showed a woman holding a naked infant on her lap while reading from a book propped on a wood stand. There were no religious symbols that Rick was accustomed to spotting in portraits of the Madonna and Child. This was simply a woman cradling her baby.

"According to tradition," Betta said, "this was painted by Raffaello and is a portrait of himself as an infant being held by his mother."

Rick studied the fresco. "There's that 'according to tradition' line again. You can't fool me."

"*Bravo*, Rick. His father was a second-rate painter, of course, so it could have been by him."

"Or somebody could have sneaked into the place one night and painted it, hoping it would be taken for Raffaello himself."

"A good forger couldn't make any money that way. But it does have some of the features that Raffaello became known for later, like the long neck and the delicate features. Who knows? Maybe it really was painted by him. That's what the people who run this place would love to have proven."

They walked into another room, an antechamber with one door leading out to a courtyard and the other into the kitchen. Going into the kitchen first, they found that an open fireplace took up most of one side. Like everything else in the room, it was clean and neat, with only a few lines of soot which could have been spray-painted on for effect. The hearth was rigged with an ancient gadget of weights and pulleys that looked like something from a grandfather clock, but was in fact an ingenious system to turn a spit. Rick studied it before they walked through the open door into the *cortile*. The rough brick walls of the building closed in the four sides of the courtyard, its coldness softened by the green of potted plants in the corners. Against the wall nearest the kitchen sat a well, covered by a metal grate. Rick leaned over and could not see the bottom through the darkness, though he suspected there would be coins to be found if anyone ventured down the shaft.

"With all the wonderful views in this town, it's unfortunate that Raffaello's family didn't have one from this courtyard," he said and looked up at the shuttered windows of the top floor. "Maybe from up there the view is as good as from Morelli's living room."

Betta was staring at one of the potted plants, though her eyes were not focused. Suddenly she fumbled in her purse and pulled out her phone. "You got it, Rick. Why didn't we think of that sooner?" She looked at the small screen, found what she was searching for, and pressed the button.

"What did I say?"

"I'll explain. Let me get through to Alfredo."

—

Betta's eyes darted up and down the street, unsure from which direction DiMaio would come. "Let's go in—I can't wait any longer."

"Why don't you call him again?"

She shook her head. "Look, Rick, we figured this out, and the missing drawing is my case. An officer from the art fraud squad should be the one to arrest him. I want to see his face when we confront him."

"Betta, this isn't only an art fraud case."

She wasn't listening. When she pulled roughly on the door handle they heard the faint ring of the bell somewhere in the back of the shop. Rick held open the door, and they walked inside. It all looked the same as when they had been there twenty-four hours earlier, including the case of miniatures. If any had been sold yesterday to some passing tourist, Bruzzone had replaced them with others. The door to the office in the back of the gallery was open barely a crack, and

Rick thought he heard the voice of the owner, though it was so low he couldn't be sure. When the door opened, Bruzzone stared at them with a lack of recognition but quickly composed himself. He was dressed in the same suit, shirt, and tie as the previous evening, and he pulled a handkerchief from a pocket and quickly cleaned his glasses. Stubble on his face competed with the neatly trimmed goatee. The bandage on his forehead was new, but the blue edges of the gash were visible at its edge. Mechanically, he raised his hand to cover it.

"Dottoressa Innocenti, Signor Montoya. You have come by to check on me? How kind of you. As you can see, I am recovering nicely."

He stood just inside the doorway to the office and made no move to approach them. Was there someone else in the office? Betta stepped forward. "There was no guard outside, Signor Bruzzone, and we wanted to be sure you were all right."

He clasped his hands like a priest greeting his flock. "Yes, of course, the guard. I requested that he be removed. As you can imagine, having a policeman standing outside the door does not help business. Have you brought news of the missing Piero? I didn't sleep well last night thinking that it may never be found."

"We think we know where it is."

He froze but quickly recovered his composure. "Really? Why, that's excellent." His eyes started to move to his side before he looked back at Betta. "I had always thought it was tossed away by someone who didn't understand its value. Has one of your colleagues in the art fraud police found it already on the black market?"

"No, it's still here in Urbino. In fact, it is very close to where we are now standing."

Bruzzone swallowed hard and stood frozen in place. His eyes moved to Rick. "Signor Montoya, I don't understand what she's saying. Can you help?" It was as much a plea as a question.

"What she means, Signor Bruzzone, is that the missing drawing, since the night Manuel Somonte was murdered, has been in your possession."

Betta pointed over Bruzzone's shoulder at the bulletin board. "You told me that you had made a copy of the Piero sketch and very cleverly offered it to me to use in the investigation. But that drawing on the wall is the one you took from Somonte's leather case."

Bruzzone now scrambled behind the desk and pulled the sketched face off the wall, sending a pushpin flying. "Are you saying that I murdered Somonte for this?" He waved the drawing in the air while Rick and Betta stood transfixed.

Rick held up his hands. "Signor Bruzzone, please—"

Bruzzone stared at the paper in his hand and then dropped it on the desk. Keeping his attention on Rick, he reached down and opened the top drawer. His right hand came out with a dark pistol that he pointed at Rick and Betta. Still looking at them, he held up his left hand, as if keeping someone back.

"We will be all right, my dear. Stay where you are, and I will take care of these two."

"Signor Bruzzone, put down the gun," said Betta. "Inspector DiMaio will be here at any moment—you won't be able to escape. This is only making matters worse for you and your wife."

Rick slowly moved in front of Betta. "She's right—it will only make your situation worse. If you'll just—"

The door crashed open, causing Bruzzone to take his eyes off Rick and Betta.

"Drop the pistol!" DiMaio shouted while pulling his own weapon from his belt holster.

Rick shoved Betta down just as a shot rang out. As he was

dropping to the floor to cover her, another was fired. He heard a woman's scream and turned to see Bruzzone sprawled face-down on top of his desk, the pistol spinning slowly on the floor below. The woman who had screamed was now standing next to the desk, staring at his body and sobbing.

Other police officers burst into the gallery with guns drawn, but DiMaio ordered them out and told one to call an ambulance. As Rick and Betta were getting to their feet, he retrieved Bruzzone's pistol from the floor using a handkerchief and placed it on top of the glass case.

"It's fortunate he wasn't a very good shot." DiMaio looked back at the office. "I will call a policewoman to take care of Signora Bruzzone."

"That's not Signora Bruzzone," said Betta. "It is Loretta Tucci, the director of the museum in Monterchi, the Piero specialist who verified the drawing's authenticity."

As they watched, Tucci pulled the drawing from under Bruzzone's body and tore it to pieces.

—

Loretta Tucci sat in the same chair that Morelli had used three days earlier, and the same microphone was propped up in front of her. DiMaio sat directly across from her, and a female uniformed police officer stood against the wall behind her back. The bloodstained blouse and skirt she had worn when taken into custody the previous morning were replaced by a drab dress provided by the police. She did not appear to notice anything in the room but instead stared at the scratched surface of the table before her. DiMaio adjusted his microphone and stated the time, place, and participants, before centering a yellow pad in front of him and removing a pen from his jacket pocket.

"Would you like to have an attorney present, Signora Tucci?"

She looked at him as if he was speaking another language. After a few seconds she shook her head.

"Please speak into the microphone."

She leaned forward and looked at the red light on the base. "No need for an attorney," she said before leaning back. "What do you want to know?"

"Let's start with how long you have known Ettore Bruzzone."

She closed her eyes tightly, then opened them while letting out a low breath. "We met many years ago, at an art gallery in Milan owned by a mutual acquaintance. He was there looking at the work of a new artist he was thinking of putting in his shop. I was studying at the university. He was there without his wife, so he asked me if I had dinner plans. We became friends." Her voice was a clipped monotone.

"And you kept in contact after that."

"You could say that. Whenever he came to Milan he called me. After I got my degree I tried to get work in Milan but was rejected for several positions. A friend in the Cultural Ministry told me about an opening as the assistant curator in Monterchi. It didn't pay much, but it was a steady job and Piero della Francesca was my area of interest at the university. That eventually led to the position I have now. Or had, until this."

She noticed a bottle of mineral water, opened it, and splashed some into a plastic cup. DiMaio waited while she drank.

"I started seeing more of Ettore once I moved to Monterchi. We'd find an excuse to be in Florence at the same time. It was on one of those days that I came up with the plan."

DiMaio looked up from his pad. "So it was your idea."

Tucci appeared about to laugh. Instead, she smiled sadly while composing an answer. "He is not the most innovative person you'll ever meet. And looking back now, it's clear to me that I was more motivated. I was at a dead end in my life, working in a tiny museum without much hope of moving up to something better. In the cultural world you need a network of contacts, and especially someone high up who takes you under their wing. I was never good at working the system."

DiMaio almost pointed out that it was the same in police work but decided it would not look good on the transcript. He let her continue.

"This was my chance to have a better life, since I knew that at my age I couldn't hope to get to the top." She looked at the cup, as if about to take another drink of water, but instead she went on. "Ettore had told me about his client list, and the kind of art they would buy, and it seemed like a perfect scheme. Nobody has a larger ego than an art collector, Inspector. They try to give the impression it is all about beauty, but it's really about prestige." She took another sip of the water. "We were both sure the local collector would buy it. What's his name?"

"Morelli."

"Yes, of course, Cosimo Morelli. If he'd bought it, none of this would have happened. No one would ever have known. Even the old lady in Monterchi conveniently died, so that part of the operation was sealed. Instead, that damned foreigner outbid Morelli. At the time I thought it was even better—the drawing would be off in another country. But then he decided to come back and donate it to the museum in Sansepolcro, and everything started to unravel."

"Did you plan the murder, as well?"

DiMaio could see that the question took her by surprise. Did she think this was just an informal chat between friends?

"Certainly not, Inspector. When Ettore read in the newspaper that Somonte was going to donate the drawing to the Sansepolcro museum, he called me immediately. He was frantic to the point of being incoherent. I knew he was a weakling, but it surprised me that this had almost pushed him over the edge. When I finally calmed him down, I said I would come up with a plan to get the drawing, which I did a few days later. It involved a burglary, with no violence, and it would have worked."

"But it didn't."

"He couldn't wait, and decided to take the situation into his own hands. Perhaps he wanted to impress me with his masculinity." She looked straight at DiMaio. "You'll have to ask him."

"I plan to…when he regains consciousness. What about the faked attempt on Bruzzone?"

"That was my idea."

Some minutes later Rick and Betta took off their headsets and placed them on the edge of the desk. Unlike the windowless room where the policeman was wrapping up the interview, DiMaio's office was splashed with morning sunlight. They sat at the small meeting table, its surface bare except for the earphones and a bottle of water they had shared while listening to Tucci.

Betta rubbed her ears and gave her short hair an unneeded brushing with her fingers. "If the voice weren't so familiar, Rick, I'd would have thought she was a different person than the woman we had lunch with three days ago."

"She had poor Bruzzone wrapped around her little finger."

"Poor Bruzzone? The man is a murderer."

"In America we have an expression about someone being thrown under the bus. I'm not sure if it works with a literal translation into Italian."

"I get the image. She definitely threw him under the bus down there just now, as if the murder was completely his idea."

"Maybe it happened exactly the way she recounted it."

"Or perhaps she was just trying to get a lighter sentence."

They looked up when DiMaio entered the room holding his pad of paper. "There was a bus accident?"

"It's just an expression, Alfredo."

The inspector dropped the pad and sat down behind his desk. "Were you able to hear everything?"

"Perfectly," said Rick. "Even with just the audio, our sense is that she didn't come off as the weaker vessel, led astray by an evil criminal mind."

"Same with the body language." He put his hands behind his head and leaned back in the chair. "I just heard downstairs that Bruzzone is conscious and talking, so it will be interesting to compare his version with hers. But after hearing her, my guess would be that she was telling the truth. I already checked to see where she was at the time of the murder and confirmed she was visiting her mother in Milan."

"Very convenient for her," said Betta. "The dirty work of covering up her original crime is done by Bruzzone when she's nowhere near Urbino. You have to think she planned it that way."

DiMaio rubbed his neck with both hands. "I'm not sure what I think. I finally managed to have a good night's sleep, but now I could use a few days of just petty crime. This case has been exhausting."

Rick glanced at Betta before speaking. "Alfredo, I have to ask you. There is something we—"

The policeman raised his hands to fend him off. "I know what you're thinking, you two. What happened between the inspector and a certain Spanish person key to the investigation?"

Rick smiled. "You're reading our minds, Alfredo."

DiMaio had settled back into his chair. "When she was ushered in here, I was sure I could mix business with pleasure. Would it hurt to have a close relationship with someone who could give me firsthand information about the victim of the crime?

Understanding the victim is always a first step in finding out who would have a motive to kill him. Basic police procedures. But two nights ago I found that having a special relationship actually worked against it. When I dropped her at the hotel I made a simple request. Routine really. Had she been just another suspect in the case, there would not have been a problem. I simply asked her to show me her airline ticket so I could confirm that she was in fact not in Italy when her father was murdered."

"Oh, my."

"Oh, my, indeed, Betta. She exploded, saying, 'Don't you trust me?' She even raised her hand and was ready to slap me but had second thoughts and pulled it back."

"Assaulting a police officer?" said Rick. "You would have had to arrest her."

Betta shook her head. "Crime of passion. Never would have held up in court. And it may be a trait of Spanish women that they slap people when they don't get what they want."

"I think I recall hearing that," Rick said. "We're sorry it didn't work out, Alfredo."

DiMaio shrugged, and a grin wrinkled his cleanly shaved face. "As am I." He took a drink of water from a cup on his desk. "She called me from the airport yesterday."

Betta and Rick spoke at the same time. "Really?"

"She was actually quite pleasant. She thanked me for solving the case, and I pointed out that it was you, Betta, who put it all together. She sent regards to you both."

"That was kind of her," said Betta.

"She also asked me to pass on regards and thanks to you, Rick, from Lucho Garcia."

"But—"

"They were on the same flight. Signora Somonte had flown back alone a few hours earlier."

# CHAPTER THIRTEEN

"So it was a forgery." Commissario Piero Fontana studied the red color of the wine in his glass as he contemplated the significance of what he had just been told. "It makes everything fall into place, doesn't it?"

"Not exactly a forgery," corrected Betta. "More just a fake. A very clever idea, since most sketches from that period, even those done for important paintings like this one, have been lost or simply thrown away. Artists always did studies for something they were going to paint, and it was safe to assume that Piero della Francesca drew various sketches for the painting in Sansepolcro. There may even be an actual drawing of the soldier's face somewhere, but I'm sure Tucci did her research to be sure there wasn't before she created one herself. She has to be quite an artist."

Being a policeman, Rick's uncle was more interested in motive than art history. "If the donation had been completed to the museum in Sansepolcro, the sketch would eventually have been examined by specialists, am I correct?"

Betta nodded. "It's standard procedure for museums to allow scholars and other experts to study works in their collections."

"You've gone to the heart of the case, Zio," said Rick. "Eventually, it would have been exposed as a fake, and the reputations of both Bruzzone and Tucci would have been destroyed, and likely they would also have been charged with a crime. Bruzzone could have told the police that he was duped, but their relationship apparently involved more than just art fraud."

Piero took another drink of the wine, a deep red Cesanese di Olevano Romano from the hills southeast of Rome. "And the staged attempt on him was a diversion, but a very believable one since he used the same gun used to murder the Spaniard. Very clever indeed, but by doing so he was digging himself in deeper and deeper. How many times have I seen exactly that happen with someone who has committed a crime. The layers they build become clues and eventually it blows up in their face. But how did you come to the conclusion that the drawing was bogus?"

Rick and Betta exchanged smiles. "Well…" Betta began.

She was interrupted by the arrival of their *antipasti*. All three had ordered the same dish to start the meal: a large artichoke, braised until tender in wine, oil, and herbs. Like so many other Italian dishes, *carciofi alla romana* were the epitome of gastronomic simplicity. After the traditional *"Buon appetito"* exchange, they each cut off a piece of the long, tender stem and took a first bite. Conversation resumed.

"It was really just by chance," said Betta. "We were finally making a visit to the Casa Raffaello, which happens to be on the same street as Bruzzone's gallery. We were looking at a fresco on the walls of one of the rooms, a work that has been attributed to a young Raffaello but never definitively confirmed as by his hand. Rick, with his usual American humor—"

"I am all too familiar with it, Betta," said the policeman.

"Yes. Well, he joked that someone could have sneaked into

the room and painted a forgery on the wall to make it look like the master's work. A few minutes later it clicked in my mind. What if the missing drawing was in fact a fake? Once I considered that possibility, then, as you said, the motive and everything else fell into place."

"You must have immediately surmised that the woman from Monterchi was involved."

Rick put down his fork. "Since she had authenticated the drawing, she had to be. I remembered thinking when we drove behind her from the museum in Monterchi to the restaurant how it was curious that the director of a small museum could afford such an expensive car. I didn't say anything to Betta at the time, but I should have. She might have figured out their scam sooner." He pulled a piece of bread from the basket in the center of the table and tore it in two before using one piece to sop up the oil from his artichoke. "The woman who supposedly found the drawing must have been in on it as well, paid off by Bruzzone. The one good outcome of this may be that her daughter inherited the house purchased with the money."

"And now Tucci's in custody," Betta said, "with an additional charge of being an accessory to the murder since she knew about it and did not go to the authorities. I called Alfredo yesterday, and he said that her boyfriend is going to pull through. So they'll both be spending time as the guests of the Italian state." She returned to the last few leaves of her artichoke.

It was decision time. Go on to the pasta course? Skip it and order just a main dish? Have both? Piero recommended the *taglioline carciofi e mentuccia*, despite their having just finished an artichoke. The artichoke in this dish would be chopped finely and mixed with oil, wild mint, and other herbs, before being tossed in the frying pan with the fresh pasta. It sounded good to Betta, but Rick decided on spaghetti *cacio e pepe*. The waiter took the order, removed their antipasto plates, filled their glasses, and departed for the kitchen.

"What about the other suspects?" Piero asked. "From the report I read of his questioning, that olive oil dealer seemed like someone I would have loved to take into custody. I only read the transcript, but even without hearing his voice, it was easy to get a sense of the man."

"Morelli?" said Rick. "He is as oily as the product he buys and sells. I was hoping that the amphorae I photographed in his living room would turn out to be stolen."

Betta sighed. "Actually, Rick, I heard this morning from the person in our office who traces such things, that it is legitimate. The sale was even registered. Sorry about that."

"*Mannaggia,*" said Rick, lightly punching the air. "I really wanted to nail that guy."

"But in the other picture you took with your phone there was a small, bronze oil lamp. It turned out to be Roman, first century, and unique. It's worth about three thousand euros and is on the list of items stolen from a museum in Calabria three years ago."

Rick picked up his glass. "This deserves a toast. After solving the mystery of the missing drawing and now finding a precious ancient artifact, we'll soon be toasting your promotions, Betta."

"I'm not counting on it," she said as the glasses touched.

"Are you going to be sent up to retrieve the oil lamp?" Piero asked.

"No, we'll leave that to the local police in Urbino, along with collecting a hefty fine from Morelli. He'll claim he didn't know it was stolen when he bought it, but he'll end up paying."

"Local police?" Rick said. "Somebody we know?"

"It very well could be."

"Which reminds me," said Piero, "I was going to ask you

about Inspector DiMaio. You both were mentioned in his reports, so you must have been working closely with him. Is your impression of him still the same as after the Bassano case?"

Rick had expected the question. Alfredo's initial relationship with Pilar still bothered him, and he expected it might not sit well with his uncle. Yet wasn't it the job of the police themselves, not that of an outsider like Rick, to rule on the professionalism of their own officers? The memory of the exchange of gunfire in Bruzzone's shop was still fresh in Rick's mind, and he wasn't about to pay back Alfredo with even a hint of criticism. On a list of transgressions committed by police every day, this one would be considered minor, and Alfredo had learned his lesson.

"I'm sure his reports bear out our impression of DiMaio's work, Zio. I can't see how any other policeman would have done any better investigating what was a rather complicated murder. Add to that the delicate international aspect of the case, and I think he did quite well."

"I have to agree," said Betta. "It was not easy to deal with those Spaniards." Was she having the same thoughts as Rick?

Three plates of pasta were placed on the table. They were similar in their basic creamy color, but the plates with the artichoke were sprinkled with greens and browns while Rick's *cacio e pepe* showed only the white of the cheese with flecks of black pepper. Rick made a mock protest when both Betta and his uncle stole forkfuls of his pasta for a taste. He counterattacked by taking bites from each of their plates before everyone tasted their own. It was declared a tie, and they returned to the suspects list.

"Before Betta solved it," Rick said, "I thought it was Vitellozzi, the museum director. He struck me as just too smooth an operator, and he had the motive of missing out on getting the drawing, not just once but twice." He looked at Betta. "You were leaning in his direction as well, weren't you?" He didn't mention her questionable foray into Vitellozzi's office since it might have chafed his uncle's professional sensibilities.

"Either him or Garcia," Betta added. "Garcia was the assistant to the murdered man, Piero, and he seemed to have had a relationship with Signora Somonte. Or Garcia with the support of Signora Somonte. They had the most to gain from the death of Manuel Somonte."

"Along with Somonte's daughter," said the policeman. "I assume she inherited something."

"She did, Zio. She got the family business, where she was already working. There is some question in our minds whether she and Garcia might be romantically involved."

"This Garcia fellow must be quite the ladies' man." He pushed the pasta with his fork before twirling some on it. "Any other suspects?"

"There was another, the director of the botanical gardens where the body was found, but it was difficult for DiMaio to take him seriously."

"How is that, Riccardo?"

Rick told his uncle about Florio's penchant for publicity to boost his attendance numbers, and how the man's interest in crime fiction made him think that he could solve the murder.

Piero smiled. "I've had a few like that. Usually they just walk in off the street and give us their theories, hoping to get a few moments in the limelight. We have to talk to them, since—*ogni morto di papa*—what one tells us turns out to be correct."

Piero had used one of Rick's favorite phrases, "every time a pope dies," the Italian equivalent of "once in a blue moon." The policeman placed his fork in the empty dish and patted his lips with the napkin while Rick waited for the inevitable story. Having spent many pleasant lunches with his uncle, he knew when there was more to come—something in the man's expression said so. Betta sensed it as well and quietly finished her *taglioline*.

There was a story, but it had nothing to do with public-spirited citizens helping the police.

"When I heard that you were going to Sansepolcro to witness the donation of a work by Piero della Francesca, I was pleased. Several times I have planned a trip to the towns of Tuscany where his works are found: Urbino, Sansepolcro, Arezzo, and of course, Monterchi. The office always got in the way, but I'll do it eventually. Not only is he an artist who I admire greatly, I feel I have a personal connection with him. No, I am not an aspiring artist—far from it. The connection is through your grandmother, Riccardo."

Rick and Betta kept silent.

"You said you went to Monterchi to interview the woman who found the drawing. I was hoping you would go to Monterchi and that while there you would stop at the museum to see the *Madonna del Parto*. If I had known that before you left Rome, I would have insisted, but fortunately, as it happened, you went anyway."

He stopped to take a drink of his mineral water, either to clear his throat or simply for dramatic effect. Either way, he had their attention.

"You may have heard, when you were viewing that master-piece, that for centuries, when it was located in a country chapel just outside the town, it was venerated by the local women. Partly it was due to the belief, which I understand to be true, that the artist executed the work to honor his mother, a simple peasant with whom these women could identify. But also, since it was the depiction of the pregnant Virgin Mary, women who were having difficulty conceiving began going there to pray for a child. Naturally, word got around that such a pilgrimage worked, and women trying to get pregnant came from all over Tuscany, as well as farther away, to kneel before Piero's painting. One of those women, Riccardo, was your grandmother." He leaned back in his chair and awaited a reaction.

"Zio, that is a wonderful story. Can I guess where I think this is going?"

"I would expect nothing less from my clever nephew."

Rick raised his glass, which fortunately still held some wine. "Let me raise a toast to the artistic powers of Piero della Francesca, and to my uncle, who was given his name." They tapped their glasses and took their sips. After some moments of silence, Rick added, "Zio, I have to ask you—did…?"

"No, Riccardo, two years later your mother arrived without any help from the Madonna."

They decided to skip the main course and ordered fruit and cheese instead.

# THE WINE AND FOOD

Just as Le Marche does not get the tourism it deserves, the wines of the region are not as well known as those of its flashier neighbors. But don't take that to mean it is a vinicultural backwater. Among Italy's twenty regions, Le Marche ranks twelfth in acres of vineyards, tenth in gallons of wine produced, and eighth for DOC (controlled origin denomination) wines. While production is now very diversified, at one time the region was known solely for verdicchio, a white that was, and still is, mass produced. (The fish-shaped bottles of Verdicchio dei Castelli di Jesi are almost as distinctive as Chianti in the basket flasks.) The areas that produce the best verdicchio are found around the towns of Jesi and Matelica, and as with wine from any grape, its taste varies according to climate—how far up the mountain, how distant from the sea—as well as the composition of the soil, which in Le Marche is mostly limestone and clay. Curiously, the only time Rick and Betta have a white while in Urbino it is a Bianchello del Metauro, from grapes of the same name grown along the Metauro River. They apparently didn't get the memo about verdicchio.

Regarding Le Marche reds, the game is dominated by one

grape, montepulciano. Two of the best montepulciano reds, Rosso Cónero and Rosso Piceno, are enjoyed by Rick and Betta on the pages of this book. At the wine bar the last night, they also try a Focara Rosso that is made by a friend of the owner, which may indicate how obscure this wine is, even in Italy. Its main grape is sangiovese, with a bit of pinot nero.

That same sangiovese grape, along with other varieties, goes into the Cesanese di Olevano Romano that Piero orders at the lunch in Rome with Rick and Betta. It comes from the Castelli Romani, the hills southeast of Rome where Romans have been escaping summer heat for centuries. The area is best known for its whites, especially frascati, but some excellent reds like this one are produced there as well.

It will not surprise my regular readers that when Rick and Betta are in Urbino they manage to eat well and sample some of the local specialties. The sampling begins at their first lunch when DiMaio orders them *olive ascolane* and *vincisgrassi*, the latter being one of the more curious names for what is essentially lasagna. According to tradition, in this case true, it was named in honor of an Austrian military commander named Windischgratz (or Windisch Graetz), who was stationed in the area and fought against Napoleon. Most of my sources note that it is usually more rich than the *lasagne* from other regions, thanks to such ingredients as chicken livers or sweetbreads.

For their first dinner, the restaurant I had in mind when writing was Vecchio Urbino, where my wife and I had a memorable meal on our first trip to that city. All I have to do is mention the distinctive star-shaped light fixtures and she remembers it. At the meal in the book, all four diners have *gnocchetti al ragu di cinghiale*, small gnocchi tossed in a wild boar sauce. (Regular readers of Rick's adventures will recall that I extol the taste of wild boar in the first book in the series, *Cold Tuscan Stone*.)

The place where Rick and Betta lunch with Loretta Tucci the next day is also a real place, out in the country between Monterchi and Sansepolcro. My wife and I had lunch at the Castello di Sorci years ago, on a Sunday, which meant it was packed with families, and children running loose everywhere. The fare was simple that day: generous antipasto platters and homemade pasta. That's what I decided Rick and Betta should have for their lunch as well. Dinner back in Urbino that evening featured chicken breasts with one of the most famous local specialties, black truffles, something I had to include in at least one of their meals. I'm not a big fan of truffles—they're just too overpowering a taste for me—but it is something everyone should try, especially if you are in Piedmont, the region of white truffles, in the fall.

The lunch spot the next day has a specialty of grilled meats, which reminds Rick of the *churrascarias* he went to when visiting his parents in Rio de Janeiro. (By an amazing coincidence, your author spent six years in Rio.) For the setting, I again had an actual restaurant in mind when writing, though not one located in Urbino or Brazil. Coccorone is found on a narrow street in Montefalco, a town southeast of Perugia. Because of its rustic atmosphere and grilled meats specialty, it seemed the perfect eatery to move temporarily to Urbino for Rick and Betta's enjoyment. Be assured that I put it back in Montefalco, a beautiful hill town, right after describing the lunch in the book.

The last dinner in Urbino isn't much of a dinner. Ironically, given the Spanish nationality of the book's victim, the place they go to could almost be described as a tapas bar. Importantly, it gives Rick and Betta a chance to sample another famous local specialty, *formaggio di fossa*, which is described in some detail as they eat it. In addition, they once again have bruschetta with their wine. You just can't have too much bruschetta.

The traditional Rome wrap-up lunch with Uncle Piero is set in a restaurant just off Via Veneto called Peppone. It was on our regular rotation of restaurants, and not just because it was conveniently located so close to our apartment that we could have thrown water balloons down on diners sitting at its sidewalk tables. (We never did.) One of its specialties, *taglioline carciofi e mentuccia,* was a favorite of mine, so I had Betta and Piero order it. Rick has one of those simple but hard-to-do-right dishes, spaghetti *cacio e pepe,* which is pasta tossed in tangy cheese with black pepper. The hard part is getting just the right amount of pasta water when you toss it with the cheese.

# AUTHOR'S NOTE

Given Rick's knack for turning up in wonderful Italian towns, it was inevitable that he would eventually find his way to Urbino. Located in Le Marche, one of the less traveled of Italy's twenty regions, it is a true gem well worth the effort needed to reach it. The traveler must remember that if Urbino were located almost anywhere else in Italy, it would be overrun by tourists, so its isolation is a small price to pay. For the most prominent Duke of Urbino, Federico II da Montefeltro, that isolation was just fine, a splendid location to hold court when not fighting wars. Federico took seriously the "fortune" part of the term "soldier of fortune": he never formed alliances but instead fought strictly for cash. And he was good enough at warfare to amass a treasury that allowed him to enlarge his territory and create one of the most enlightened courts in Europe. The duke's greatest pride was not his considerable skill in battle but a library that rivaled those of Italy's great universities. Federico was also the patron of several of the finest artists of the time, including, of course, Piero della Francesca, whose work is frequently described in this book.

The reader will not be surprised that Piero is one of my

favorite Renaissance artists, and you can check out his paintings on my website to understand why. Naturally, this book is a
murder mystery, not an art history text, so my descriptions of
his work are superficial at best, but I tried to be accurate. The
best way to appreciate Piero is to go to Italy and seek out his
work in Arezzo, Sansepolcro, Monterchi, and Urbino, as well
as in museums in Florence and Milan. On one post-retirement
trip, when my wife was studying art history at the University of
New Mexico, we parked outside the walls of Rimini and hiked
the length of the town just to see his faded fresco portrait of
the young Sigismondo Malatesta. It is found inside the Tempio
Malatestiano, designed by an architectural genius of the
period, Leon Battista Alberti. (Alberti's final work is featured
in book five of the Rick Montoya Italian Mysteries, *A Funeral in
Mantova*.) The trek to the Tempio was worth it.

You could say that Piero actually wrote the book on perspective—*Di Prospectiva Pingendi* was the title—and he used
its mathematical principles in everything he painted, including the human figure. I have always found it fascinating that he
died on October 12, 1492, the day that, thanks to Columbus,
may have marked the beginning of the end of the Renaissance.
If you are interested in learning more about him, I would recommend *Piero della Francesca* by Marilyn Aronberg Lavin, the
book I had in mind for one scene involving Betta.

Urbino's most important native son is of course Raffaello,
whom we know in English as Raphael. The house where he
was born, now a museum, is featured in a final scene of the
story. If you want to explore it without going to Urbino, you
can do a virtual tour of its rooms and courtyard on the museum's website: casaraffaello.com. When I finished writing the
first draft of this book and was checking the veracity of some
of its details, I noticed a news item in an Italian newspaper

about some faded frescoes found in a chapel outside Urbino that one expert thought had been painted by a young Raphael. Tucked into the story was a mention that 2020 would mark five hundred years since the death of the master. I checked other sources and found that a series of major Raphael exhibits would be mounted during the quincentenary, including in Paris at the Louvre, Rome at the Scuderie del Quirinale, and of course Urbino at the Galleria Nazionale delle Marche, which is the scene of some of the action in this story. So, even though it was pure chance that I discovered it, I thought why not tie this real anniversary into the plot of a book of fiction? Obviously, I have no shame.

Sansepolcro, which Rick and Betta pass through all too quickly, is another small Tuscan city worth a visit. Most people, understandably, go there for the Civic Museum and its collection of Piero's works, but there are other things to see inside this walled town, like its cathedral and the church of San Francesco. I must note that it has another famous native son besides Piero: Luca Pacioli, the mathematician who invented double-entry bookkeeping. Well, famous among accountants. West of Sansepolcro is the town of Anghiari, mentioned in the book as the birthplace of Somonte's Italian mother. On the plain below the town, the Battle of Anghiari took place in 1440, one of the more famous engagements of the period, fought between a Milanese force and an army of Florentine and Papal troops. The victory was so important for Florence that it commissioned Leonardo da Vinci to paint the action on a wall in City Hall, but the work never got beyond the drawing stage and is still the subject of conjecture among art historians.

At one point in the book Rick is looking at a painting and wishing he had his book of Christian symbols to help him appreciate it. The book he refers to is one I have recommended to many a traveler to Italy, *Signs and Symbols in Christian Art* by George Ferguson. Why does the baby Jesus have a piece of coral hanging around his neck? Who is the saint filled with arrows? What's the significance of the number seven? Ferguson explains it all. The book comes in paperback, so it's easy to carry when walking through museums.

There is frequent reference in this book to the great Italian crime writer Andrea Camilleri. Just as I was finishing it, the news came that the author of the Montalbano series had passed away in Rome at the age of ninety-three. Whenever people ask me about other crime novels set in Italy that they should read, I always recommend his books, and I do so here.

My thanks go out to my good friend Richard Draper, a true Italophile, whose menu suggestions found their way onto the pages of this book.

As always, my wife, Mary, kept my feet to the fire and was the perfect sounding board for ideas and plot lines. She also helped with key details about the artists mentioned on these pages. I can't write these books without her.